PRAISE FOR *FLOWERS FOR SARA:*

"*Flowers for Sara* is a beautiful story that is wonderfully told by the author, Davina Kotulski. It has many layers that transport the reader back in time just long enough to remind us that we sometimes need to look at our past to envision the future. And the current-day adventure of the main character, Dani, keeps you guessing as to what she might find out next. I wholeheartedly recommend it."

—Gayla Turner, author of
Don't You Dare: Uncovering Lost Love

"I thoroughly enjoyed this book. The author makes you feel you are right there with the main character, Dani, in Italy. A great love story with twists along the way, and I learned some history while being entertained. Bravo!"

—Sudi (Rick) Karatas, author of *Rainbow Relatives* and
How Catering Sucked the Life Right Out of Me

Flowers for Sara
A Novel

Davina Kotulski

Red Ink Press / Davina Kotulski
www.davinakotulski.com

Disclaimer: This is a work of fiction. All characters, with the exception of some well-known historical figures, the gondolier, and the cemetery keeper, are products of the author's imagination and are not to be construed as real. Where historical figures appear, the situations, incidents, and dialogs concerning those persons are entirely fictional and not intended to depict actual events or change the entirely fictional nature of the work. In all other respects, any resemblance to actual people, living or dead, or to businesses, companies, events, institutions, or locales is completely coincidental.

Copy editing and book production Stephanie Gunning
Cover design by Davina Kotulski and Gus Yoo

Library of Congress Control Number 2023903118

Flowers for Sara / Davina Kotulski —1st ed.

ISBN 979-8-9876262-0-7 (paper)

CONTENTS

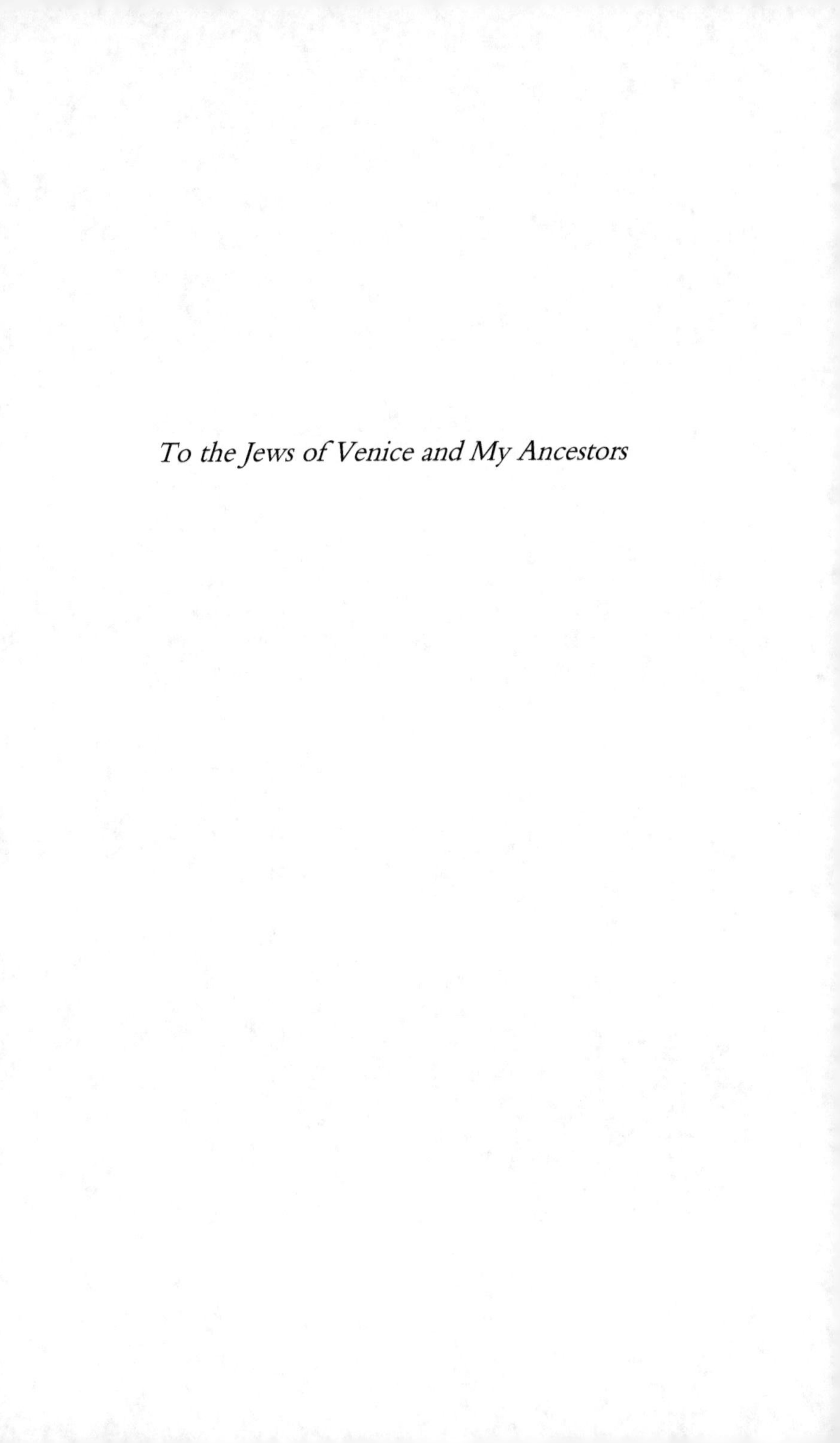

To the Jews of Venice and My Ancestors

UNO

The phone startled Dani awake. She reached across last night's tattooed blonde femme and fumbled for the cordless phone on the nightstand. *This better be important.*

"Happy twenty-fifth birthday, Dani," the voice on the other end whispered.

"Michelle?" The name stuck in her throat.

"I just wanted to call while I had the chance," Michelle said.

Dani eased out of her bed, trying not to wake the blonde. Her hands trembled as she gathered her striped boxers and the black tee-shirt from the floor. She held the phone to her ear with her shoulder and dressed.

"How . . . how are you, Michelle?" she stammered.

Michelle spoke. Her voice sounded different from the last time Dani heard it, softer maybe, transporting Dani back in time to warm summer afternoons and the scent of fresh-cut grass. She closed her eyes wanting to linger there, but Michelle asked her a question that brought her back to the present and her cramped San Francisco studio apartment.

Dani took a deep breath and sighed. "I need some time to think about that."

"I miss you," Michelle said and hung up.

Dani closed her eyes trying to recapture the feelings of those late summer afternoons, but they were gone. She turned towards the window. "Did you hear that, Fern?" she asked her one potted plant, a maiden fern that hugged the ledge of the windowsill.

"What?" the blonde asked, still half-asleep.

Dani stifled a laugh. "I'm talking to my plant."

"Oh, OK." The blonde rolled over and went back to sleep.

Dani stood staring absentmindedly at the books on her bookshelf—mostly classics, a few modern novels, several books of poetry. *Ugh, so much dust,* she thought.

Then she caught her reflection in the window. Her short brown hair was mussed. She wondered if she looked her age or still looked like a "cute sixteen-year-old boy" as Michelle used to say. She tried to shake off the butterflies she hadn't felt in years. It was a strange sensation. *So adolescent,* she thought as she got back under the covers. She wrapped her arms around the attractive stranger nestled in her bed, comforted to have something beautiful to hold on to.

DUE

Michelle's unexpected proposal reverberated through Dani's mind, distracting her as she made lattes at Common Grounds. It was a queer-friendly café in the Mission where she lived, a predominately Latino and lesbian district of San Francisco. She loved the two-story Victorians, *taquerias,* and the Chicano art culture that flourished there. The name came from the Mission Dolores, a Catholic Mission built in 1776.

The Castro, San Francisco's gay-borhood, sat adjacent to the Mission District. She loved the Castro, but rents were so high there that most of the lesbians she knew could not afford to live there.

Dani had moved to the Mission in the summer of 2003 and had noticed things changing rapidly in the three years she'd lived in "the City," as San Francisco was referred to by locals. Since the recovery from the dotcom crash of 2000—the demographics were rapidly changing. Her friends would talk nostalgically about the good old days in the late Nineties, when you could find aging Mexican cowboys and lesbian punks enjoying the best burritos in any one of the dozens of taquerias in the area and residing under the same roof.

The Mission was morphing, as hip vegan restaurants and wealthy dot-commers were moving in and buying up buildings, more and more lesbians and Latinos were being forced from their coveted cramped apartments and relocating to the East Bay, especially Oakland and Berkeley. The East

Bay, the designation the locals used to refer to all the cities on the east side of the San Francisco Bay, was full of homes built in the 1920s with much more affordable rents, though many of the most affordable ones were in decrepit and dangerous neighborhoods.

Dani wanted to stay where the action was. She was grateful that her apartment building was rent controlled. Gentrification wasn't impacting her the way it was some of her old work friends from Good Vibrations. Good Vibes, as it was colloquially known, was a women-owned adult sex shop. She worked there until she got canned for demonstrating the merchandise on a customer. In her defense, it was a willing customer and she'd made the sale, something that seemed inconsequential to her boss. It was the longest job she'd ever held and came with some great perks.

Dani liked working at Common Grounds too, for different reasons. The owner, Serena, supported local Latino artists by hanging their colorful and controversial paintings on the walls. The café served organic, fair-trade coffee. The clientele reflected the neighborhood: starving artists and writers, yuppies, San Francisco General Hospital staff, self-righteous students from New College. Dani listened to the students argue while they sipped cappuccinos and lattes. She enjoyed their spirited discussions on post-modernism and "deconstruction." The guys especially would deconstruct their deconstructions until there was nothing left to deconstruct. Their endless debates on Foucauldian discourse analysis in the presence of female students who would never sleep with them made her smile.

Dani was brewing another round of house blend when a twenty-something brunette with blonde highlights and piercing blue eyes, wearing a colorful dress with Origami cranes, white platform shoes, and a shiny gold nose ring walked in. The girl took out her Hello Kitty coin purse and approached the counter.

"Nonfat latte?" Dani asked, anticipating her order, the most common for her demographic.

"Do you think I'm fat or something?" The girl looked worried.

"Not at all. You seem like the healthy type."

The girl smiled. "Yes, I'll have a nonfat latte please."

Dani held in her eye roll. She noticed the girl's Chinese characters tattooed on her wrist and changed the subject. "I like your tattoo."

The girl looked at her wrist with a sense of pride. "Thanks, it's the Chinese character of crisis, but it also means—"

"Opportunity," Dani finished her sentence.

"How did you know?"

"Lucky guess." Dani lied. She'd heard that adage many times. She moved quickly to the espresso maker, emptied out the portafilter, smacking the old grounds into the garbage can, and then wiped the filter clean with the dish towel.

"You go to New College?"

Hello Kitty looked surprised. "Yeah, do you go there?"

"No, just another lucky guess." Dani smiled. *Honey, you are so cliché,* she thought as she ran the grinder and filled it up with fresh ground beans, tamped down the fluffy pile, and then locked the portafilter snuggly in the espresso maker.

Hello Kitty read the bulletin board postings while Dani made her latte.

"Isn't it ironic that this café is in a predominately Latino community, yet how many working-class Latinos can even afford a three-dollar latte?" Hello Kitty mused, outraged by her own white privilege.

Dani leaned in and held Hello Kitty's gaze. "Deeply ironic," she said.

Flirting for Dani was as automatic as breathing. She poured the espresso into a to-go cup and added the steamed milk. "Here you go," she said, summoning Hello Kitty.

Hello Kitty took the cup and smiled at Dani. "What do you do?"

"I'm a writer," Dani sniffed after she said it, a tick she had when she was trying to look like a badass.

"Really? That's cool," Hello Kitty said. "I want to write something for you." Hello Kitty took out a piece of paper and wrote her number on it. She was about to hand it across the counter to Dani when a bookish brunette with caramel skin sashayed up to the counter, her silver bracelets clanking on the countertop.

"And speaking of writers, it's Veronica Mendolsohn, San Francisco's award-winning food writer," Dani said.

Veronica truly looked the part of an eccentric writer: long brown hair, black-rimmed glasses, bright red lipstick, wearing a burgundy lace dress with a vintage butterfly brooch pinned to her thigh-length black sweater. Veronica epitomized vintage chic. "How does it feel to be twenty-five?" she asked.

"About the same as twenty-four but with more awareness that my ten-year high school reunion is only three years away and I've done—literally speaking—jack shit."

Veronica gave Hello Kitty a why-are-you-still-standing-here look.

Dani turned back to the girl. "Did you need anything else?"

Hello Kitty handed Dani the paper with her phone number. "Call me if you want to talk sometime," she said and sauntered towards the exit.

Dani watched her saunter away while Veronica rolled her eyes.

"If you're here to give me crap for being charming—," Dani began, but Veronica castrated her confidence in one fell swoop.

"Emily got a book contract."

Dani's mouth fell open. "What? For what? That breeder clit-lit romance novel, *Smooth and Lovely?*"

Veronica nodded. "With a six-figure advance."

"They'll publish anything with a throbbing . . . It's total crap! She read it at open mic. I'm not kidding, it's terrible!"

Veronica stood there, cool to Dani's theatrics. "Tell me how you really feel?"

"It reads like every cheesy paperback romance."

Veronica raised her eyebrows and gave Dani a quizzical look. "And how many paperback romances have you read exactly?"

"Exactly none." Dani shook her head. "I just know."

"Nevertheless, she finished said 'cheesy paperback romance.'" Veronica looked squarely at Dani. "And it shall be published."

Dani turned away from Veronica, grabbed a dish towel, and began obsessively cleaning the espresso machine. "I'm a quarter-century old and I have nothing to show for it and that chick with her schmaltzy romance novel is getting a major book deal."

The front door creaked open. A well-groomed man with short dark hair walked in and got in line. His sweater was tied around his neck. He looked like a life-size version of Yacht Club Ken. Dani cringed. He reminded Dani of the kids she despised in high school, rich preppies with their nauseating blandness and overabundance of money. She had acquired an aversion to these kinds of guys. *He can wait,* she thought.

Veronica, unrelentingly, delivered the second blow. "And Random House is picking it up."

"Random House?" Dani exploded incredulously. "Random-freaking-House?" Dani tossed her barista towel across the room.

The man stood impatiently at the register and cleared his throat.

Dani glanced over at him and his expensive-looking gold watch and his perfectly tanned arms. She slow walked to the register and smiled tightly at him.

"How can I serve you?" she asked, sarcastically.

"I'd like to order a cappuccino," he said, shaking his head, confused about the attitude he was getting.

"One cappuccino," Dani said. She rang him up and then walked to the espresso machine and went to work.

On the other side of the counter, Veronica continued adding fuel to the fire. "There's even some talk about her agent selling the movie rights to Lifetime."

Dani emptied out the portafilter, smacking it hard against the garbage can. "Did you say a movie?"

"Excuse me," the man interrupted. "My cappuccino please."

Dani glared at him and sidestepped to the grinder with decaf beans. "Yes, I'm making it now," she said, engaged in a quiet passive-aggressive retaliation against him.

"I'm going to go before I get you in trouble," Veronica said, beelining for the door. "See you tonight."

Dani began to steam the milk while she waited for the shots to pour. Lattes were easy, but she had never figured out how to finesse foaming for cappuccinos and the milk sprayed everywhere. She wiped the milk from her shirt and the machine. *Oh well, I didn't get this job because I was good at it,* she thought. She poured what remained of the foam into the cup and handed it the man. He took a sip and spit it back into the cup.

"What is this?"

"A cappuccino."

"No. This is not a cappuccino. This is a decaf with nonfat milk. I've had better cappuccinos from vending machines."

Serena, the owner, shot out from the back room dressed in a tight purple shirt and black yoga pants. *Serena always looked good in those yoga pants, but she looked even better with them off,* Dani thought.

"What's going on?" Serena demanded.

Dani began to apologize, but Yacht Club Ken interrupted. "Your barista thinks his customers can wait while he catches up on the latest gossip with his girlfriend. I'm late for work now."

"I'm so sorry, Mister . . . ," Serena said, trying to repair the situation and remember the man's name, and ignoring the fact that he had misgendered Dani.

"It's 'doctor,' Doctor Fischer," Yacht Club Ken corrected.

"I'm so sorry, Doctor. Fischer." Serena shot Dani an angry look, opened the cash register, retrieved three dollars, and gave the man his money back. "Your next coffee drink is on us."

The man looked mildly appeased as he pocketed the money. He walked by Dani and glared at her. "You better get your head out of your ass if you ever expect to make something of yourself," he said.

Dani's face flushed with anger. He struck a nerve. "Blow it out your ass, Herr Doctor," she said under her breath. He didn't hear her, but Serena did.

Serena motioned Dani to the back room. Serena's attractive face contorted in a scowl.

Dani followed her. "How was yoga?" she asked.

Serena turned on her heels, glaring at Dani. "I'm not going to let you destroy my business."

"What do you mean?"

"You're fired!"

"Oh, come on, you're overreacting. That guy was a total douche." Dani moved towards Serena and brushed a wisp of her hair behind her ear.

Serena pulled away. "You can't even make a cappuccino right."

"Who gives a rip," Dani said. "I have other talents. That's why you hired me."

"I'm tired of you using your job to snag trollops." Serena pouted.

"OK, I understand that, but Veronica Mendolsohn is not a trollop. We were discussing writing and that entitled prick was impatient." Dani began kissing Serena's neck.

"Don't play me. I know she wants you."

"Veronica?" Dani laughed at the thought. "She's just a friend. I'm not even her type." Dani pulled Serena towards her, gripping her ass. "How can you be so jealous when you have such a hot body?"

Serena's icy resolve melted.

Dani kissed Serena, backing her up to the desk. "I need to do my morning worship of the sexy yoga goddess."

Serena sat on the desk and Dani slipped off Serena's shoes.

Dani kneeled and pressed her lips to Serena's crotch and blew a hot breath between her thighs. Serena moaned.

"Let me see that beautiful altar," Dani said and eased Serena's yoga pants off. She bit and licked the inside of Serena's thighs, making her way to the yummy center. Serena's body writhed with pleasure as Dani buried her face between Serena's legs and worshipped her.

Serena arched her back. "Oh god, you're so good," she moaned, climaxing.

Dani backed away, smiling. "Feel better?"

"Yes," Serena sighed loudly, "much better. But you're still fired."

Dani looked confused. "Are you freaking serious?"

"Uh huh," Serena said, grabbing her pants off the floor. "I'm going to find someone who can foam milk."

"You do that. I'm gonna go find something to take the taste of skank out of my mouth." Dani grabbed her brown plaid jacket and black messenger bag from the door hook. "This place is riddled with roaches and cafés like this are the first step in gentrification," she yelled to the confused customers as she stormed out of the café.

She walked several blocks before stopping to take in what had just happened. She looked up at the dull gray sky with contempt. This was not the California of her dreams. The California of her dreams was always sunny and warm. She'd moved to the darkest part of California. San Francisco weather, with its thick fog, was as overcast and dreary, as the Seattle suburbs she'd left behind.

"Shit!" she screamed to the pigeons swirling around a nasty garbage dumpster and kept walking. What she was going to do now, not only for money, but with her day? Nothing about the day looked like how she'd fantasized her life would be by the time she hit this milestone birthday. She figured by twenty-five she would be a published novelist, traveling around the country on book tours and speaking gigs. She'd have a steady girlfriend and they'd be arguing over whether to stay in San Francisco with the rising rental market or to save up to buy a house in the East Bay. Instead, she was walking home in the middle of the day to her empty studio apartment, jobless and far from the published author she dreamed of being as an angsty Seattle teenager.

She walked down the dirty Mission District sidewalks, speckled with remnants of gum and dog shit, and considered her options. A shop caught her eye, Botanica Yoruba.

Dani crossed the street and walked towards the storefront. A string of gold bells on the door handle chimed brightly as she opened the door to the *botanica*. The store smelled like *nag champa* incense and sage. She loved that smell.

In front of her were floor-to-ceiling shelves lined with cylinder-shaped glass candles. She picked three with solid colors: red, black, and purple. Each candle had a magical power or intention. Red for passion and vitality, black to banish negative energy, and purple to enhance psychic abilities. She didn't believe in magical powers or psychic abilities, but she loved purple. In her mind, purple was the color of masculine and feminine energy combined. It was the color that represented gay people and people like her that were neither male nor female but some amalgamation of both. Banishing negative energy right now and increasing passion couldn't hurt. She took the candles to the counter.

"Do you have something specifically for good luck?" she asked, surprising herself as she asked it. "My luck has totally sucked today."

The gray-haired Latina behind the counter reached out to Dani, her wrist wrapped in woven bracelets and her stubby fingers adorned with silver rings. She put one of her thick hands on Dani's shoulder.

Dani felt an odd, tingling sensation at the old woman's touch. It made her uneasy. She pulled back.

The grandmotherly woman looked at her with sad eyes. "*Su papá,* he want you to know he love you," she said in broken English.

Dani eyed the woman suspiciously. "*Señora, lo siento.* Can you just ring me up, *por favor?* I'm in a hurry. *Tengo prisa,*" Dani lied. She didn't want to get suckered into a psychic reading.

The woman mumbled something and shook her head. She walked to the shelves and returned with a gold candle with black specks and an image of a lion with wings. Dani thought it looked really cool.

"This one is good. It calls to you," the woman said, placing it on the counter.

"Sure." Dani nodded and smiled politely. "I'll take that one too."

The woman wrapped the candles in tissue paper and carefully placed them in a paper bag, then looked up and met Dani's eyes. Dani felt the same weird tingling sensation again.

"*Su papá* says he is sorry to leave you so soon and wish he could have taught you more about *su cultura.* He is happy you are wearing his *chaqueta,* his jacket," she said, stumbling over the English pronunciation.

Dani flashed back to the last night of her father's life. They'd played chess in front of the fireplace and he let her win. Her mother had brought them hot chocolate and they'd all sat on the couch watching the fire. Dani had fallen asleep nuzzled next to him. When she awoke the next morning, he'd covered her in his brown plaid jacket, the one she was wearing now. It was a pleasant memory, but it hurt to think of him and how suddenly he had disappeared from her life.

How could she know?

Keep the change," Dani said and threw a twenty-dollar bill on the counter. She hurried out of the store as quickly as she could.

TRE

Dani stood outside the four-story apartment building on Valencia Street and pressed the button for "Mendelsohn, V." There was a loud buzzing sound and then the lock released. She rode the elevator to the fourth floor and stepped into a hallway filled with the scents of onions, garlic, and rosemary.

"Hi, honey, I'm home," she said, walking through the open door to Veronica's apartment.

"In the kitchen."

"Smells great. What's for dinner?"

Veronica stood in the narrow kitchen fixing dinner. She was wearing her favorite vintage cherry blossom cotton apron. "Seafood paella." She smiled proudly.

Veronica's apartment was a cozy one-bedroom, but it seemed luxurious compared to the 275-square-foot studio apartment that Dani could barely make the rent on each month. Veronica's home décor was even more flamboyant than her vintage clothing. The living room was jungle themed. Her futon was leopard print, draped with a leopard print throw and tiger-striped throw pillows. The curtains were zebra striped.

Her kitchen was midwest mid-century: Multicolored polka dot curtains hung above the kitchen sink window, a red and white gingham tablecloth covered the kitchen table, and her yellow oven mitts with cherries on them dangled from the handle on the gas range.

Going to the bathroom was like taking a trip to a tropical beach. The moment you switched on the hula girl light plate your eyes glimpsed the coconut toothbrush holder next to a full-size pineapple soap dispenser, and then were drawn upward to a colorful painting of blue, green, and red parrots on the wall behind the toilet. While you sat to pee, you could enjoy the tropical scene printed on the shower curtain: a sandy beach with palm trees. Dani always joked that Veronica should keep a blender in there for self-serve *piña coladas.*

All together the décor was a freak collision of patterns and textures exploding into a discordant cacophony of pure garishness. But Veronica made it work. It had even become a bit homey to Dani.

Dani took a seat at the kitchen table. It was set with two votive candles, a few wildflowers in a blue bottle, and two steaming plates filled with Veronica's homemade paella.

"Wow, this looks amazing. Mussels, clams, calamari—"

"And shrimp from the Pacific Northwest," Veronica interrupted.

Dani took a bite of the paella, nodding her approval. "Delicious."

Veronica smiled at her from across the table. "Happy birthday, Dani."

Dani set down her fork and sighed. "Not my happiest."

"What do you mean?" Veronica asked, setting her fork down too.

"I got fired this morning."

Veronica looked crushed. "Oh my god, Dani, I'm so sorry. It's my fault isn't it? I knew I shouldn't have bothered you at work."

"It's a shitty café anyway." Dani shrugged. She picked up her fork and took another bite of the paella. "Wow, this is soooo good."

"My superpower."

Dani smiled. "You know, you're the best thing to come from my working there."

Veronica gave Dani a quizzical look.

"Our friendship."

"That's right. The night I was doing the reading for my second book, *The Perfect Thyme.*"

Dani smirked. "I learned so much about natural aphrodisiacs. Not sure I ever thanked you for that."

"Of course, that's what you remember," Veronica laughed. She used her knife to scoop a helping of paella onto her fork, but didn't eat it. She looked at Dani wistfully. "I can't believe I thought you were trying to pick me up with all those refills because I thought you were too shy to ask me directly."

"Yeah, that's hilarious. Me? Shy?" Dani laughed. Then her mood darkened. She felt annoyed that their conversation about Emily this morning had cost her job. She felt bad thinking it.

Veronica was her best friend in San Francisco. Intelligent and attractive, a "nice Jewish girl," as her mom might say. "A nice Mexican-Jewish girl," Dani would have corrected. But there was some ingredient missing that kept them "just friends." Veronica had a sarcastic edge that Dani appreciated, and she was certainly Dani's type—long dark hair and big brown eyes—but ultimately, she was too brash, too intense for Dani's taste. It was never going to happen between her and Veronica.

Still, they got each other's jokes and were there for one another, and that was enough to keep them both full while they snacked on the fluff of the San Francisco dating scene.

"Something else big happened today." Dani took a sip of her tea. "Michelle called me this morning."

Veronica's lip twitched. "One of her flying monkeys go missing?"

Dani smiled and played with a loose string on the tablecloth. "She asked me to come back to Seattle. She misses me and wants to get back together."

Veronica burst into laughter. "That's hilarious!"

"I'm not sure why you find that so amusing."

"Wait, you'd seriously consider going back to her?"

Dani took another sip of her tea and set the cup down, her face softened. "Yeah, I told her I'd think about it."

"So, wait, she just calls you every now and then for phone sex for the last few years and then she says jump and—"

"It's more than that."

"I see she gets you revved up and you take it out on all the unsuspecting Bay Area femmes." Veronica rolled her eyes. "She's so Lucy and you are so Charlie Brown."

"Screw that, I'm more like Schroeder."

"No, he's more serious about his craft than you are."

"Ouch!" Dani clutched her heart.

Veronica got up and collected the dinner plates and took them to the kitchen.

She returned with a chocolate cake with a single flickering candle on top. "Make a wish."

Dani closed her eyes, made a wish, and blew out the candle.

"I hope your wish was to finish your novel."

"Must we go there?" Dani groaned.

"What's happening with that?"

"This cake looks beautiful. I bet you had one of those pink Betty Crocker Easy-Bake Ovens when you were a kid, didn't you?" she asked, changing the subject. She didn't want to talk about her novel and there was no way she was going to tell Veronica her wish. She knew Veronica wouldn't approve. It was the same one she had made every year since she was seventeen, when Michelle gave her a tiger's eye necklace on her birthday.

"No." Veronica shook her head. "I had two Easy-Bake Ovens. One for breads and one for desserts. Later it became one for meat dishes and one for dairy."

Dani looked confused.

"Kosher. Are you sure you're a Jew?"

Dani shrugged and Veronica nodded. "That was a pretty Jewish shrug. You've been working on that novel for what, two years now?"

Dani was about to take a sip of tea but reconsidered, it seemed too hot. "Closer to three," she said, blowing on the tea to cool it.

"How many pages do you have, not counting the table of contents?"

"I really need to get these polished," Dani said, staring at her shoes, but there was no escaping Veronica's interrogation.

"How many pages?" Veronica asked.

"Are we counting the ones I deleted?"

"Perfectionism is a lame excuse for procrastination."

"You should put that on an angry fortune cookie or an inspirational coffee mug." Dani laughed then receded into her thoughts. "It's just, I can see the story, but I can't make it come alive. I'm blocked. I can't dive deep enough into the protagonist's motivation."

"I don't know anything about writing fiction, but I do know from writer's block. It happens to all of us." Veronica sipped her tea.

Dani could feel the waves of a familiar melancholy roll in. "Maybe my dreams are unrealistic." She sighed.

Veronica brightened. "When I was finishing writing my cookbook *The Culinary Landscape,* I couldn't write one more word about bok choy or baby bib lettuce. I was totally blocked and not going to make my deadline."

"I can't imagine you missing a deadline."

"Yeah, because I didn't, Smarty Pants. I was in Vermont doing a freelance piece for *The Chronicle* and I kept passing these roadside farm stands with autumn squash: acorn, butternut, blue Hokkaido pumpkins, and corn with the husks still on. Oh, and the blackberries, those blackberries—best ever! It lit me up."

"I can see that. Do you need a cigarette?" Dani laughed.

"I was on fire writing about tempting basil elixirs and . . . " Veronica's eyes narrowed in on Dani with laser-like intensity.

"What?" Dani asked, starting to feel uncomfortable in Veronica's gaze.

Veronica nodded her head knowingly at Dani.

"You're kind of freaking me out, Veronica, what are you thinking?"

"You should go to Venice," Veronica said.

Dani felt a chill come over her body. "Muscle beach?" Dani asked, trying to process the non sequitur. Veronica usually argued with focus.

"No, Venice, Italy," Veronica said, still not blinking.

"What are you talking about?" Dani asked, almost choking on her tea.

"You're always talking about how you want to travel."

"Yeah, so?"

"You should travel."

"Are you trying to get rid of me?"

"No, not at all."

"Then why are you telling me to go to another country?"

"Because you're not going to be the best version of yourself if you just stay here."

"Wow. That stings. Why would I go to Venice?"

Veronica reached for a small picture book on the shelf behind her. Veronica opened the book and flipped through a few of the pages showing Dani pictures of old buildings.

"OK. It looks neat," she said, feeling the strange chill again.

"Neat!" Veronica threw the book down. "No, this doesn't even do it justice. You have to go there. Venice is magical. It's mystical. You have to feel it. In fact, it's the perfect place to get into your senses. God, I loved it there. I loved Vermont too, but in a different way and I don't think Vermont would do you any good. Venice really helped me to connect with a deeper part of myself. It just brings out your inner artist. You'll fall in love with the city and it will get your creative juices flowing. Can I be honest with you?"

"What do you call this?"

"When you've read your stuff at an open mic, I can see you're writing from your head. That's why it's flat. Your heart and soul need to be in your writing. Go to Venice, surround yourself in beautiful architecture, and eat some sensuous food. It will change your writing. It will help you find your voice."

"May I remind you that I just got fired!" Dani said, nonplussed.

"From your day job! Are you a barista or a writer?" Veronica shrugged her shoulders. "You want to finish your novel, don't you?"

"It's been my new year's resolution for the past three years."

Veronica groaned, "Right, you have too many distractions here. You know what I'm talking about."

"Why not Paris?"

"Venice is where all of the great writers go for inspiration. Trust me." Veronica haphazardly put her teacup on the table sloshing the amber liquid on to the checked tablecloth and began listing writers on her fingers. "Dickens, Byron, Hemingway, Henry James, Thomas Mann. Shall I go on?"

It was an impressive list. Dani had read works by each one of them. She'd always admired Byron's romanticism, but Dickens was by far her favorite. She took a sip of her tea and fiddled with the string attached to the tea bag. "No, I think you can stop dropping names now. I'm not going. If I move back to Seattle I'm going to need every penny." It was a bit of an exaggeration since she knew her mother would be thrilled to have her living at home again. It was true that she'd always wanted to travel, but traveling now would be absurd, especially if she was going back to Seattle. She looked at Veronica and her tone softened a bit. "You can come visit me. We've got great food up there. The smoked salmon is to die for."

Veronica looked incensed. "Dani, you're my best friend and you're selling yourself short by abandoning your dreams. If you can't stay here and write, then go to Venice. Just don't go back to Seattle. Because if you do, you'll never finish your book. Moving back to live with your mom is a step backwards."

"You don't know that."

"Yes, I do. Seriously, you owe it to yourself. Listen to me. If not because you think I'm right but because you respect my authority."

"Your authority?"

Veronica locked eyes with Dani. "I'm published."

Dani leaned back in her chair and sighed. "Touché."

The two sat in silence for a moment and then Dani reached out and put her hand on Veronica's hand. "It's my birthday. Can we push pause on this? I know you love me and I appreciate that. Can we just eat the cake? What kind is it?"

Veronica relented. "Yes, of course. It's chocolate with raspberry filling and it's frosted with chocolate and hints of blood orange."

"Oh, my god. Can I have a piece now?"

Veronica took off her black-rimmed glasses and looked soberly at Dani. "She must be amazing in bed."

Dani remembered holding Michelle in her arms and softly kissing her lips. She felt her face redden. "She was my first love. She's special."

"There's nothing special about a closet case," Veronica said, rolling her eyes.

"Hey, be nice."

Veronica walked into the kitchen and returned with a carving knife. She looked at Dani with a devilish grin. "About that girl?" She smiled as she sliced into the cake. "Never!"

QUATTRO

Dani unpacked the candles and put them on her dresser. She decided to light the one with the winged lion, the one the woman gave her for luck. She needed some good luck.

Before going over to Veronica's, she had spent hours thinking about Michelle and obsessively cleaning her studio apartment. It looked like an Ikea showroom with her perfectly made bed and the immaculate black nightstand and matching black dresser. The décor was stark—functional and masculine. It included a torchiere floor lamp adjacent to the couch, a bookshelf with the CD player perched on the middle shelf, and a CD holder with all her CDs in alphabetical order. The only touch of color came from the large glass candles on her dresser. The candle with the winged lion flickered brightly.

Dani sat on the couch and turned on her aging laptop. The cursor blinked on the empty screen. She typed a few sentences, then stopped and read them.

"Schmaltzville," she said and stabbed the DELETE button three times, an overkill.

"What am I going to do now, Fern?" Dani asked the plant. The plant didn't respond. "Giving me the silent treatment again?" she said and walked over to her bed. She reached underneath the bed and pulled out a shoebox. She took off the lid. It was filled with keepsakes: childhood photos, cards, letters, and a few maps that once belonged to her dad, who was an avid traveler. She collapsed on the bed, pouring out the contents of the box. A faded brown map with drawings of boats and a lion with wings caught her eye. She looked over at the candle and then back to the map. *Strange coincidence,* she thought and pushed it aside, shaking her head.

She picked up a picture of Michelle hugging a tree, her blue eyes sparkling. There was handwriting on the back of the photo. She read the words out loud, "Dani, I love you. You know the real me, the parts of myself I never even knew existed." The words hurt her now, reminding Dani of what had followed those words.

She stuffed the photo and the rest of the keepsakes back into the box and shoved the box back under her bed. She beelined to her dresser and put on a fresh black tee-shirt and a pair of black jeans. Then she grabbed her jacket and keys and headed out.

Dani walked into the Lexington, a lesbian pub in the Mission District. It was about an hour before midnight. The place was dark and smoky, filled with a young, hip, queer crowd. Dani sat at the bar, drinking a beer, and watched a couple of bois playing pool. *Bois* were biological women who wore their hair short and used masculine pronouns. They dressed and identified as young men and were attracted to masculinity in its various forms. Bois were different than the trans guys who had top surgery and were taking hormones. Trans guys often frequented the bar because they felt safe in the crowd and connected with the queer community.

The bois sometimes made passes at Dani because she was butch. It didn't bother her, because they were sweet, but she wasn't the least bit interested. She was one hundred percent attracted to femmes, which meant she slept with a lot of bi girls and the more than occasional curious straight chick.

A Latina femme with long brown hair and luscious red lips sitting on a barstool near the bar counter caught her eye. She smiled at her. The Latina femme smiled back. Dani strode confidently across the room towards her.

"You're a cute one," the Latina femme said, smiling.

"I'm glad you noticed."

"Uh-huh," the girl said, biting her lip.

"What are you drinking?" Dani asked, checking the girl out.

"A cosmo."

Dani tried to flag the bartender. He held up his finger, giving her the one-minute sign. She felt a tap on her shoulder and turned around. An attractive redhead in a shaggy fake fur coat stood facing her.

"Why haven't you returned my calls?" the redheaded femme asked.

Dani stared. "Hey, you."

The girl's eyes bulged with rage. "My name is Amanda."

"I know," Dani lied. "Been busy working on a novel, Amanda. How you been?"

"You're an asshole," the girl said and walked off.

Dani shrugged, not bothering to defend herself. She turned to face the Latina femme. "So, what's your name, smexy?" she asked.

A sour look formed on the girl's face. "I'm Salvadoreaña," the Latina said shaking her head in disgust. "We're not all the same." She stood up from the bar stool.

"My bad," Dani said, embarrassed by her presumption. She knew better than that. *"Espera, lo siento."*

The Latina stopped and looked at Dani. *"Serio?"*

"Sinceramente, perdonme," Dani apologized. *"Por favor, tu eres una diosa. Como te llamas, diosa?"*

"A goddess, huh?" The girl smiled. "My name is Marisol."

"Marisol, sientese. Por favor?" Dani continued her apology and seduction.

The bartender approached Dani. "What can I get you?" he asked.

"A cosmo for the goddess and an Anchor Steam for me."

Marisol returned to the bar stool. The bartender opened a bottle of beer and set it and a glass down in front of Dani and went off to make the cosmo.

Dani filled the glass with beer, and sidled up to Marisol. Marisol was beautiful. And yet, even as she sat flirting with this hot Latina femme, memories of Michelle flooded her mind like a torrential Seattle downpour. She couldn't escape it: Michelle's call had opened Pandora's box.

CINQUE

Dani liked Michelle Ellison from the moment Michelle spoke to her at the start of their sophomore year of high school.

"When am I ever going to use this?" Dani blurted out, slamming her math book shut, rather than confess that she was completely lost.

Michelle happened to be sitting next to her in class that day. The popular cheerleader regurgitated all the reasons one would need to know algebra, "Baking, building furniture, landscaping projects . . . " She recited at least a dozen reasons, none of them compelling.

"Yeah, because I've always dreamed of mowing lawns for a living." Dani laughed, trying not to stare at Michelle's full lips and sparkling blue eyes. She was beautiful.

"What do you dream about?" Michelle asked.

"You really want to know?" Dani asked, surprised by Michelle's sincerity.

"Yes." Michelle waited attentively.

Dani softened. "I'm going to be a writer."

"Who is your favorite writer?"

"Depends. Poetry: Anne Sexton. Plays: Tennessee Williams and Edward Albee. Fiction would be a tie between Charles Dickens and Charlotte Brontë. Don't think any of them needed algebra!"

"But you do need good grades in math if you want to get into a good liberal arts college. I could help you in math if you help me with my Spanish?" Michelle offered and Dani suddenly felt a budding interest in learning algebraic formulas.

"Por qué no?" Dani said casually, hiding her surprise that a cheerleader wanted to hang out with her. The other popular girls treated her like a pariah.

"My house tomorrow?" Michelle asked.

"If you insist," Dani joked.

"See you then," Michelle said, smiling a perfect smile that made Dani quiver inside.

The next day, when school let out, Dani walked with Michelle to Michelle's house—a beige two-story on a quiet cul de sac. They sat at the kitchen table studying. Dani tried to pay attention to the algebra lesson, if for no other reason than not to look stupid in front of Michelle. But she was easily distracted by Michelle's beauty. She wanted to run her fingers through Michelle's long, curly blonde hair.

Michelle was a much better pupil. She seemed legitimately engaged in their conversations in Spanish and in conjugating verbs. Dani was grateful that learning Spanish was easy for her.

Their friendship grew during those afternoons spent studying at Michelle's house. The lessons began in the kitchen, eventually moving upstairs to Michelle's frilly pink bedroom, the walls covered with teen magazine pinups of Johnny Depp, Leonardo DiCaprio, and Hootie and the Blowfish.

Dani could not relate to schoolgirl crushes on these teen heartthrobs. Her stomach fluttered for the first time when she saw a *Friends* episode of two women getting married, which led to the realization that she liked girls—not boys. She kept the realization and her feelings to herself. She felt she had no choice. So, it was Michelle who began dropping hints—sitting closer to Dani on the bed and brushing against her as they studied. It was Michelle who told Dani how handsome she was and commented on her "soulful amber eyes."

Dani pretended not to notice all the cues, which became more frequent with her lack of response. She knew that to do otherwise might create problems for them both. Michelle's father eyed her suspiciously when he arrived home from work and found them studying. She felt like a criminal in his presence though she'd done nothing wrong.

Then one day, Michelle invited her to spend the night while her parents were away for the weekend. Dani knew she should decline the invitation, but didn't.

The evening began innocently. She found her usual place at the kitchen table with her back to the framed and handstitched, "The Lord is my shepherd . . ." biblical passage that hung on the wall. It creeped her out. She didn't like the idea of anything "maketh-ing" here to do anything. She propped open her algebra book and began reading.

"A quadratic equation is an equation in which one or more of the terms is squared but raised to no higher power, having the general form $ax^2 + bx + c = 0$, where a, b, and c are constants." She shoved a handful of grapes into her mouth. "Seriously, what the hell does that mean and why should I care?"

"Put that away for now," Michelle said. "I rented *Thelma and Louise.*"

"Your parents would freak out if they knew that."

Michelle rolled her eyes. "Come on, we can study later." Michelle patted the couch for Dani to sit next to her.

Dani closed her algebra book, picked up the bowl of grapes, and joined Michelle on the black leather sofa in front of the widescreen television.

Michelle pressed the remote and leaned back against the couch. Dani could smell the jasmine scent of Michelle's hair. It distracted her, she tried not to focus on it, or on the way her stomach flip-flopped when Michelle reached over her to get a handful of grapes from the bowl.

Somehow, she managed to pay attention to the movie and to keep her nervous excitement under wraps, at least until Thelma kissed Louise before gunning the engine and driving off the cliff. She tried to play it cool, but she felt herself blushing.

"Man, that was really great."

"Except that they die," Michelle said sarcastically.

"Yeah, except that. Totally reminds me of Kate Chopin's book *The Awakening*. The protagonist, Edna, swims out to the ocean to commit suicide after an encounter with her lover because she knows she can't stand going back to her regular life."

"You're such a brainiac, Dani." Michelle shook her head and got up to turn off the TV. When she returned, she sat closer to Dani. A wave of heat rushed through Dani's body. She'd wanted Michelle for a long time, but had stifled her desire. Dani started to shift away from Michelle, but Michelle turned towards her. "If you think that was great, tell me what you think of this?" Michelle leaned in to kiss her.

Dani stopped her before their lips touched. "Are you sure?" Dani asked. Her heart beat fast in her chest. She'd never kissed a girl before. She'd never kissed anyone.

"More than anything," Michelle said and leaned in and kissed her.

It was electric.

Dani kissed her back. Then Michelle opened her mouth and their tongues found one another. It was awkward at first, then they entwined in a rhythmic dance that their bodies somehow already knew the music to.

It was dizzying.

Dani had to stop and catch her breath. As she did, she was overwhelmed by the sweet fragrance of Michelle's hair—intoxicating, addictive. Her awakened body trembled with yearning for Michelle. She ran her fingers through Michelle's silky blonde hair, then buried her face in Michelle's curls, kissing her neck, and fumbling awkwardly with the clasps on Michelle's bra.

Michelle pulled one of the shoulder straps through her shirtsleeve and then the entire bra through the other. Dani ran her hand up Michelle's shirt, feeling Michelle's nipples harden under the touch of her fingertips.

Michelle moaned, sending waves of electricity through Dani's body. "I love you, Dani," she whispered.

"I love you too, Michelle," she'd whispered back, pulling Michelle closer.

SEI

Dani woke to a loud buzzing. She tried to ignore it, but it continued. She reached over Marisol for the purple vibrator. It was off. The noise continued. She realized it was her apartment doorbell. She hoped whoever it was would go away, but the buzzer buzzed insistently. She pushed the covers off and got up. Her head hurt from the beers and tequila shots from the night before. When the bartender found out it was her birthday he'd given her a free shot, and when she'd shared the story of how she'd gotten fired, he gave her free drinks all night. She was a loyal customer.

Dani walked across the room and pressed the intercom button. "Hello?"

Veronica's voice blared over the speaker. "Dani, come downstairs."

"Maybe when the room stops spinning," Dani whined into the intercom.

"Get. Dressed. Now," Veronica insisted.

"I have company."

"You got yourself a birthday present, huh?" Veronica asked, the annoyance in her tone was clear. "I'm not leaving."

"You're relentless." Dani released the intercom button. She begrudgingly threw on last night's jeans, a fresh tee-shirt, and a black sweater, then gently nudged Marisol awake.

"*Buenos días,* sexy. Time to get up," she said.

The girl woke up and smiled. "Mmm, *buenos días.*" She went to kiss Dani, but Dani stopped her.

"I'm sorry, hottie, but I gotta go, which means you gotta go."

Hurt and a bit confused, Marisol got out of the bed and began looking for her clothes.

Dani picked up Marisol's lacy red panties and tossed them to her. "You don't want to forget these," she said.

Marisol muttered something in Spanish that Dani couldn't make out as she went to the bathroom to pee.

Dani made the bed and laid the rest of Marisol's clothes on it. Marisol returned from the bathroom looking pissed. She quickly put on her bra and her sexy dress that was never meant to see the light of day.

"Last night was amazing," Dani said, grabbing her jacket and ushering the girl out of the apartment and into the elevator.

Marisol caught a glimpse of her mussed reflection in the elevator mirror. She pulled a lipstick from her purse and did her best to apply it.

"You're really hot!" Dani said, smiling at her.

She didn't smile back.

As soon as the elevator door opened, Marisol stormed out. The sight of Veronica standing by her red moped waiting for Dani was the ultimate indignity. "*Pinche pendeja,*" she yelled and flipped them both off hurrying down the street as fast as her high heels would take her.

Veronica looked at Dani and shook her head. "Taco Tuesday, huh."

Dani mean-mugged her. "That's racist and totally insensitive."

"Uh, I'm Mexican. I can make that joke."

"It was Marisol Monday!"

Veronica held out a white helmet with a pink RIDING BITCH sticker. "Get on."

Dani reluctantly took the helmet, put it on and tightened the straps. "Was dominatrix one of the top three ranked careers on your high school aptitude test?"

"Yeah. Was yours gynecologist?"

"I prefer to be more selective than that occupation allows."

Veronica shook her head. "Could have fooled me."

Dani straddled the shiny red moped and wrapped her arms around Veronica. "Where are we going?" Dani asked.

"You'll see."

They rode to the Embarcadero and then up to North Beach. Veronica parked in front of Stella's Italian Bakery.

Dani took off the helmet. "A bakery?"

"I always come here when I'm depressed," Veronica said.

"I'm not depressed, I'm unemployed. It's different."

Dani got off the moped. They walked to Stella's. She opened the door for Veronica. "After you."

"Snag us a table. I'll get the cappuccinos." Veronica beelined for the pastry counter.

Dani sat down at the table by the window and stared out at the passing cars. They were going somewhere. They had purpose. She felt like her life was going in circles, or worse, circling the drain.

Veronica placed two cups with saucers on the table and sat down. "I'm sorry I got you fired."

"It wasn't all your fault," Dani said, stirring the foam in her cappuccino with a small silver spoon. "It was because I couldn't make a decent cappuccino like this."

Veronica looked into her eyes. "Please go to Venice."

"To learn how to make decent cappuccino?"

"No, to finally write your novel."

"Seriously, Veronica." Dani set the spoon down and stared at her friend. "Are you *loca?*"

Veronica took Dani's hand in hers. She looked into Dani's eyes with a softness Dani hadn't seen before. "Please go. I'll take care of your plant."

"Her name is Fern and she needs to be talked to every day, so I can't go."

"I'll take care of Fern and I'll talk to her. I owe you."

Dani cupped her chin in her hand and starred at the table. She couldn't hold Veronica's gaze. "I'm going back to Seattle."

"Finish your novel first. Please," Veronica persisted. It made Dani uncomfortable. She wasn't letting this go. "What about that ring your dad gave you? I'm sure it's worth a lot. Sell it and use the money to go to Italy and finish your novel. I'm telling you, Dani, Venice is the perfect place to write."

"I'm gonna live with my mom for a few months and look for a job. That's more practical."

"When did you become so basic? Wouldn't your dad tell you to follow your dreams if he was alive?"

"Well, he's not and I'm not sure why everyone's invoking his ghost lately."

Veronica looked confused. "What do you mean?"

"Nothing, my dad is dead. Can we move on and talk about something else? Your favorite scone recipes, perhaps? New ways to devil an egg?"

"I'm sorry, Dani, but you told me your dream was to be a published novelist by your twenty-fifth birthday."

"Yeah, well dreams die too."

Veronica slapped her hand on the table, causing the cappuccinos to spill and the saucers to rattle. "Maybe if you put half the energy into your writing that you put into trying to sleep with every girl in San Francisco, you'd at least have a first draft. And if you go back to Seattle now, you'll never write. You'll just be her plaything. She's never going to take you seriously."

"Jeezus, Veronica! Thanks, for the pep talk. I sure feel better now."

Dani stared out the window.

Veronica shook her head. "You know what your problem is, Dani. You went deep with Michelle and you got hurt, so you're unwilling to go deep with anyone and that includes your writing. It's like you're committed to never letting anyone get close to you again. You refuse to be vulnerable. You refuse to really feel anything. When artists refuse to feel, they get stuck or they make shitty art. You need to get back into your broken heart and stop playing with everyone else's."

"You make me sound like a pathetic cliché."

"Then stop acting like one, and go to Venice. You need to get back into your senses, into your real emotions." Veronica reached out her hand and placed it on Dani's. "Don't you see? The Universe is setting you free to focus on your writing."

"Nope, I definitely don't see that." Dani picked up a cannoli and took a bite. It was sweet and creamy. "Oh my god, this is good." She licked the cream from the corner of her mouth and took another bite. She tasted hints of cinnamon and orange rind. "This is delicious," she said, her mouth full of pastry, "almost as good as sex."

Veronica gave Dani a seductive look. "If you think cannoli is almost as good as sex, then you need to have Italian gelato, *IT IS* as good as sex."

Dani rolled her eyes. "Nothing is as good as sex, Veronica."

"Gelato is. It's like the nectar of the gods."

"Seriously, is there a word for people who have erotic feelings towards food?" Dani cocked an eyebrow. "*Nymph-food-maniac?*"

Veronica smiled. "The word is *foodie,* and I'm trying to tell you, Venice is like a sexy woman who will get your creative juices flowing. You're creatively constipated."

"Are you calling me a shithead?"

"I didn't become a Chronicle Books bestselling author just by eating good food. I know how to seduce my muse, Dani, and you don't."

"What do you mean? I'm a great seducer."

"You know how to seduce women. That's not the same as seducing your creative muse. Being a creator. Bringing things to life. You're just fucking away your potential. Spilling your proverbial seed. Venice can change that for you."

"Wow, you are relentless." Dani starred at her.

Veronica's words stung, but she couldn't argue with Veronica about writing. Veronica was successful. She essentially had Dani's dream jobs: writing part-time for the *San Francisco Chronicle* and penning her own books. She'd already published three books and she was only two years older than Dani. Veronica was highly regarded when it came to food lit. But she wasn't sure Veronica's advice would translate to her own stalled-out projects. She'd struggled for years trying to construct a realistic plotline for her novel.

Still, maybe Veronica was right, maybe time away would give her the space to outline the bones of her novel and really give it flesh. Get it touch with whatever it was that was missing from her writing.

"What is gelato anyway?" Dani asked, hoping to lighten the mood.

"I can't believe you're Italian and you've never had gelato."

"Well, I'm Jewish too and I'm sure there's a ton of Jewish food I've never had either, like . . . what's that stuff . . . guff-filter fish?"

"Gefilte fish." Veronica made a gagging noise. "You're not missing anything there, but gelato . . . ," she paused for a moment. She looked wistful.

Dani tried not to smirk. It always cracked her up when Veronica talked about food like someone would a summer romance.

"Gelato is Italian ice cream, and it's even better in Italy where it's like the fifth food group. The *stracciatella* is the best chocolate chip ice cream you've never had. Rich velvety chocolate and sweet milk. Then there's the *coco,* the smoothest coconut ice cream. Oh god, and then there's orange chocolate gelato and pistachio gelato. And Oh. My. God. I almost forgot my favorite: whipped ricotta with caramelized figs. It's like eating a velvet cloud."

"Down girl!" Dani said, feeling slightly aroused, and at the same time flustered, by Veronica's public display of affection for this mystery dessert.

"You have no idea. When I'm in Italy I have it three times a day. There's after lunch gelato, afternoon gelato, and evening gelato. It's the only way to experience all the flavors."

"Is there somewhere here in North Beach where we can get some?"

"Of course."

Dani looked playfully at Veronica. "If gelato really is as good as sex, and I do mean *as good as sex,* I'll sell the ring and go to Venice. But if it's not, you can never say another bad thing about Michelle ever again. Capeesh?"

Veronica looked at her flatly. "Are you making a joke or a wager?"

Dani pursed her lips and looked defiantly into Veronica's eyes. "A promise, beyotch."

SETTE

45

Dani couldn't believe she was standing in Marco Polo Airport in Venice, Italy. "Damn gelato," she murmured.

OTTO

Dani could have reneged on the bet, but she'd learned early on from her father that when you give your word you follow through. Veronica was right about that gelato: It was as good as sex. Not better, but the chocolate with peanut butter was at least as good.

It was a fourteen-hour flight from SFO to Marco Polo. During the last two hours of the flight there was so much turbulence no one could get up to use the restroom. As soon as she deplaned, Dani looked around for the bathroom with the symbol with the dress. It always made her feel uncomfortable. Gender-neutral bathrooms were rare and she had to pee—she didn't have the luxury of time to go exploring for one. She took a cautious first step through the entrance, relieved to find the bathroom empty.

Dressed in masculine clothing, with cropped hair, Dani was often mistaken for male. It never bothered her; she was a proud butch, after all. But it had its hazards when it came to public restrooms.

Dani quickly wheeled her suitcase into the stall closest to the entry and sat down. She heard the sound of high heels clicking through the bathroom and then it was quiet. Relieved to be alone, she peed. Within moments she heard a man's voice saying something in Italian, then she saw a broom come under the stall door. She realized that he was yelling at her in Italian as he was whacking at her feet with the broom. She didn't understand what he was saying, but she could assume.

Dani flushed the toilet, buttoned up her jeans, and opened the door. She pointed to her breasts and glared at the man.

The man realized his mistake.

"*Mi dispiace,*" he said, repeatedly, lowering his head.

Dani wheeled her suitcase out of the bathroom and tried to reorient herself toward the airport exit. The flow of traffic from the plane was gone now and the green signs that hung from the ceiling were in Italian—totally useless to her.

Dani had charged the plane ticket on her credit card, called an apartment rental company, got an expedited passport and an international adapter/plug-in jack for her computer, and gave Veronica a key to her apartment to water Fern. "She better be alive when I come back," she'd warned Veronica.

Now here she was in Europe for the first time, in Italy, with no knowledge of Italian. She looked around for a sign for the ferry, but everything was confusing. *I should've listened to those damn* Learn Italian While You Drive *CDs on the plane,* she thought. Instead, she'd loaded her iPod with the newish Everything But the Girl *Adapt or Die* CD and listened to their extended remixes from the last decade. She also indulged in two newly released inflight movies: *The Devil Wears Prada* and *The DaVinci Code.* The movies made the long flight bearable.

She approached a ticket window. "Hi, where is the ferry to Venice."

The young woman behind the counter seemed annoyed by the question. "There." She pointed to a sign with a drawing of a boat with blue waves and an arrow pointing to a pathway. "You walk left. Seven minutes to waterbus."

Dani made her way down to the pier. The path seemed endless. By the time she arrived, she was overheated. She took off her plaid jacket and sat down on a bench on the floating dock. A young couple on the bench across from her were entwined in each other's limbs. They looked so in love. She felt overwhelmed with jealously as they laughed and spoke intimately in a language that was unfamiliar to her.

She took out her father's yellowed map that she found in the box under her bed. She used it now to block their public display of sexuality in honor of Eros. She noticed an area circled in pencil: the Venetian Ghetto. She couldn't remember anything specific about her father's travels in Venice, or any other part of Italy for that matter, only that he loved it and promised to take her with him when she graduated from high school. A promise he couldn't keep.

She didn't tell Veronica this. It was too sad to think about and such a strange coincidence. Besides, she wasn't going to give Veronica one more reason to pressure her into going. Dani wasn't much for new-age synchronicities, like Veronica was. Veronica was always finding coincidences and secret meanings in things. Numerology this, astrology that. Dani was more practical. The gelato was simply the final confirmation that convinced Dani that she really should go and give herself time to write and finally complete her novel. Then she could go back to Seattle with something to show for herself.

The pier began to rock. Dani looked up from the map. Through the fogged-up windows on the enclosed floating pier,

Dani saw a white boat approaching. As it approached, it rocked the pier with a greater ferocity, almost knocking over a woman standing next to her. The boat docked and a flood of people and baggage disembarked—a chaotic medley of language and luggage.

"Is this the boat to Fondamente Nove?" she asked the waterbus driver, glancing at the paper from the apartment rental company.

"*Prego,*" he said, motioning her on board.

She handed him the exact amount of euros the apartment rental company told her it cost for a one-way fare on the *alilaguna,* the special waterbus that took passengers from the airport across the lagoon to Venice. She stepped on board and took a seat near the boat's exit. She was glad she exchanged her money at San Francisco Airport. Her mother had insisted she do that when Dani called her to say goodbye from the airport payphone.

"Do you have the address and directions of where they are meeting you and the phone number of the apartment rental company in case your plane gets in late?" her mom asked.

"Yep."

"Your tickets and your passport?"

"Mom, I couldn't have gotten this far into the airport without them."

"Did you exchange your money?"

"I'll do it when I get there."

"No, do it now! You don't want to show up empty handed. Get some Italian liras before you go."

"It's euros now, Mom. If I get liras, I'm really gonna be in a bind."

"You know what I mean," her mother said, the irritation in her voice plain.

"Fine, I'll get some now."

"Get a phone card now too and call me when you get there!" Her mother insisted.

"I'll call you when I land."

"No, call me after you settle in wherever you're staying."

"I love you too." Dani hung up the phone quickly before her mother thought of anything else that hadn't been accounted for.

Dani knew she should be more sensitive about her mother's worries. Travel of any kind triggered her mother's anxiety and memories of her father's death. During a business trip he had stopped to put on chains during a snowstorm and was struck by a car that skidded out of control. He was killed instantly. Dani knew her mom was handling her traveling as best she could, but still, all the fussing made her feel smothered.

The boat traveled across the water leaving white waves in its wake. The ocean breeze felt good on her face. She loved the scent of the salty air that filled the boat's cabin, the smell reminded her of walking the stalls at Pike Place Market in Seattle and meandering the tourist stops at San Francisco's Fisherman's Wharf, places where she'd felt inexplicably at ease. She wondered what it was that drew her, almost unconsciously, to these cities where land and sea met and mingled, not with the force of the ocean, but the quietude of a coastal bay. They all ached with a dull gray.

She pondered that momentarily until the boat began passing several dilapidated buildings that looked like warehouses. *Surely these are not the "architectural delights" Veronica promised.* The misty haze on the horizon, coupled with the grayish buildings, evoked a sense of loneliness in her. A feeling she'd managed to stave off since leaving Seattle. She turned her head and looked away.

On the other side of the boat, she saw a fifteen-foot-high brick wall that ran the perimeter of the island and what looked like floating streetlamps in the water near the island's shore. As the boat edged closer, Dani noticed that the lamps were mounted on poles that protruded from the water and didn't seem to be configured in any particular pattern. Their chaotic arrangement disturbed her sense of order.

"*Cimetero,*" the waterbus driver said and pointed to the island.

Is that wall to keep us out or to keep them in? she wished she could say in Italian, not wanting to miss an opportunity for a bad joke.

As she reflected on the mixed fortune of the dead having their own island, the other passengers suddenly reached for their belongings.

Dani turned around and the city came into view. It was nothing like she could ever have imagined. The buildings were painted brightly—some were cotton candy pink and yellow pastel, others were dark red, deep orange, and mustard—and they were all mirrored in the water. It was like the buildings were floating, the blue-gray water meeting their foundations. The structures delighted her. Her eyes were drawn to white wooden terraces intricately carved into shapes and designs that one might see peering into a kaleidoscope: four-leaf clover patterns, crosses, repeating arches. The architecture was beautiful and unique. Domes and steeples dominated the skyline. *This is what Veronica was talking about!* She took an expansive breath feeling the city cast its magic upon her.

The waterways were full of life. Sleek brown wooden speedboats plowed past them, each sporting an Italian flag and a yellow banner with the word *TAXI* in all caps taped to the side of the cabin window. There were several other boats in the waterway that resembled city buses filled to the brim with passengers. A few boats chugged along carrying cargo, one with endless crates of milk and another loaded with vegetables.

Her boat docked alongside an enclosed floating pier painted white and yellow. One of the crewmen hoisted a thick braided rope over a steel dock cleat, anchoring the boat to the dock. He drew back the metal gate and the seasoned passengers moved quickly off the boat.

As she shuffled off the boat with the much slower tourists lugging their luggage, a beautiful dark-haired woman briefly caught her eye. She seemed familiar. Dani was trying to make the connection of who this woman reminded her of when her eyes landed on a sign with her name on it. The sign was held by a man who wore his sunglasses on top of his head, which made his thinning, grayish brown hair appear slightly thicker and had the unintended effect of protecting that part of his scalp from the afternoon sun. He was dangling the sign haphazardly with one hand while his other held a freshly lit cigarette.

"Maurizio?" she asked.

"*Sì,* Daniela Riman?" Maurizio exhaled, blowing smoke to the side of Dani's face.

"Dani," she replied, stepping further to the left in case the smoke decided to follow her. It would be awkward to try and shake his hand since he was smoking.

"You come here alone?" he asked.

"Yes," she said. Not sure what his question was implying.

"*Va bene.* How was your flight?" Maurizio asked, but didn't bother to listen to Dani's reply. He dropped his cigarette on the walkway and took hold of her black suitcase.

"I got it," she said and wrangled it back from him. She could manage her own luggage and wasn't going to accommodate his male cultural prescription to carry her luggage.

Maurizio shrugged and hailed a water taxi. The boat beelined for the dock. Maurizio held out his hand to assist Dani into the boat. She pretended not to see it and got into the water taxi unassisted.

"Riva di Biasio," Maurizio instructed the driver. He turned to Dani. "It's only a short ride."

As the boat edged into the canal, she glimpsed her first gondola—a sleek, black, coffin-like boat with a petite velvet love seat and red-fringed pillows. The boat was guided by a man in a black-and-white striped shirt sporting a wide-brimmed straw hat with a red ribbon. She watched the boat skim effortlessly over the water.

"This is the *Canale Grande* of *Venezia,*" Maurizio said.

Dani craned her neck to look at the buildings they were passing.

It was beautiful. *The kind of place you'd go on your honeymoon,* she thought. The thought depressed her.

"*Fa bel tempo, no?*" the driver asked Maurizio.

"*Si, la primavera è bellisima.*"

Dani knew the word *bellisima* meant "beautiful," and she felt confident that they were not describing her.

Most men were not really sure how to take Dani, which had led to some interesting chances to eavesdrop into the lives of men. Once in college, a fellow classmate thought he was talking to one of the guys and offered up his assessment of their teacher's anatomy. "Man, she ain't much too look at, but she's got some nice tits. Don't you think?" Dani laughed at him. She appreciated women and boobs, but not the male propensity to reduce women to their parts.

"This is it." Maurizio stood up before the boat docked and grabbed Dani's luggage before she could. "*Andiamo.* We go."

Dani followed behind him, enchanted by the cobblestone walkway. Maurizio turned left down a cramped alley that couldn't have been more than three-feet wide and led to a blind corner. They turned the corner and the narrow passageway opened up to a less restrictive alley about eight-feet across—wide enough to relieve her previous feeling of claustrophobia. It led to a hemmed in courtyard of four-story apartment buildings that Dani guessed were at least three hundred years old. They were painted brightly in solid yellow and orange hues. The stucco of the building was chipped in several places, exposing a pink and red brick structure underneath.

The antiquity of the buildings had a magical, dreamlike quality in comparison to the edifices in the suburbs where she grew up. By contrast, the courtyard had a somberness to it. It was bricked up and, with the exception of a handful of window boxes freckled with red and pink geraniums, it lacked nature. It felt stoic and cold, like a prison rec yard.

"How do cars get down these streets?" she asked.

Maurizio shook his head. "No cars in *Venezia*. We are built on lagoon. We are one hundred and fifty canals here. Our transport is boat or walking. This street is called Calle de Figher. You see sign there?" Maurizio pointed to the white street sign with black capital letters affixed to the building.

"Do you have bicycles?"

"On Lido, yes, but Venezia no. With so many *pontes*—you say *bridges*—a bicycle would be useless." Maurizio stopped in front of a faded yellow, four-story building with white wood-framed windows. "We are arrived." He pointed to a second-story window with a green-and-white striped awning. "That is you."

Dani looked up at the building. Sheets, shirts, and socks hung on a clothesline coming from a third-story window. *This is authentic Italy,* she thought. It delighted her that she was going to be sleeping in an apartment building from the seventeenth century.

Maurizio unlocked the thick wooden front door. "Come," he said and stepped inside the darkened alcove. "Light for hallway," he said, pointing to a switch on the wall, but not turning it on. He ascended the stone steps, still carrying Dani's suitcase.

Dani gripped the cold metal handrail as she climbed the stairs, following behind him. He stopped at the top of the first flight of stairs. There were two doors leading to two apartments.

"Your *casa,*" he said, fumbling for the keys in his pocket and unlocked the door on the right. He held out his hand to invite her in.

Dani walked inside. The apartment was as cramped as the streets they'd taken to get here. There was a narrow hallway that led to a bathroom-sized kitchen with a sink, an undersized stove, a three-quarter-sized refrigerator, and a dining table pushed against the wall with a cute flowering plant on it. One person could fit comfortably in this kitchen, two not so easily.

Maurizio left the keys on the marble-topped counter and continued with the tour of the tiny apartment. The bedroom here and the bathroom." He pointed to both rooms from the hallway. "Is good?" Maurizio asked. He seemed anxious to leave.

"Yes, this is good," she said, though struck by how small the apartment was. There wasn't even a living room, not even a couch. She wasn't sure how it was possible, but this one-bedroom apartment seemed even smaller than her studio back in San Francisco. Still her heart fluttered with excitement. She was a traveling writer now, prioritizing her craft. This would be her sanctuary.

"OK, you need anything, you call." Maurizio opened the door to leave.

Dani looked around. "Where is the telephone?"

"You must go around the corner to DeLucia's Café. There is payphone in *campo.*"

"*Campo?*" Dani asked.

"What you call a 'square,'" he explained.

It took a moment for Dani to register what he'd said as his accent was so thick. "The big courtyard?"

"*Sì. Ciao,*" he called out, shutting the door behind him.

"*Ciao,*" Dani answered back.

Travel weary, she walked into the bedroom and put her laptop bag on the handmade, ancient-looking wooden desk by the window, then dropped in full yawn on the bed. It was low to the ground, like it was missing a box spring. She plumped up the two white pillowcases behind her head and wrapped herself in the flower print bedspread that seemed to clash with the stone mosaic floor, a mixture of black and white marble fragments and gray stones. Her eyes took in her new surroundings. The walls were pink with one framed painting of a gray vase with pink flowers. A fluffy white lace curtain covered the window and two simple wooden nightstands flanked the bed, one held a frosted glass lamp.

It was a bit girlie for her tastes, but she appreciated that it was minimalistic and clean, which meant fewer distractions. She felt confident that here she wouldn't get caught up in binge cleaning, a habit that often kept her from focusing on her writing. At home, she would turn on her laptop and then suddenly find herself dusting the tops of the baseboards or reorganizing her closet. Sometimes it reached obsessive heights. One day she'd powered up her laptop, sat down to write, and within two minutes had abandoned her computer and was sitting in front of the bookshelf arranging the books according to their size and thickness, some sort of feng shui aesthetic she'd read about. *There will be none of that,* she thought.

She was relieved that there wasn't a television, telephone line, or modem in the apartment because that would have led to numerous distractions like emailing friends or watching indecipherable Italian television shows. It was just her and her unwritten novel. Maybe now she could finally focus on it. She felt both grateful for the space and suffocated by it.

Dani got up to change into her version of pajamas—black sweatpants and a sweatshirt. She reached up to unclasp the green agate and tiger eye necklace she wore. She took it off and held it in her hand. She felt its weight.

Michelle had given Dani the necklace in the new part of the old pioneer cemetery where Dani's father was buried. It was Dani's seventeenth birthday and she wanted to celebrate it with her dad and Michelle. Michelle thought it was a bit weird and dramatic, but then Michelle was always teasing Dani about the morbid things she did. They'd taken a picnic basket and a blanket and sat next to Dani's father's headstone eating Hostess dessert pies—chocolate and coconut—Dani's two favorite flavors.

Michelle had told her to close her eyes and then kissed her deeply before placing a wrapped package in her hand.

"What is it?" Dani asked.

Michelle smiled. "Open it."

Dani unwrapped the present, the necklace. She loved it immediately. Dani wasn't a fan of jewelry, but something about the look and the feel of the reddish brown of the tiger's eye stones appealed to her. She ran her fingers over the smooth stones. "It's beautiful," she told Michelle.

Michelle helped Dani put it on. She beamed at her. "When you wear it, Dani, you'll feel my love and know I love you." Michelle had said so earnestly.

Dani ran her fingers over the polished stones on the necklace, remembering that moment. Now when she wore it, the weight around her neck was a constant reminder of how sweet love could be, and how cruel. She put it on the night-stand and looked at the clock. It was only 6:16 PM, but she was so tired. She got into bed and closed her eyes hoping to fall asleep so she could wake up early and start writing her novel.

NOVE

Dani startled awake in the unfamiliar bed. A wave of panic rushed over her. She hadn't called her mother. *Oh god, I'll never hear the end of it.*

She dressed quickly, grabbed the keys, and hurried down the darkened stairwell to the café that Maurizio had told her about. It was still light out and she easily found the café, but without a phone card, the payphone was useless. She went inside. A man was wiping down a glass pastry cabinet full of tarts, croissants, and cream puffs that sat atop a marble counter. The pastries looked delicious, but she wasn't hungry.

"Do you know where I can find a phone card?" she asked him.

The man looked to be in his mid-fifties. He might have been mistaken for Marlon Brando in his later years, though he had a slighter build and seemed more affable than Brando.

"*Sì, il tabacchi,*" the man said.

Dani grimaced. "Sorry, I only speak English and *un poco español.*"

"*Non capisce? Un momento, per piacere.*" The man turned from Dani. "*Gina, Gina,*" he called out.

Dani could see a young woman chopping vegetables in the back room.

"*Che padre?*" the woman called back continuing to chop vegetables.

"Ho bisogno di un interprete." The man beckoned. *"Americano."*

The young woman washed her hands in the kitchen sink and wiped them on a towel before coming out of the back room. She had long brown hair with reddish highlights, brown eyes, full pink lips, and a slender figure. She looked a little like the actress in that movie Dani had watched on the plane, Anne Hathaway.

The young woman approached Dani. "Can I help you?" she asked, looking a bit surprised.

Dani recognized the look. It was that "Sir, I'm so sorry, ma'am" look.

"Americana, padre," she said to her father, emphasizing the 'a' at the end."

"Scusi," her father said, his cheeks turning a darker shade of red.

Dani shifted uncomfortably. "I need a phone card," she said. "Do you know where I can get one?"

"Yes, at the *tabacchi,"* the woman replied.

"The *tabacchi?"* Dani said, trying to pronounce the word right.

The young woman smiled and repeated the word again like an adult would when teaching a child. *"Sì,* go over the bridge and walk until you can't go any farther, then go right again." She traced the air with her finger. "Then go left until you see the pizzeria. At the pizzeria, go left."

Dani thanked her and walked out of the café. She tried to remember the directions the young woman relayed to her as she crossed the bridge. She turned right and then kept walking, looking for the pizzeria and for the *tabacchi.* She saw neither. After about thirty minutes of going up and down the narrow alleyways, she stopped a gray-haired woman, her arms loaded full of groceries.

"*Tabacchi?*" Dani asked, hoping she was pronouncing the word correctly.

"*Sì, a sinistra,*" the woman said and tried to point to the left without dropping her groceries.

"*Gracias,*" Dani said, offering her thanks in Spanish. She walked a few more blocks and seeing nothing, asked a man walking a butterscotch cocker spaniel. The dog barked at her and wagged its tail excitedly.

"*Tabacchi?*"

"*Diritto,*" the man said and pointed forward. "*È vicino.*"

Why didn't I listen to those damn CDs? she thought. She followed the line of his finger and noticed a big wooden sign with a "T" on it. *Please let this be it!*

Dani opened the door to the building. A bearded man sat behind the counter reading a newspaper and smoking a pipe. *This looks right.* She approached the counter.

"Phone card?" she asked.

He put down his paper, but not his pipe, to retrieve the card from the cash register. "*Quale?*"

Dani stared at him not knowing how to answer. "English?" she asked, embarrassed.

"International or Italian?" the beard asked flatly.

The door opened and customers took their place in line behind her. She could feel their irritation. "International," she said, reduced to speaking in one-word sentences.

"Five euros," he said and abruptly placed the card and a receipt on a glass tray on the counter.

Dani fished in her pocket for the money and handed it to him. She had to squeeze by the other patrons who were not interested in making her exit easy. She pushed past a backpacker, wearing a blue bandana. He reminded her of one of the jocks from her high school. She hated jocks. She had good reasons to. He gave her the stink eye as she passed. She assumed it was because she was gay, but he could have been annoyed with her like the others were for slowing the line down. They all seemed to lack patience for bumbling tourists.

Outside of the *tabacchi* she was disoriented, forgetting which direction she'd come from. Another flutter of panic passed through her. She looked around and mentally retraced her steps. Most of the buildings looked the same: sporting red, yellow, or pink stucco, with whole sheets of stucco torn away, exposing red and gray bricks. She'd never seen buildings this old in her life. The oldest building in Seattle, the Ward House, built in 1882, was only 124 years old. The Ward House seemed modern compared to the buildings in Venice; these were at least 300 years old (three centuries old).

As she looked around, Dani realized that every building in Venice was built before the United States was even a glimmer in the Founding Fathers' minds. She tried to imagine the generations of children raised in those apartments and the dramas that unfolded in the cobblestone streets around her. She wondered how the women were treated, especially women like her, and how they survived. It boggled her mind to think about the weight of history.

She continued walking and wondered if she was anywhere close to the apartment or if she was wandering farther and farther away. She heard her mother's voice scolding in her head. *I told you to buy that phone card before you got on the plane.*

Dani was grateful when she spotted DeLucia's Café. It stood out to her now like a land mass to a sea-weary sailor. She scratched off the metallic covering on the card as she walked towards the payphone. She made several unsuccessful attempts to call her mother, unable to figure out what sequence of numbers to dial. Then she saw the country code for the United States listed with other country codes on a plastic frame on the phone. She dialed again. This time it rang and she was relieved to hear the sound of her mother's answering machine pick up.

After the beep, Dani said, "Hi, Mom, sorry I missed you. I'm here. The apartment's good, clean and everything. There's no phone, so I can't leave you a number. You have the number for the rental company so if there are any emergencies you can call me there. I'll call again in a few days. Love you."

Dani hung up the phone thrilled to have avoided a litany of questions about her trip and with the fact that she was not obligated to anyone. She looked around and smiled at the ancient buildings. She'd done it. She'd taken a huge leap of faith by not filching on her bet with Veronica and here she was in this beautiful city on the sea. She sauntered back to the apartment feeling triumphant.

Once inside the apartment, she took out her laptop and placed it on the table. She also pulled her blue spiral notebook and favorite pen from her suitcase and laid them next to the laptop. "All right, Venice, work your magic," she said, then crawled back into the bed and turned off the light to sleep.

DIECI

Around 5:00 AM, Dani woke up shivering. She got out of bed and went to look for the thermostat, the words *non toccare grazie* were handwritten on it. She knew that in Spanish *no tocar* meant "don't touch," but it was freezing in the apartment so she moved the lever anyway and waited. Nothing happened. The room stayed cold. The cold marble floor added to the chill she felt in her bones. She opened her suitcase and threw all of her clothes on top of the covers, got back in bed, and pulled the covers tighter around her.

Dani lay in the bed, wide awake. She wanted to sleep, but she couldn't stop thinking about Michelle, and thinking about Michelle meant thinking about Sean.

Sean McMurty was their high school's cherished football champion. He was six-three and 211 pounds, with short brown hair, blue eyes, and, except for the gap between his two front teeth, a perfect smile. Sean was the school's running back and linebacker celebrated in the *Komo Sports* newspaper for "scoring twenty touchdowns for the Rough Riders and rushing 1,377 yards on 198 carries." *Whatever the hell that means?* Dani thought when she'd read it. Sean's football accomplishments had been the cover story for their lame school newspaper—*The Rough Rider Reader*—on multiple occasions.

Dani wrote for the newspaper and thought there were more interesting stories to write about. She had proposed a piece on the Sheryl Crow album banned by Walmart because it had a song blaming Walmart for selling ammo to kids who killed people. Dani also proposed a "Where are they today?" story about American citizens of Japanese ancestry who were forcibly taken from their homes in and around Seattle and interned in camps during World War II. Her classmates summarily dismissed her ideas. They wanted to write about Sean's impressive performance on the field compared to other football greats at his age. She resented him and his success. The world was given to him on a silver platter and it still wasn't enough. He had to come for the scraps life had given her.

One memory that stuck in her mind and skipped like a broken record in a deep groove was the afternoon she'd gone to meet Michelle at her locker and found Michelle and Sean deep in conversation.

"Why are you hanging out with that freak?" she'd overheard him ask.

"Her math has improved a lot because of MY tutoring her, Sean," Michelle had replied.

Sean combed his fingers through his hair. "Michelle, you're a saint. I remember when we were in Sunday school and you found that baby bird that had fallen out of its nest and you asked me to help you put it back in."

"You remember that, Sean?" Michelle had asked coyly.

"Yeah. I have a lot of good memories from back then."

Sean had grinned so wide that Dani had wanted to punch his teeth out. "Well, I gotta get to practice. Let me know if she tries to go lezzie on you. I don't usually hit girls, but Riman doesn't count." Sean sniffed and then rubbed his nose like a prizefighter.

Dani had stood there frozen in the empty hallway until she heard the squeak of Sean's shoes coming in her direction. Sean saw her as he rounded the corner. He intentionally bumped into her with his shoulder as he passed, knocking her off balance and out of his way.

"Watch it, jerk!" she'd yelled, stifling her desire to shove him back. If her cards had been dealt differently, and she'd been born male, she would have whipped his ass. She tried to regain her composure and walked towards Michelle's locker.

"Hey, Michelle, what's up?" she asked louder than she had expected. She tried to compensate by looking solemnly at Michelle and slumping James Dean-style against the row of gray lockers, trying to downplay her anger. She'd wondered if Michelle had meant what she said or if she was just trying to throw Sean off.

Michelle had turned to face her. "Nothing. You ready to hit the books?"

"Seems like something's up." Dani had felt her heart beating hard in her chest. "I'm your charity case, huh, your charitable project?"

"It's not like that," Michelle had said, smiling her perfect cheerleader smile. "I'm just trying to get him off my case. I have a reputation to uphold!"

"Yeah, and clearly you don't want it connected with mine," Dani said as she slung her black backpack over her shoulder.

Dani had tried to be compassionate and understanding and not take Michelle's fears of being "outed" personally. She had always known that Michelle's Evangelical Christian parents were barely tolerant of Michelle hanging out with someone who didn't go to church and that at one point her father had become highly suspicious about their relationship.

The memory stung. It had been so perfect early on. She wondered why things had had to change. Her mind wandered back to the December of their senior year in high school and she felt a pain in her stomach, the wound still fresh despite the fact that it was several years ago.

Sean had ruled Jock Corner, an unsupervised school hallway near a wall heater where the Junior Varsity and Varsity Football players liked to hang out. Junior and senior girls coveted the lockers close to Jock Corner so much that the school had created a lottery system to get one. While most of the other high school girls were gossiping about the high school jocks, Dani was sublimating herself in poetry and classical literary fiction. They were memorizing the birthdays and astrological signs of the varsity football team's quarterback and wide receivers, none of whose names she knew at the time, while Dani was memorizing the rhythm of iambic pentameter and heroic couplets. Dani didn't want to be anywhere near Jock Corner.

Unfortunately, she had to walk by it to get to biology class.

As Dani approached Jock Corner, she saw Sean surrounded by some of the other players. She walked at a relaxed pace, her black backpack slung over her left shoulder, and a can of Dr. Pepper in her right hand. She was almost through the gauntlet when the name-calling started.

"Nasty dyke!" Sean's voice was easily recognizable to her.

She felt her right leg give way. One of the jocks had come up behind her and kicked her hard behind the knee. Her leg buckled and she fell to the ground, spilling the Dr. Pepper all over her clothes and smacking her face on the hard floor. Dani tried to get up, but Sean pushed her back down. He grabbed her wallet from her back pocket and started thumbing through it.

"What's this?" he asked, brandishing a picture of Michelle.

"Give that back!" she yelled. She could feel the blood rush to her face.

Sean proudly held out the confiscated picture Michelle had given her. "Sick ass freak! Does Michelle know you jack your clam to this?" He put the picture in his pocket.

Dani got up and shot him a look that should have killed him on the spot, but it didn't, so, with trembling hands, she grabbed her wallet back from Sean. Then, ignoring the laughing and heckling behind her, she walked calmly to the water fountain and began filling the empty soda can with water, all the while a subterranean anger was welling up inside of her. Once the can was filled with water, she turned and walked back to Jock Corner. "You back for more?" he asked, surprised to see her standing there.

She stood there defiant staring him down and then threw the water ejaculation style into Sean's smug face. He hadn't expected it. None of them had.

For a moment she was triumphant, enjoying watching Sean wipe the water from his shocked face. "I'd rather be a dyke than a dickhole!" she said.

The bandana-wearing jock grabbed Dani by the hair and Sean punched her in the stomach, knocking the wind out of her. She doubled over.

"Smear the queer," a redheaded jock shouted. Luckily for Dani, the bell for sixth period rang and the jocks scattered to class, high-fiving each other on the way.

Dani may have lost this one, but she was glad she fought back. She could feel her left cheek swelling from where her face had made contact with the hallway floor and decided to skip the rest of her classes.

Back home, she lay on her bed listening to an Everything But the Girl CD. Shakespeare jumped on the bed and began nuzzling her. She stroked his back and he licked her cheek, purring loudly.

"Thanks, boy," she said, kissing the top of his head. The phone rang and a startled Shakespeare skittered out of the room.

"Hello," she answered gingerly. It hurt to talk. She held the receiver slightly away from her left cheek.

"Where were you? I waited for you for twenty minutes." Michelle sounded angry.

"I went home early." Dani pushed the PAUSE button on the CD player.

"Well, thanks a lot for telling me you weren't going to meet me."

"I had planned on meeting you," Dani groaned, her stomach still hurt, but she was grateful Sean hadn't hit her any higher, otherwise she might be in the hospital with broken ribs.

"What's going on? Why do you sound so weird?"

"Ask Sean."

"Dani, talk to me. What happened?" Michelle waited out the long silence, listening to Dani's breathing on the other end of the line.

Dani didn't want to tell Michelle what happened. She was torn between wanting Michelle's sympathy and not wanting Michelle to see her as weak. Finally, she admitted, "Sean and his jockstraps started some shit with me today. They were messing with me and Sean grabbed my wallet, and when he saw the picture of you . . . ," she hesitated, "well, he just went ballistic."

"Oh shit!"

"Sean McMurty is such a huge asshole! But I got him back." She told Michelle about her brief moment of revenge before getting tackled in the hallway.

"What did you think they'd do, Dani? You provoked them. Of course, they had to take it to the next level. Don't give them another reason to mess with you."

"Another reason? Me just being me is not giving them a reason to kick my ass. Whose side are you on here anyway?" Dani asked, surprised by Michelle's comment.

"I'm sorry that happened. They're stupid boys. Next time walk away. You could have gotten really hurt."

"I am hurt. Sean punched me so hard it knocked the wind out of me. My face is banged up too from that jock ass tripping me. Anyway, forget about it, you want to come over Saturday?"

"I can't. I promised Jennie and Shannon I'd get together with them to go over our new cheerleading routine."

"OK, how about Sunday?" Dani asked, surprised Michelle had made plans without telling her. They usually spent time together every weekend.

"Yeah, maybe Sunday. I gotta go, my mom is calling me." Michelle hung up.

Dani had called Michelle at least three times that Sunday, but never heard back from her. On Monday, she found Sean standing with Michelle at Michelle's locker. She waited until he walked off, then she approached Michelle.

"Did Sean come to confess to you what a total jerk off he is?" Dani asked sarcastically.

Michelle was looking into a flat makeup mirror affixed to the inside of her locker door and brushing her hair. She didn't look up. "No, he didn't." Her tone was matter-of-fact, like she was an expert witness giving professional testimony.

"What did he want?" Dani asked, leaning up against the open side of Michelle's locker.

Michelle continued examining her appearance in the mirror, fixing the collar of her lime-green shirt, and straightening her beaded necklace. "He invited me to the Winter Formal."

Dani felt a lump taking form in the back of her throat. She tried to get a glimpse of Michelle's face in the mirror. "You said no, right?"

"I said yes." Michelle focused intently on her lipstick.

"What? Why did you do that?" She couldn't believe what she was hearing. Dani touched Michelle on the shoulder, hoping to appeal to her. It backfired.

Michelle pulled away and her voice got quieter and even more professional. "How would I explain to my parents why I'm not going to my senior Winter Formal? Your mom can figure out why you're not going, but my dad is always asking me questions about you. I'm tired of having to come up with excuses about why I don't have a steady boyfriend. This will get them off my back for a while."

"But Sean?" Dani implored. It felt like she'd been punched in the stomach again, only worse.

Michelle stared back at Dani, her blue eyes icy. "Sean is the captain of the football team. He's a Christian. He's the kind of guy I should be seen with." Michelle shut her locker. "I have to go to class."

Michelle left Dani standing in the corridor, fighting hard to swallow the lump in her throat. Dani clenched her jaw and covered her face with her hand. She knew Michelle felt she had to hide their relationship. Still, she didn't understand how Michelle could have stooped so low. She would have gladly taken another physical beating from Sean and the other jocks if it would keep Michelle from going with him to the dance, but there was nothing she could do to stop it.

UNDICI

DeLucia's Café smelled of rich, earthy coffee and fresh pastries. *Veronica would love this place,* Dani thought. She surveyed the café and noted the table by the window bathed in the morning light. It was the perfect spot to write. Unfortunately, there was a businessman sitting there, reading his paper and leisurely sipping a cappuccino. She'd have to wait until he left to snag it.

Writing was hard enough as it was, she needed an ideal place to write. The perfect spot for inspiration was one where she would have minimal interruptions from the patrons. She hoped the guy would hurry up.

The young woman from the day before, Gina, was standing at the counter near the pastry cabinet, her reddish-brown hair pulled back in a ponytail. She wore a green apron over her tan pants and a white button-up blouse with the top two buttons left undone, revealing a silver cross. She was attractive, but a little younger than the women Dani dated. If she couldn't write, she could certainly flirt. Dani approached the counter.

"*Buongiorno,*" Gina said, smiling at her. "Did you find the *tabacchi?*"

"I did, thank you." Dani beamed back at her. She decided not to tell her how it took her over thirty minutes to find the *tabacchi* and that if the girl had just told her to look for a wooden sign with a "T" on it she would have found it right away. Dani studied the pastries behind the glass case. "Can I get a nonfat latte, one of those plain croissants, and a glass of orange juice?"

"*Non capisco*. Nonfat latte?" The young woman looked confused.

"Yeah, I'm trying to watch my girlish figure."

The young woman sized Dani up. "You will have *cappuccino.*"

Dani didn't want to be rude, but she knew she didn't need the extra calories. Weight gain made her body take on a more feminine appearance, a shape that troubled her.

"Where are you from?" the young woman asked, wiping off the silver milk steamer of the espresso maker with a coffee stained dishtowel.

"The United States," Dani said and thought she saw the girl trying to hide a smile.

"*Sì,* I mean where in United States?" She handed Dani the cappuccino in a white cup with a saucer and a small spoon.

Dani took the cup in her hand. "San Francisco, California."

"Ah, San Francisco, the Golden Gate Bridge, trolley cars, and the sea lions."

"You've been there?" Dani asked.

"*Sì,* my mother's uncle's cousin had a restaurant there."

"So, you're close? "Dani asked, sarcastically.

"We went for many summer times, but there are too many *heals.*"

"Heals?"

"*Sì,* not good for walking."

"Oh, *hills,*" Dani corrected, stifling a laugh. She thought the girl's accent was sweet.

"*Sì.*" The young woman put a croissant on a blue-and-yellow-patterned plate and poured Dani a glass of orange juice. "What brings you to *Venezia?*"

Dani put down the cup and reached into her pocket. "How much do I owe you?" she asked, pulling a bill out of her wallet, and hoping to avoid the question.

"*Sette euro,*" the girl said and fired off another question. "You are here on vacation?"

"Not exactly. I'm here to work on some writing."

"Writing? Like book?"

"A novel," Dani said sheepishly.

"What's it about?"

Dani bit the side of her cheek. She hated having to explain what she was writing about. "It's kind of complicated."

The young woman grabbed the dishtowel to wipe down the marble counter. "I can handle complicated," she said.

"It's about a female bank robber who hears a crime victim's story while she's in prison and it triggers her guilt over what she's done so she goes to therapy to deal with it and her childhood abuse. In the end she gives up her life of crime to help others."

"I like she heals her abuse and helps others. I would like to read it."

"You would?" Dani asked, laughing. "It sounds a little schmaltzy to me, plus I just made it up."

"What?" The young woman looked confused. She went to throw the dishcloth at her but stopped herself. "Are you here to write novel or to play tricks on Venetians?"

"I never considered that as an option. I might be better at that then writing."

"So, you are really a writer?"

"I'm trying to be. I came here to write. Too many distractions back home."

"Now I distract you. Please, sit down. I'll bring these to you," the woman said, referring to the croissant and orange juice she held in her hands.

Dani wondered if she had offended her with the joke. Veronica, on the other hand, would have laughed so hard at her faux novel. *Humor doesn't translate,* she thought. She walked to a table in the middle of the café and begrudgingly sat down. The businessman was still occupying the window table she wanted.

She tossed her notebook on the table and took a sip of the cappuccino, getting the foam all over her lips. It was heavenly. She shook her head in self-disgust. She'd never made a cappuccino this good. Not even close. The trick of foaming the milk right had always seemed to elude her. She'd been a total failure as a barista and a total failure as a writer. The only thing she'd ever been good at was sex. Luckily, she was damn good at that.

Dani studied the young woman at the espresso machine. She envied her skill. She'd mastered this simple art form. This foam held its shape, while hers quickly melted like a deflated soufflé or a loaf of bread that failed to rise. This cappuccino was formidable. After tasting the smooth, foamy cap she pledged she would learn to do it right when she returned to

San Francisco or Seattle, wherever she ended up, and vindicate herself.

Dani started to inhale the croissant, having gone to bed without a proper dinner. Midway through, she stopped and gave it her full attention. This croissant was different. It was warm and flaky, with a delicious sweetness to it. Nothing like the big, bloated croissants she'd eaten at Starbucks in Seattle, which tasted mostly like puffy air. This one was thinner, with a crispiness to it. It melted in her mouth. She dabbed at the crumbs on the plate with her fingers, then took a last sip of her coffee. Physical need sated, she opened her notebook and stared at the empty page. Nothing came to mind. She drew flowers. She wrote Michelle's name, then crossed it out. She wrote it again: Michelle Ellison. Her leg began to shake. She was fully caffeinated now. *Think, think,* she told herself. But nothing came to mind. Nothing, but Michelle. *Maybe I'm too jetlagged to write right now.* She exhaled loudly and got up from the table.

Gina was waiting on another customer who was speaking rapidly to her in Italian, but she waved goodbye to Dani when she saw that she was leaving. Dani smiled and waved back. *Yep, there is one thing I am good at.*

DODICI

Dani dug through her suitcase and found the *Learn Italian While You Drive* package. She pulled off the plastic sheathing, took out the first CD and put it into her portable CD player, then put on the headphones, crawled back into bed, and pressed PLAY.

"Good morning," a man's voice announced.

"*Buongiorno,*" a pleasing female voice returned in Italian.

"*Buongiorno,*" Dani echoed, overdoing the accent, and sounding more like a cartoon character of a waiter in an Italian restaurant.

"Good evening," the man said.

"*Buena sera,*" the woman replied.

Dani repeated her.

"I sell fish." The man confessed.

"*Io vendo pesce,*" the woman responded.

Even selling fish sounds poetic and beautiful in Italian, Dani thought. She worked diligently to approximate the accent and learn the words she felt she would need to get around in Venice. Maybe if she felt more comfortable in her surroundings her creative mind would emerge relaxed and she could finally focus and write.

Two hours later, she had memorized several Italian phrases that helped her when she finally wandered out of the apartment to *el mercato*.

The market was at the edge of the campo. She picked up a basket to put her groceries in and meandered down the aisles. She figured she'd make her favorite bachelor meals: PB and J and tuna casserole. She picked up a loaf of bread, then walked to the aisle with jam. Blood orange marmalade caught her attention. She put a jar in her basket.

Dani searched the shelves for peanut butter, but she didn't see any, only a jar of something called Nutella. She picked it up. It looked weird, but she decided to try it. Then she grabbed a jar of olives, a can of tuna, and a box of macaroni and cheese. She was headed to the frozen foods section for peas when a wave of emotion hit her. It surprised her. *I've had it a million times without feeling sad before, so why now?*

Tuna casserole was her dad's favorite. It consisted of mac and cheese, tuna, and peas. It was a dreadful combination, but Dani's dad loved it and she loved it too. She smiled as she remembered an evening her mother had cooked the casserole for him. He was so delighted, heaping large helpings of the casserole on his plate and then lovingly kissing her mother. There was so much love in the house back then. She was swimming in it. And then, just like that, it was gone. All gone. His death had taken the light from their lives, leaving an empty darkness.

The casserole usually evoked feelings of comfort and being so far away from home she needed a little of that, not this strange melancholy.

Dani wiped away the tears gathering in her eyes and walked to the frozen bins to see what else she could take back to the apartment to cook. She examined the packages of frozen foods:

There was calamari, pasta with black squid ink, pizzas made with corn, tuna, and potato—things she never imagined combining together—things that sounded even more disgusting than her mom's tuna casserole. One package startled her, *cavallo,* horse meat; the discovery made her stomach turn. She thought she might throw up. She quickly moved to the section with frozen vegetables and reached for a bag of peas then hurried to get in line for the checkout counter.

By the time she returned from the grocery store and put away the food, it was already three o'clock in the afternoon. She felt dizzy and tired. Her empty stomach growled, reminding her that she'd only eaten a croissant and that was hours ago. She glanced at her laptop and felt a twinge of guilt. Even though she hadn't done any writing yet, she decided to go out for another cappuccino and lunch. She would write better on a full stomach.

As she walked down the cobblestone alleys, she admired the metalwork on the decaying brick buildings. The colors of the buildings captivated her—the stucco painted in deep mustard and marigold, burnt orange, wine red, and coral, and the rooftops with their terra cotta shingles. Even buildings with the stucco stripped away, exposing the innards of pink brick, mesmerized her. She was enchanted by the arched, white window frames and the buildings accented with the vibrant swashes of colorful laundry hanging out to dry. The windows with forest-green shutters that shut from the outside and their flower boxes filled with blooming red geraniums delighted her too. It was all pleasing to her senses. The day was so perfect she could not fathom weather that would warrant anyone to close those external green shutters sealing themselves off from the magnificence outside their windows. It was unimaginable.

Dani was falling in love with Venice, as Veronica had predicted. Venice was a magical, floating city, its waterways pulsating with life. Dani loved water. She loved Seattle's Elliot Bay and living close to the San Francisco Bay. She imagined her love of water was because she was a Pisces. While the yawn of an ocean bay gave her wanderlust, there was something about Venice and its watery canals that snaked through the city that relaxed her. She even noticed that she was breathing more deeply as she crossed the bridge over the canal by DeLucia's Café and entered Campo San Giacomo dell'Orio, the famous square outside a beautiful old church.

For a moment, she felt a deep sense of peace, then she glimpsed the perfect empty table outside a trattoria in the campo. Overlooking a quaint and serene scene, it sharpened the edges of her loneliness.

Loneliness was a feeling Dani kept carefully at bay with her regular conquests. Somehow traipsing through this exquisitely enchanting, romantic city, reduced her to a state of sap and schmaltz. She was aware of pangs not felt since her days with Michele. It unnerved her.

Dani ran her fingers through her hair and took a deep breath, hoping to will away the empty feeling in her gut. She knew it wasn't hunger—not for food anyway—but she hoped a good meal might fill the uncomfortable emptiness just the same. She strode over to the restaurant to peruse a menu perched on a music stand. She paged through it, noting photos of fifteen types of pizza with their toppings described in Italian,

German, French, Spanish, and English. She picked up the menu and took a seat at the table. A waiter approached with a cloth napkin and bread sticks.

"*Prego?*" he asked.

She pointed to a picture of a pizza with basil and tomatoes.

He nodded. "*Margherita pizza. E bere,* to drink?"

"*Cappuccino and water.*"

"*Acqua minerale con gas?*" the waiter asked.

"Excuse me?"

"With bubbles?" he asked, sounding annoyed.

"Just regular water please."

"*Senza gas.*" The waiter scribbled on his notepad and walked back inside.

Dani was thrown by his clipped tone. *Everything here is so damn fancy.* She just wanted a glass of water. She placed the yellow napkin on her lap and chewed on a bread stick. She was going to need to learn more Italian if she was going to survive in this city.

The waiter returned and placed the bottle of water, a glass, and the cappuccino on the table with little fanfare. She poured the water into the glass and took a sip, enjoying feeling the warmth of the afternoon sun on her face. The people in the square caught her attention and made for mild entertainment. She chewed at the bread sticks and watched them as if she was eating popcorn and watching an artsy foreign flick.

There were three men in their late sixties gathered around a park bench. Two sat, while the third, a thin man wearing a brown hat and jacket, stood over them. They laughed and watched a little boy blowing bubbles with his mother. She studied the boy and his mother. She'd never wanted kids, but Michelle had. Dani had imagined a cosmopolitan life filled with travel and dinner parties while Michelle seemed to dream no bigger than the cul de sac she grew up on.

The boy who couldn't have been more than three years old, quickly lost interest in the bubbles when a woman in a fur coat wrapped her dog's leash around the park bench and walked inside the store. The little boy made a beeline for the black and white terrier. His mother ran after him, reaching him before he could touch the animal. She scooped him up and distracted him by throwing crackers to the pigeons. This also caught the attention of several brown sparrows that had been circling Dani's table since her pizza arrived. They all flew off in the direction of the crackers, except one sparrow that had the audacity to walk across the checked turquoise and green tablecloth towards her plate. She appreciated its bravado, but shooed it away. She wasn't sharing today.

Dani cut a slice of the pizza and tasted it. It was mouthwatering, with fresh basil, mozzarella cheese, and the most delicious tomatoes. She hadn't seen a tomato with this rich red color since she was a kid, and couldn't remember when she'd tasted one this good. The tomatoes back home were tasteless. *Veronica was right, the food, the canals, the cobblestone streets, the architecture, it is mind-blowingly beautiful.*

Dani cut off another bite of pizza and watched a black cat leap to the top of a well in the campo to sun itself. A lump formed in her throat because it looked like her dead cat, Shakespeare. She thought about sweet Shakespeare and the tragic end of his life. She wiped a tear from her eye noting yet another chink in her armor. She was losing it.

As she tried to pull herself together, she heard joyful squealing coming from the table across from her. She looked over and recognized the amorous young couple from the airport. The young woman held out her left hand to show the waiter her new engagement ring.

"Congratulazioni! Tempo per festeggiare," the waiter gushed. He hurried off to retrieve two champagne glasses and a bottle. *"Proseco,"* he said, pouring the bubbling liquid.

The couple toasted and kissed a long, deep kiss that made Dani want to yell, "Get a room." She had no patience for their love.

"Bravo." The waiter applauded.

Dani felt a surge of adrenaline rush through her body. "Check please."

The waiter waved his hand at her and disappeared inside. She took a sip of water and waited impatiently. She could feel her cheeks flush.

The waiter returned, but not with her bill. He had a plate of bruschetta for the happy couple. *"Sulla casa!* On the house," he said and placed it on their table. They began feeding the bruschetta to one another like it was wedding cake.

Embittered by their display of affection, Dani threw down twenty euro, more than enough to cover her meal, and fled the scene.

She stopped at the canal near DeLucia's Café and stared into the calm water. The surface of the water gently rippled. The mirrored reflection of lamplight from the blown-glass chandeliers in the buildings along the canal danced on the water. The multicolored pendant lamps hanging outside the *pensione* were particularly appealing to her. She watched the speckles of color shimmer and took a deep breath trying to quiet her mind.

It was useless. Despite her efforts to soothe herself, a painful memory rose to the surface and flooded her with sadness.

TREDICI

It was March of her senior year in high school. She'd been in the library after school, working on the spring issue of *The Rough Rider Reader.* As she walked to her car, she caught Sean and Michelle leaning against his cherry red Mazda Miata in the parking lot, kissing—Michelle in her cheerleader outfit and Sean in his football uniform.

Her throat tightened. "What a fucking cliché!" she screamed at them before she could stop her emotions from taking over. She ran to her car not knowing if they heard her and sped home. She barely made it to her bedroom before the tears came rushing down. She threw herself on the bed and sobbed. It was one thing to know Michelle was playing both sides, quite another to see it. It absolutely crushed her.

Dani reached beneath her bed and pulled out a shoebox filled with letters and cards Michelle had written her. She took one out and began reading it.

My dearest Dani,

I love you with all that is true in my heart. You know the real me.

"You fake-ass bitch!" she said. "What would Sean think if he knew the truth about us? I could ruin you." Her threats filled the empty room as her tears fell on the letter, smudging the ink.

Dani knew she would never "out" Michelle. *She's just trying to survive the viciousness of high school,* she recognized. *Once we graduate things will be different.*

Looking back at that terrible afternoon, Dani remembered how she had minimized Michelle's choices. How she had tried to calm and reassure herself to take the sting out of the betrayal. She'd put the letters away and decided to drive to the bookstore. Books about love were better than the real thing. *Maybe a good book could help?* she'd thought.

As she backed out of the driveway, she heard and felt a thud under the back wheel. She got out and saw her cat, Shakespeare, lying crushed in the driveway. She stood still, trying to will the vision away but blood began to pool around him. There was nothing she could do. His body was mangled. He was gone. She knelt down to clutch his lifeless black body to her chest. Her own body shuddered with sobs. She struggled to breathe. Giant tears fell from her eyes, staining her clothes and leaving wet splotches on the cement. She felt cursed.

In shock, Dani walked back to her car, flipped the visor down, and pushed the garage door button that was clipped to it. Her mother wouldn't be home for several more hours. She couldn't wait. It would only be worse. She went inside the garage and grabbed a shovel. This was probably the first time anyone in the household had held the shovel since her father died. It was his tool.

Dani dug a two-foot-deep hole on the remote side of the house. Then she went to her bedroom and took her favorite red flannel shirt from her dresser. She lifted poor Shakespeare's broken body from the red-flecked driveway and tenderly wrapped him in the flannel. She kissed his head and looked at those green eyes. His eyes, vacant now, and his fur mottled with blood broke her. She began to cry again.

"Goodbye, my little friend," she whispered, choking on the words, then gently lowered Shakespeare's cold body into the earth. She didn't think her heart could be any more broken, but it was.

After the burial, Dani got back in the car and drove on autopilot to the bookstore where she sat on the floor in the used classics section and thumbed mindlessly through a paperback copy of *Great Expectations*. Her eyes were wet with tears.

A guy with long, sandy blond hair came around the stacks. "May I help you?" he asked, startling her.

She quickly wiped her eyes and snapped the book shut, hoping he hadn't noticed her crying. She looked up at him. "Can you bring my dead cat back to life?"

The guy pursed his lips. "Shitty day, huh?"

"The worst." She shook her head. "Unless we're counting the day my dad died when I was ten."

"Damn, that does sound bad," he said, sighing. "I'm sorry to say I can't raise the dead. Anything else I can help you with?"

Dani pursed her lips. "Know any rich benefactors?"

The guy shook his head.

Dani sighed. "OK, how about this. Can you help me figure out why Pip continues to pursue Estella?"

He struck a contemplative pose. "Aw, yes Pip. Well, we always pursue the ones who treat us cruelly when we feel we don't deserve better."

"I guess it's better to be teased and taunted than to be Miss Havisham," Dani said.

He shrugged his shoulders. "Depends on how you look at it."

"Studying psych at U-dub, Matt?" Dani asked, reading the guy's green name tag.

Matt sat down on the circular step stool and raised an eyebrow. "Girl trouble?" he asked.

Dani nodded. She bit hard on the inside of her cheek to damn the flow of tears threatening to burst through again. The acrid taste of blood filled her mouth. "And I just ran my cat over." The tears came anyway.

"Ouch," Matt said. "I'm so sorry."

Dani wiped her eyes with her shirt sleeve. "My girl is leading this guy on so that no one suspects were together, and he's a real jackass."

"She sounds like a coward."

Dani's eyes widened as she considered Matt's remark. "I never thought of it that way. She wrote me these romantic letters and all I'd have to do is show him. That's it! She's taking this charade way too far. She was kissing him in the parking lot today. What the hell is she thinking?"

"Certainly not about your feelings," Matt said.

"No, not at all." Dani was surprised again by Matt's quick responses and his affinity for her predicament. She hadn't expected to find a sage and an ally in the used classics section of the bookstore. "I just want to shove the letters in his face. I mean, man, she picked the biggest jerk!"

Matt swiveled on the stool. "Do you think showing him her letters would solve your problems?"

Dani slumped over. "No, but I wish she'd tell the truth. I mean, it's 1999. They're going to have gay marriage in Vermont soon and people will be able to get married there and come back and have their marriages recognized here. Things are really changing for the better, but she keeps hiding."

"Be grateful you can tell the truth. Maybe you're stronger than she is. Maybe she's confused. Maybe your family gives you more support and freedom than hers does." Matt looked at her solidly, his eyes unflinching.

Dani looked away and traced Michelle's name with her finger in the dust on the black-and-white checked floor. "I don't feel stronger. I feel like she's a great actress, she's got them all fooled about being straight. But I guess she had me fooled too. I thought she was only into me."

"Ah Pip, you sit on the floor grounded in your truth, and your girl, Estella, she has a long way to fall off that pedestal. Be grateful."

Dani exhaled a wave of melancholy. "Yeah, well, I wouldn't want them to tear her up like they did me."

"Kids at school? Yeah, I remember how brutal high school can be. It gets better." Matt raised his eyebrow. "You will survive."

"I don't feel like I have any other choice," she said, holding her chin in her palm.

"Well, as they say, there are other salmon in the Pacific."

She looked up at him meeting his gaze. "Yes, but there's no one like her."

"That's the point." Matt got up from the stool and walked over to her, he put his hand on her shoulder. "Cheer up, Pip, this will work itself out. I have great expectations for you."

Dani groaned, "And you were doing so well."

QUATTORDICI

Dani couldn't shake the angst she felt about her writing. It crept alongside her as she walked back through the narrow streets
of Venice to the apartment. It was a sick feeling. A feeling of empty promises, aborted dreams, and unorthodox desires. She was never going to amount to anything if she didn't write this novel.

Away from the bar scene of San Francisco, she was starting to feel those old feelings she thought she'd left behind in Seattle after high school ended. Her sexual conquests in the years since then gave life variety and flavor and kept the bigger feelings of disappointment and failure at bay. She had become a master at seduction. She knew what women wanted. She knew their bodies, their desires. She'd give them just enough to leave them wanting more. But that was all. Anymore was too much. It was a winning formula.

Dani climbed the steps to her rented apartment, and once inside turned on the stove to boil water for tea. She hoped a cup of tea would restore some sense of calm and help her focus. She needed to clear her mind of the ugly memories that damned love-sick couple had triggered. She needed a clear mind to write—a sharp and focused mind. She needed to start writing. Twenty-four hours had passed since she'd arrived and she hadn't even turned on the computer to write. No more excuses!

She took her laptop out of the case. In the computer world, her laptop would have been considered a dinosaur. It was at least nine years old. She had convinced her mother to buy it for her freshman year of college. It was a gift without gender drama, unlike too many other gifts from her mother who had never completely let go of "Daniela," her imaginary feminine daughter. Her gifting of clothes to Dani was a painful ritual. Dani would offer up a thank-you and then later a request for a return receipt so she could get something she actually liked— which she knew would hurt her mother's feelings once she found out. She felt worse though if she kept the girly item because her mother would expect her to wear it. Dani's own tastes were more masculine. If she kept the clothing, it was only long enough to donate it to Goodwill.

The computer was a drama-free purchase. It was top of the line when her mother bought it for her. The best gift her mom ever gave her. Unfortunately, six years later, it was unable to support the software needed to make a USB port accessible, so Dani was forced to lug a five-pound external floppy disk drive to back up her writing just in case the computer crashed.

She unlatched the cover and fired up the machine. Then she moved the laptop to the desk by the window, opened a Word file, and began reading what she had last written.

A maiden born and raised in a divided world is plain and ordinary until, one day, her fate turns and her name becomes known to many in her land. It starts when a mysterious stranger, who has come a great distance, happens upon her tiny village. He impresses the villagers with his stories of adventure, his expensive garments, and other fineries that have accompanied him and his journeymen on their travels.

The villagers were not used to visitors of his stature. Some travelers would pass through on their way to the township on the other side of the mountain, but most avoided the tiny village, thinking that there was nothing to be gained from the heathen peasants. The cloak of mystery that surrounds the traveler intrigues the maiden as well, and she finds ways to be in his company. They pass many days together and she relishes his attention and he enjoys the food and drink that she generously provides him.

"Such crap!" Dani said, disgusted, and slammed the lid of the laptop down. She remembered her college writing teacher telling the class about her internalized "evil editor," a sort of dominatrix in thigh-high black boots with a punishing whip. *If the evil editor saw this, I'd be due for a good ass-whipping.* She imagined the evil editor cracking her whip at the open laptop, the leather thong catching the computer's edge and snapping it smack against the wall.

There was something satisfying about the thought.

She picked up a pen and her notebook and tried to think of another idea or to find a way to rewrite the story with more gravitas. She couldn't concentrate. All she could think about was Michelle. It made her stomach churn. It reminded her of that gut punch. Not the physical one from Sean. The one she felt the day that Michelle told her that she was going with him to the dance. That was the day Dani began to lose herself, the day she buried her heart and stopped letting people see what really mattered to her. She put on the first layer of the protective mask she wore, a mask that had morphed and perfected itself until it had subsumed the one who'd made the terrible mistake of falling in love with Michelle in the first place.

She slumped in the chair.

Why is she calling me now? I thought I was done with that chapter of my life? But Dani knew she wasn't. She'd managed to push Michelle to the back of her mind, but here she was, still in her heart. No matter what Michelle had done to her, she couldn't stop loving her. It was why none of the other girls she dated could hold her attention. She didn't want to hurt them; she just didn't have any room in her heart. Michelle had a strangle-hold on it still.

Dani had read about the power of intermittent reinforcement being the most powerful connector in her Psych 101 class. Every now and again the thought of it popped into her mind. It was what hooked gamblers and made lab rats push levers to death. It was an unsettling thought that Michelle's behavior had such a powerful grip on her. *Surely, Michelle loves me. Even after all this time with Sean she still wants me. She can't quit me. And the fact that she called me on my birthday and begged me to come back to Seattle proves it.*

Dani dreamed about finding a girl who loved poetry and cafés like she did. A girl who would walk with her hand in hand, out in the open, for whom what the world thought of them being a couple wouldn't matter. The only thing that would matter would be their love.

The thought pierced her. She choked back tears and got into the bed. It felt harder somehow, the pillows too. The room was cold again.

QUINDICI

Dani walked down a dark alley. She turned the corner and found herself at a dead end. The cobblestone walkway came to an abrupt stop above a canal dammed up by a brick wall. Below her, piles of trash and seaweed swirled in the canal water and thrashed against the brick wall. Then, all at once, a swell rose up and swept her into the murky water. She struggled with all of her might to break free from the whirlpool that threatened to suck her under.

Then she woke up. She'd been dreaming.

Disoriented and unnerved by the dream, she glanced around the apartment, trying to ground herself. Once she got her bearings, she was anxious to get the day started and forced herself out of bed. She dressed quickly and hurried out of the apartment towards DeLucia's Café.

Dani wondered if the isolation of traveling alone was getting to her, because she was much too happy to see the young woman in the café making espresso while her father worked the cash register.

"*Buongiorno,*" the young woman warmly greeted Dani.

"*Buongiorno,*" Dani replied, more confident of her Italian today.

"Nonfat cappuccino?" the woman asked, smiling.

"Now you're playing tricks on me." Dani laughed. There was no such thing as a nonfat cappuccino in Venice and just the mention of it probably sounded ridiculous. Italy was a country that celebrated flavor. Many of the Italian women were extremely slender and she imagined they might resort to bulimia rather than cheat their palate.

"Your writing—is going well?" the young woman asked.

The question darkened Dani. She wished she'd never shared her reason for coming to Venice with the young woman. She leaned up against the marble counter like it would bolster her sagging self-esteem. "It's coming along," she said, hoping that would be sufficient to change the subject.

"*Buon appetito.*" The young woman handed Dani the plate with the croissant and the cappuccino and then squinted like she was looking into the sun. "So rude am I. I ask of your writing, but not your name. *Chiamo,* what's your name?"

Dani touched her hand to her chest. "I'm Dani. Nice to meet you, Gina." Dani smiled.

The young woman looked surprised. "How do you know my name?"

Dani pointed to Signore DeLucia. "Your father said it when he called you to come out from the kitchen the other night."

"Ah, *sì.*" She nodded her head. "That's his nickname for me. My full name is Regina."

"Oh, I'm sorry," Dani said, her face slightly reddening. *So much for paying attention,* she thought. Usually, women responded favorably when she remembered their names and were infuriated when she forgot them. She remembered the redhead in the bar. *Aman-duh!* she reminded herself.

"Nice to meet you, Regina." Dani smiled and held up her cup to toast Regina.

"*Piacere,* Dani. Nice to meet you." Regina smiled, pleased.

Dani took a sip of the cappuccino and observed that the foam was even thicker than the one Regina served her yesterday. "Does your mother work here too?" Dani asked, knowing to be on the lookout for a Catholic mother who might not approve of her talking to her daughter.

Regina sighed. "My mother passed a few years ago. It's only me and my father."

"I'm so sorry." Dani set her cup on the counter. She felt bad for her previous thought even though a disapproving mother was a real thing she needed to consider. "I know how hard it is to lose a parent. My dad died," she blurted out, surprising herself with this unexpected emotional revelation. She never shared deep things with strangers, but Regina seemed so easy to talk to.

Regina lifted out the silver cross that hung under her shirt. "This was hers. When I wear it, I feel she is still with me."

Dani felt a lump form in her throat. She hugged her plaid jacket tighter around herself and nodded sympathetically. After her dad died, she would wrap herself in his jacket and try to remember his voice and how he smelled. His smell was long gone, but the jacket was still a reminder of happier times. She couldn't let it go.

"How is your dad doing?" Dani asked. Her mind wandered back to the days and months after her father died. Her mother was a neurotic mess after the accident. At first, she tried to control everything, especially Dani. Dani had the feeling that the car accident had only exacerbated her mother's preexisting fears. Her father's death had given her mother's fears a focus, rather than being the catalyst of them.

Dani knew enough Jewish history to know that there was a pipeline of fear transferred from one generation to the next; still, she couldn't seem to muster a consistent level of empathy for her mother. She felt that if she did, she would be smothered by the weight of her mother's fears. She fought back with a callous disregard of her mother's worries, openly mocking her.

Regina looked in her father's direction and lowered her voice, which was strange since he didn't seem to understand English when she'd asked him for help the other night.

"He's very lonely. He pretends he is not because he doesn't want to upset me."

Dani nodded. She knew her mother must be lonely too. Though it was never something she'd ever discuss openly with her daughter. Dani wished her mother had remarried. She was glad that she kept herself busy with her work and her friends, but she felt like a huge part of her mom had died with her father.

Regina gave a concerned look in her father's direction. "I'm getting married in *Settembre* and I know it's going to be very hard to leave him alone here."

Dani's ears perked up when she heard Regina saying she was getting married in a few months. *Oh damn! This isn't going to go anywhere. Nothing wrong with flirting*, she told herself.

"So, you'll quit working after you're married and have babies?" Dani said, a bit coolly. She assumed that most women in Italy didn't work after marriage and went right into breeding mode.

"Oh, no. I keep working here. For a while anyway. I meant moving out of the apartment. We live upstairs." Regina pointed to the backroom.

"Oh." Dani glimpsed a staircase for the first time.

"You want something more?" Regina asked.

"An orange juice would be great."

Regina went to the counter and began squeezing the oranges through a juicer. *They even go the extra mile with fresh juice here,* she thought, pleased now with her decision to come to Venice and with finding a great café and barista so close to her apartment.

As she waited for her juice and sipped her cappuccino, some brochures scattered on the far left corner of the counter caught her eye. She picked up one with photos of Venice attractions and scanned it. *Avventure Serenissima, Tours of Venice— Grand Canal Boat Tour, Doges Palace Tour, Best of Italian Cuisine, Art Lovers Tour* it read.

"You should go on ghost tour," Regina said.

"A ghost tour?"

"*Sì.*" Regina smiled.

Dani picked up the brochure for the Venetian Ghost Tour. She read the bolded text on the brochure aloud. "A fascinating walk through the dimly lit backstreets of Venice illuminated by legends and ghost stories from Venice's past and present.' That sounds intriguing. Maybe I can add a ghost to my novel or the legend of a knight whose ghost haunts the lands."

"Yes, I think it will help your writing."

Dani looked at her perplexed, not sure how it would help her writing. *Certainly, couldn't hurt it,* she thought.

Dani flipped through the brochure some more and then returned to the tour page and read the description out loud. "'Venice by night is a place of romance and mystery. The streets dimly lit and deserted are a place where long shadows loom and footsteps echo in the distance. On this walking tour through narrow calli and campi, the ghosts of the past and present day will keep you company as our guide introduces them to you, telling all their secrets.' Yeah, that sounds kind of fun."

Regina smiled. "Venice is very beautiful at night. You will see."

"Touring the city at night with a group sounds safer than just wandering around by myself not knowing where I'm going."

Dani considered asking Regina to join her, but now knowing that Regina had a fiancé, inviting her out seemed a little bold. She was not on her home court and Venice was way too small. Even if she could seduce Regina, which she supposed she could, the idea seemed a bit reckless. She needed to have a neutral spot to write outside of the apartment. *Stay focused on your writing,* she told herself.

"Sit, I will bring your breakfast to you," Regina said, noticing a large group of people coming through the front door.

After Dani finished her breakfast, she opened her blue spiral notebook and began jotting down ideas for her story. She started to articulate the plot and was finally finding the story arc. The mysterious stranger would lure the maiden away from her village and then betray her. He would become the antagonist. Then she would meet a handsome duke who would help her return to her village unscathed, well maybe slightly scathed, but redeemed, nevertheless. She would up the romantic element. Romances were popular and big sellers. *Emily can write clit-lit if she wants, but I'll write something even better,* she thought.

Every once in a while, she looked up from her writing and glimpsed Regina and her father talking to customers and serving espresso. There was something delightful about Regina. She had a sweet innocence that was refreshing, different than the shallow cluelessness or jaded edginess of most of the girls she came across in California.

At one point, Dani noticed an attractive, muscular guy with a chiseled face, green eyes, and wavy short brown hair leaning on the counter talking to Regina. He had a thick build. She looked like a bread stick standing next to him. Dani wondered if this was Regina's fiancé. She saw him point in her direction and say something. Regina laughed and playfully hit him with a dishtowel. She took off her apron and they walked outside with their cappuccinos. The way he threw his shoulders back when he laughed reminded her of Sean. The couple shared a confident body language. They seemed at ease with expressing their sexuality and fondness for each other openly.

Dani enviously watched them through the window. They were laughing as they sipped cappuccinos at an outside table in the campo. The gondolier who was posted at the canal's edge walked over to them, lit a cigarette, and chatted with them. From time to time, he would call out to the passing tourists, who seemed more interested in taking pictures of the boat than riding in it.

An idea for her book popped into her head, so she started writing in the notebook again. When she next looked up, Regina and her fiancé were gone. She glanced at her watch. *Where has the time gone?* She never understood how time could fly by so quickly when she was writing, or in this case writing and rewriting plot ideas and chapter outlines.

She got up from the table and wandered over to the counter, surprised that Signore DeLucia had never brought her the bill. The man was making something akin to sandwiches. These were triangular in shape with no crust on the bread and he was filling them with things that she didn't think should be mixed together, like shrimp and eggs. Regina was nowhere in sight.

Signore DeLucia finally noticed Dani standing at the counter and made his way toward her. "*Sette euro,*" he said and handed her the bill.

She paid him, then walked outside. She pulled the ghost tour brochure from her pocket and walked to the payphone, which looked like a pregnant robot. She played with the phone card, tapping it against the phone's big gray belly while the phone rang.

"*Pronto, Avventure Serenissima,*" a woman answered.

"I'd like to go on the ghost tour tonight."

"*Certo,* you are in luck, we have one spot left," the woman told her. Dani gave her credit card information, and then the woman said, "Wait at the top of the Rialto Bridge at sunset, on the side facing west, and your tour guide will find you."

Dani finished the arrangements and hung up, pleased with her evening plans. She felt a sense of contentment and walked leisurely back to the apartment enjoying the palette of colors reflecting off the buildings and the canal in the late afternoon sun. She thought she could feel her luck changing.

SEDICI

Back at the apartment, Dani opened the refrigerator and reached for the jar of olives. She ate them standing over the sink, a habit she'd developed as a teenager, having eaten so many meals by herself when her mother had to go to work early or stay late. She never liked sitting alone to eat. Dani put the lid on the olive jar and grabbed her map of Venice and spread it out on the kitchen table.

She searched for the Rialto Bridge. "Ah, there it is," she said aloud, mentally noting the streets she would need to take to get there: Lista Dei Bari, Calle Larga Dei Bari, Calle Dei Boteri, Calle Becarrie. They all sounded the same, and twisted across the page like an unsolvable maze. She would just have to pay really close attention on her way there and hope she didn't get too lost.

Dani carried the laptop into the kitchen, set it on the narrow table, and squeezed into the chair wedged between the table and the kitchen wall. "OK, thirty minutes butt in chair," she told herself.

She turned on the computer and tried to think of what to write. She painstakingly typed out a few sentences. The words flowed like frozen molasses. She just continued typing, trying not to judge herself, and more importantly, not pressing the backspace button to delete it all. She kept at it for about an hour and then read a few passages out loud.

The mysterious traveler, Remarco, invited the young maiden, Malandria, to depart with him. The town was shocked he had chosen such a plain girl. There were many young women in the village with much more to offer the wealthy stranger in looks and talents. Remarco enjoyed Malandria's company because she was deferential and listened intently to his stories of conquest and danger. She herself was hungry for adventure and to see the world outside of the village. The girl's parents were pleased to be marrying off their last daughter and grateful that destiny had brought this fortune to their tiny village.

When the time came for the maiden and the man to depart with his entourage, she kissed her family goodbye and took one last look at the village and the mountains that surrounded it. She thought she felt a sickness in her heart, but she brushed it aside and smiled self-consciously, a bit ashamed by the chip on her front tooth. With outstretched hand, he pulled her up onto the back of his steed and they rode out of the village in the direction of the township.

Dani stopped and smiled, pleased with herself. It sounded just like those fairy tales that people loved. She knew she was hitting the marks and the plot points of those romances that sold. Like Emily's book that was picked up by Random House, this story had a chance of going somewhere. She could feel it. It excited her.

I can write ridiculous epic romances too, she thought, and noticed the red light on her laptop. That meant the battery was almost dead. She went into the other room and removed the cord from the laptop bag with the U.S. flat prongs and took out the European adapter, then returned to the kitchen. She plugged the cord into the laptop, then into the wall. The machine made a loud, popping noise. The screen flashed and went dead.

"What? No, no, no!" Dani yelled and quickly unplugged it. The room filled with the smell of burning plastic.

Dani kick-punched the air. "Good luck candle my ass!" she cursed. She stormed out of the kitchen to the bedroom where she punched the pillows. "I can't believe this shit," she screamed. "I'm so screwed!"

She'd spent the last eight hours perfecting the lines in her manuscript. She was finally making headway and now everything she'd typed into her computer was inaccessible. She'd have to start over.

Dani grabbed her jacket, snatched up the keys and map, and slammed out of the apartment.

The sun was setting as she stormed down a wide cobblestone street in the direction of the Rialto Bridge, her hands balled into tight fists. *I can't believe the bullshit luck I have. The Universe didn't set me free to write. It set me free to find another way to screw me over,* she thought.

Dani turned into a square with a corner market, a café, and a *gelaterria.* She scowled at the bins of gelato. *You did this to me,* she thought. It did look good though. She'd make sure and get some tomorrow, but she didn't want to be late and miss the tour.

She looked around the square, trying to orient herself. With the exception of the night when she got lost searching for the phone card, she hadn't walked more than a couple of streets from the apartment.

There were numerous exit points from the square. She pulled out her Dad's old map and tried to match the street names on the map with the yellow street signs on the brick buildings.

Her eyes darted from sign to map, map to sign, and back again. Then she saw a yellow sign with the words *Per Rialto* painted on it and an arrow pointing to an extremely cramped alleyway. She was relieved to get her bearings, but her sense of relief quickly dissipated as she followed the arrow into a blind alleyway. She felt her body tense as the narrow passageway led to a darkened corner. She moved quickly down this dark corridor and into another equally dark alley. It felt inevitable that she would get lost in this claustrophobic and confusing labyrinth.

As she continued walking, Dani's eyes were drawn to a window display of masks. They were ornate with long, wispy feathers and creepy eyeholes. The store was shuttered, and the eerie faces of the masks unnerved her. *This is like the beginning of a horror movie,* she thought. *Minus the organ music.*

She walked briskly, trying to take in the details of her path to help her remember the way back. She made mental notes: *Vacuum cleaner store, art store with orange and red paintings, hanging clock, antiwar protest sign, creepy doorknob in the shape of the head of a screaming woman . . .*

She became more apprehensive the farther she walked from the apartment, realizing that getting back was going to be much more challenging than she could have expected.

Some alleys she walked down were so empty that the only sound was her footsteps on the cobblestone streets. But as she neared the Rialto Bridge, there was a growing buzz of voices that comforted her as she walked through the darkness.

As she reached the ancient arched white bridge, which was swarming with people, she welcomed the sound of their voices booming in Italian, German, English, and Japanese. She loved hearing all of the accents. They delighted her. Her mood shifted.

Dani took in the magnificent bridge with its arcade of shops and decorative railing made of white stone. On the map she'd noticed that only three bridges crossed the Grand Canal—the main freeway for boats. The Rialto Bridge was one of those three, and clearly a major intersection for locals and tourists. It was about five car lanes wide and half of a football field long.

The bridge had three staircases. The middle staircase was the widest, flanked by the arcade of covered tourist shops on either side. The outer two staircases were teaming with tourists enjoying the view of the Grand Canal and posing for photos. Tourists crossing the bridge wove in and out of the stores. At the top of the bridge was a well-lit portico where tourists could stop to catch their breath and get a glimpse of the view from both sides of the bridge.

At the foot of the bridge, where she stood, were artisan booths filled with touristic objects; postcards of Venice, tee-shirts with the word *Venezia* and pictures of gondolas on them, and ornate blown-glass ashtrays and vases. Her eyes milled over the dried multicolored pasta she imagined Veronica would appreciate. She was especially drawn to the writing quills made from large red and purple feathers.

Dani made her way through the throbbing crowd of people as she ascended the outer staircase. There was a young boy selling long-stemmed roses, tourists snapping pictures, a German couple in their mid-thirties studying a paper map, and a group of Italian college students, probably on spring break from their university, who were really drunk and singing loudly in Italian.

Dani stopped at the crest of the bridge. She leaned over the railing made of white stone and listened to the waves lap against the mossy cement steps alongside the canal. The water shimmered with the red lights from the *vaporetti*. The Grand Canal was lit up like a Christmas tree reflecting lights from the buildings that flanked it. It was breathtaking. Her eyes were drawn to a gondola that swept silently over the water below. She watched two figures nestled together in the slender boat and thought about how romantic it would have been if it was her and Michelle. It was a sweet thought that quickly darkened her mood. She knew if she wanted to be with Michelle it had to be in the shadows.

As her hand moved unconsciously towards the necklace Michelle had given her, she felt a pressure on her shoulder. She turned around and saw a small-framed woman with long dark hair. The woman who looked to be in her early forties, was dressed in a copper-colored silk dress that exposed ample cleavage. Dani tried to avert her eyes, but the woman's necklace, a gold ring looped through a gold chain, caught her eyes. The gold ring landed perfectly in the space between the woman's bosom.

"You look like you could use a guide," the woman said with a thick accent. "You are here for ghost walk?"

"Yes, I am," Dani replied, meeting her gaze.

The woman smiled. "My name is Sara. I will be your guide. Let us start."

"Where is everyone else?"

"*A lora,* you get special, how do you say, V-I-P service." The woman spoke in formal, but broken, English.

Dani sized up the woman, trying to figure out if she really was a tour guide or some kind of scam artist. She looked more like a librarian than a criminal, and the brochure had seemed legitimate. It was plausible that "only one spot left!" was their sales pitch to get you to commit right away to buy the tour. It had worked on her. Maybe most tourists preferred the art and cathedral tours, over a late-night ghost walk tour?

"Don't worry," Sara said, seeming to sense Dani's apprehension. "I am not intending to hurt you. Come, we start tour here where it is quieter."

Dani ignored the funny feeling in her stomach. "Alright," she said, apprehensively.

"*Buono.*" The guide gestured to her. "Follow me."

Dani followed the tour guide to the other side of the bridge where there were hardly any tourists. She casually moved her wallet from the back pocket to the front pocket.

"Venice was built on lagoon by people hoping to escape barbarian raids of the Visigoths in the fifth century. It is believed that the city was founded Twenty-fifth of March, Four hundred-twenty-one. Saturday is *Venezia anniversario.* She will be one thousand, five hundred and eighty-five years old."

"Dang, this place is almost sixteen hundred years old," said Dani.

"*Sì, molto vecchio.* Very old."

"Did Noah park his ark here?" Dani couldn't even imagine the world back then. It blew her mind. She thought it was cool she was here on the anniversary of Venice's founding.

"Is question or joke?" the guide asked, uncertain.

Dani grinned. "Joke."

The guide nodded then continued her *spiel.* "We go now to the sight of our first ghost story, Campiello del Remer."

Dani followed the tour guide down the steps of the Rialto Bridge, to what seemed like a main *calle.* Then she turned left and Dani followed her through a poorly lit alleyway that opened up into a darkened empty campo alongside the Grand Canal. Most of the *campi* had a café or a tavern with tables outside. This one did not. It was empty of tourists and shops. All of the windows on the surrounding buildings were shuttered.

It suddenly dawned on Dani that the tour guide had lured her into a trap. She was surrounded by brick buildings on three sides and the canal on the fourth. If the passageway into the square was blocked, the only way to escape would be to jump into the water. Dani stood frozen, a sick feeling of panic in her stomach.

"This was the site of . . . ," the woman began, but Dani had stopped listening. She was too focused on her survival and weighing her chances of escape. Should she run through the passageway now and fight off the woman's accomplices? Or should she jump into the cold canal and swim until she found another area with stairs where she could climb out and get away safely? If she jumped into the canal, she might drown before she found a way to pull herself out. If she went back through the passageway, she would be mugged or worse. Maybe she could flag down a boat.

What the hell was I thinking following a stranger into an alleyway? She immediately started to blame Veronica for her current unlucky circumstances. *Great idea, Veronica. First my computer, and now this?*

The guide continued speaking in her soft alto voice and pointed to the canal. "And so, you see, at midnight on nights where there is a new moon, you can see the ghost of Fosco in the water holding the severed head of his wife, Elena."

Dani looked onto the Grand Canal but there were no boats or gondoliers to flag down. She decided it was safer to fight off this woman's accomplices in the alleyway than risk drowning in her heavy clothes or getting hypothermia.

"And if you listen, you can sometimes hear the sound of hoofs in the square."

"Um-hmm," Dani said, mentally preparing herself for battle.

"We go now to our next spot." The guide walked briskly across the campo and into the dark alley.

Dani followed her, clutching her wallet, ready to fight or flee. She could hear the chatter of people ahead, but the passageway seemed empty.

The woman stopped and turned to Dani. "Some people see ghosts. Some don't."

Dani barely heard her. She was vigilantly watching the dark corners of the square and the alleyway in case she needed to take an action.

"Are you OK?" the guide asked, studying Dani.

"I'm fine," Dani lied. Her palms were sweaty and her heart raced in her chest.

The guide could see that Dani was unnerved and took her arm in hers. "No need to be frightened of ghosts," she said. "The dead won't hurt you. Little fun with you, yes, but not to harm you."

Within moments they were back on the main thoroughfare without incident. Dani was relieved there hadn't been anyone waiting to rob her. She'd never been so grateful to be in the presence of other tourists.

"This canal is called the Rio de la Fava," the guide said.

This time Dani heard her. *Rio, like "river,"* she thought, translating from Spanish. Her only association to fava was the bean. *River of the Bean?* She shrugged and looked down at the dark water. Dani noted the reflection of the buildings on the surface. These buildings were much older than the one where she was staying. The window frames were tall with thin, ornate pointed archways. The lights in the nearby cafés and bars comforted her. She began to relax into the tour and tune in to what the woman was saying. *OK, maybe this is legit,* she thought.

"Here you see the back of Teatro Malibran. It is very tall building," the guide said.

The building was five stories, which Dani noticed was considered tall by Venetian standards. Most buildings were no higher than four stories.

"This building, we call Gothic, is home of Marco Polo, the greatest adventurer of all time. You've heard of him, no?"

Dani nodded. "Yes, of course. This was his house?"

"*Sì,* Marco, set sail to the Orient at only seventeen years of age."

"Overachiever," Dani mumbled to herself, as she turned to look at the building. It was ancient. There were three window frames with five circular reliefs above them, each one with a different carving. One was a star, another was a woman, and she couldn't make out what the others were. The building looked like it had been haphazardly remodeled several times.

"He returned after being away from Venezia for two decades with a wife from the Orient. Her name was Haldong. Venetians treated Haldong poorly and Marco Polo's family refused to recognize her as his wife. They did not like her Oriental features."

Dani bristled at her use of the old-school word for an Asian, but the guide didn't notice.

"Marco left her in Venezia and went on trade voyage, but was captured by Genoese, rivals of Venetians, and imprisoned. His family learned the news and his sister despising Haldong told her that Marco was killed on the voyage."

The guide continued, "Brokenhearted and wanting to be with her husband, Haldong took action that was customary to widows in her culture. She set herself on fire and jumped off this building into the canal."

"Barbaric custom," Dani said shocked, "but what loyalty to her love."

The guide nodded her agreement. "People say they can hear her singing around seven in the evening. Some claim to have heard her cries of anguish and seen her floating in the canal holding a candle trying to find her way back to her country."

Dani gazed at the canal, grateful not to see the ghost of Haldong floating in it. As she looked into the water she noticed how it beautifully reflected the light from the windows in the Teatro and mirrored the white wooden balcony on the building across the canal from where they were standing.

The story touched her deeply. It was more poignant than *Romeo and Juliet,* which was so over told that there were cartoon parodies of it, and of course, reflected the foolishness of young love, impetuous and self-absorbed. This story was fresh and so much like the one she wanted to tell. A love story cut short not by the lovers themselves, but by a society that despises their love and denies them the right to love because of some external immutable feature, in this case race.

"I wish I could write a story like that," Dani said, and let out an audible sigh.

The guide's voice softened. "You are writer?"

"Well, I'm working on it."

"I am also writer." The guide grinned.

"Really? What kind of writing do you do?"

"I am poet."

"That's cool." Dani felt stupid the minute the words came out of her mouth. She looked at the woman more deeply now. "What did you say your name was again?"

"Sara," the woman said, smiling.

"Sara," Dani repeated. "You really know a lot about Venetian history." Dani felt foolish for worrying that this woman would rob her.

"*Certo.*" Sara nodded, smiling. "Let's continue." Sara began walking.

Dani followed behind Sara, whose black boots clicked and clacked on the cobblestone as she walked. Sara was the kind of woman Dani might have overlooked if she had met her in any other context. Sure, the woman had to be at least fifteen years older than her, but it wasn't Sara's age that she would've dismissed. It was a tendency she had that Veronica teased her about to "gravitate towards women who wear their sexuality on the outside like 'born-agains' wear their crosses." When Veronica pointed it out, Dani knew she couldn't deny it. Veronica was right. Her relationship with Michelle had conditioned Dani to go towards women who were openly sexual and flirtatious.

Sara did not seem to be that kind of woman to Dani. However, as she stood in the lamplight telling stories about Venetian ghosts, something inside Dani stirred. Maybe it was just that she was relieved that she hadn't made a huge blunder and gotten robbed; or maybe it was something about Sara who she could now see more clearly as an individual.

Sara's brown hair was pulled back with a simple silver barrette, except for a few strands that had somehow broken free and now brushed against her pale cheek. Dani studied the delicate features of Sara's face, her olive skin, the smile lines above her pink lips, the freckles near the corners of her eyes.

Sara took her to the water's edge and then continued out onto a narrow wooden dock before stopping. For a minute Dani thought she was going to walk right into the water. Dani stayed on the quay.

"This is the *Canale Grande,*" Sara said, in reference to the large waterway. This is main route for boats." Dani noticed that they were in front of a four-story building that buttressed the canal. "And this is Palazzo Malipiero." Sara pointed. "Notice the beautiful water entrances."

Dani cautiously walked across the wooden-planked dock towards Sara so that she could turn around and take a look at the façade of the building from the vantage point of the canal. This side of the palace was designed to be the front of the building. It took her breath away. It was like a castle on the water's edge.

The first floor had two large doorways that were partially submerged. Dani realized that those were the original front entrance doors. She wondered what it would be like to be a Venetian and row your boat into the water entrances hundreds of years ago when Venice was a wealthier city. The thought delighted her.

The second floor had nine Romanesque windows topped with white statuary heads. Five of these rounded windows opened to a beautiful, white-columned terrace in the middle of the edifice. Two side windows bookended the ones that opened onto the terrace and flanked the building. She loved how the light streaming from these windows cast its glow on the canal and danced on the rippling water.

Dani imagined how the former inhabitants might take their meals on the terrace in the warmer months, enjoying the fresh ocean air, or on mild evenings, watch the setting of the sun as it quietly melted into the horizon.

She loved it. It was beyond romantic. She knew Veronica would love it too. It was the kind of scenery that totally appealed to Veronica's gaudy sensibilities. Though it was not gaudy, not ostentatious, the palace was impressive in its beauty and dignified, majestic even.

"This is gorgeous," Dani blurted out. "It's like a castle on the water."

"*Sì,* a *palazzo* is like castle. This palazzo was once home of Count Farussi. Born in Venezia in Seventeen-twenty-five April. He is known as Giacomo Casanova."

A boat went by, causing a wave of water to rock the dock. Dani steadied herself by grabbing hold of a wooden pole that arose out of the water near the dock. "Casanova, the womanizer?" Dani asked.

Sara nodded. "He knew love once. A young woman he loved for her beauty and intelligence, but she rejected him because he did not have the social standing. It darkened him."

Dani felt a surge of anger rush through her body. "I can understand that," she said, her voice straining to keep its grip on the emotion threatening to surface, "social standing shouldn't get in the way of true love." *And neither should sexual orientation or gender,* she thought, but kept it to herself.

Dani looked down at the canal, the sound of the water lapping against the dock calmed her a bit and she took a deep breath. "But it always does," she said with a sigh.

Sara glanced at Dani and nodded in agreement. She turned and looked into the shimmering water. "But Casanova had his revenge. He liked to play—how do you say? —evil jokes, on people."

Dani perked up a bit and returned her attention to Sara. "Like what?"

"He was known to summon midwives with false reports of women in labor and priests to come for dying souls in need of last rites."

"He invented crank calls?"

"He once dug up a body and cut off the arm, then he snuck the arm into the bed of his enemy while he slept. When the man awoke to find a dismembered arm in his bed, his heart almost stopped from fear. He lived, but . . . ," Sara paused and pointed to her head. *"Pazzo,* he was never the same."

"Yeah, who would be?" Dani shook her head. "Casanova sounds devilish."

"He was imprisoned for this, but he was smart and escaped. To this day, his ghost is known to untie gondolas to let them float away."

Dani shrugged. "I guess that's one way to stay relevant."

"Casanova was also writer, but he spent much time causing mayhem. He wrote a book about his years in Venezia before he was exiled. He was brilliant man, but people don't remember him for his writing, only for his indulgences of flesh and gambling."

"Indulgences of the flesh are another way to stay relevant," Dani said, "but gambling, I've personally never understood the allure of that."

"Gambling is big problem in Venezia, even for Jewish rabbis."

"Are there a lot of Jews in *Venezia?*" Dani asked, trying to pronounce the Italian.

Sara hesitated. "Not anymore." Sara brushed the brown and silver strands of hair from her face. "I am Jew," she said.

"I'm Jewish too," Dani said. "Not religious though."

Sara smiled. "Yes, I know."

"How?" Dani asked, brushing her nose unconsciously.

Sara ignored her question. She stepped off the wooden dock and back on to the quay and continued her tour spiel. "In the seventeenth century, there lived a famous Jewish rabbi in Venezia: Leon Modena. Rabbi Modena had twenty-six jobs."

"Why twenty-six jobs?" Dani asked, following Sara back to dry land. She loved the water but was happy not to have to steady herself against the waves and worry about slipping into the water.

"He needed all these jobs just to pay his—how do you say? —debts."

"Sounds like he was a great gambler, but a terrible winner," Dani joked.

Sara walked into a narrow alleyway and continued talking. "He was rabbi, teacher, music director, writer of epigraphs on tombstones, writer of religious and political texts, and poet. But he was secretly known for being a Kabbalist."

"He was a closeted *shoemaker?*" Dani asked, confused.

"Not *cobbler. Kabbalist.* A Jewish mystic. Jewish mystics study Zohar."

"The Adam Sandler comedy?"

Sara stopped walking and squinted at Dani, as there was clearly a cultural disconnect. "Zohar is mystic teaching from Rabbi Simon ben Yohai of second century. He hid in cave in Israel for thirteen years because Romans wanted to kill him. Jewish mystics believe in reincarnation, numerology, and a—"

"Reincarnation? Like past lives?" Dani interrupted.

"Yes. They believe a person returns to learn lessons they fail to learn in past lifetimes. They had to hide this from the Romans and Catholic Church or they could be killed. They also practiced alchemy. You know alchemy? The alchemy takes the lead to turn to the gold."

Dani raised her eyebrow. "If he could turn lead into gold, why the twenty-six jobs? Sounds like he was a really bad gambler and a terrible alchemist too."

Sara laughed for the first time, a quick nasal laugh.

Dani smirked. The iceberg was finally thawing just a little. She liked the sound of Sara's laugh. It was cute. Veronica, on the other hand, would have loved her witty remark so much she would have snorted uncontrollably. Dani loved how much Veronica appreciated her humor.

"Many believed it was possible to take lead and turn it to gold, but when the rabbi's son tried, he was poisoned by the fumes and died. Rabbi Leon's other son was murdered in the ghetto."

They entered into a campo and Dani looked up at the moon and sighed, as she reflected on the litany of suffering Sara had just shared with her.

Only a Jewish tour guide, she thought.

"Leon knew many hardships. Yesterday, in Sixteen-forty-eight, was the day he himself left this earth. May his memory be a blessing."

"You just mentioned a ghetto?"

"Yes, the Jewish ghetto."

"What does that mean exactly. I saw it on the map, but I can't imagine a ghetto in a place as beautiful as Venice. I thought ghettos were a modern, inner-city thing."

"We are the first ghetto, here, in Venezia. We are model for ghettos of which you speak. Venetian Jews were forced to live in ghetto, not far from here." Sara pointed past the Rialto Bridge where they were headed.

"I don't understand. What do you mean forced, like in the Holocaust?"

Sara's face twisted in anger. "Five hundred years ago, Jews were forced into the *Ghetto di Venezia.* Jews were not allowed to live among the Christians. The Franciscan friars did not approve of Jews and Christians living as equals. On Twenty-nine March, Fifteen-sixteen, during the holy week of Passover, seven hundred Jews living in Venezia were forced to move to—how do you say? —the 'little' island."

"That's horrible." Dani shook her head.

Sara quickened her pace as they walked past some official looking buildings along the water's edge, one building had a gold plaque on it with black embossed letters that read: COMUNE DI VENEZIA.

"Next week, ghetto will be four hundred-ninety years old. It was once metal foundry. Any Christian living there had to move, and Jews were forced to leave their homes and live on little island, isolated from Christians. We pay three times more than Christians to live there."

"Wow, that's kind of like what happened to the Japanese in Seattle, where I'm from," Dani said, hoping to sound halfway intelligent since she had totally blown it by being clueless about alchemy. "During the Second World War, the Japanese were taken from their homes and locked up in internment camps out in the country isolated from other Americans because the government believed they threatened national security."

Sara shook her head. "You are very smart. I know. Now you learn about *your heritage,* about friars who say Jews contaminate Christian minds with our bodies and religion. Jews were removed from San Polo and Sant' Agostino and locked inside ghetto after sunset until morning sunrise. We were confined there until Napoleon liberated us in Seventeen-ninety-seven."

"That's so wrong," Dani said, trying to keep up with Sara who walked at a clipped pace past a stop for a *vaporetto,* the public transportation waterbus, with a few tourists and their luggage, likely heading for late-night flights.

"We were not the only ones," Sara said, stopping abruptly at the foot of the Rialto Bridge, her face contorted in anger. "The Germans who came to Venezia to sell their goods, friars didn't want them to convert Catholics to Protestants or have advantages over local businesspeople, so they lock them here at night." Sara pointed to a large white building with a sign that read: FONDECO DE TEDESHI. "*Tedeshi* is Venetian word for Germans," she continued. "Tedeshi could sell their goods at market in daytime, but at night they were locked in. *A lora,* that ends our tour."

Dani looked at her watch. An hour had passed. It had gone by so quickly, well maybe the last part with the extra history lesson had dragged on a bit, but the time did seem to fly.

"See you are safe and in one piece." Sara smiled again.

Dani laughed embarrassed that Sara had recognized her apprehension.

"Have you had enough of Venetian ghosts for tonight?" Sara's eyes glinted under the lamplight.

Dani had enough talk of ghosts, but she wasn't sure she'd had enough of Sara. "Yes, *grazie,* Sara. Very interesting tour." Dani played with the loose change in her pants pocket trying to think of what to say or ask to keep Sara talking a little longer. She wanted to avoid going back to the tiny apartment and her smoldering laptop. *Think, think, think, gelato!*

"Would you like to get some gelato?" Dani asked.

Sara shook her head no. "If you like, I can take you on a tour of Jewish ghetto tomorrow."

Dani didn't want to hear about all the horrible shit that happened to Jews five hundred years ago. She wanted to finally try some Venetian gelato and hone her seduction skills on Italian women. Hell, that's why she'd come to Venice: Veronica and her damn gelato. But on the other hand, Sara's brown eyes glinting under the lamplight and her sumptuous cleavage were so sexually compelling she just couldn't refuse the opportunity.

"Yeah, that sounds great!" Dani said, a little too enthusiastically. She felt disappointed at her lack of sophistication tonight with Sara. Her seduction was slightly off. First misreading her, then her "like totally" too casual West Coast speech, which wouldn't have bothered the punk femmes in San Francisco, but sounded really stupid when she was speaking with Sara. She needed to pay more attention to how she spoke and not revert to her default mode of speech.

"I'm definitely interested in learning more about the tensions between Catholics and Jews. Where should I meet you?" Dani took the map out of her jacket pocket and stepped closer to one of the streetlamps to read.

"It is in the District of Cannaregio."

Dani searched for the Cannaregio District on her map. "OK, found it."

"From here at the Rialto . . . ," Sara pointed to the image of the Rialto Bridge on the map, "you go left down the street where we started our tour. It is called San Giovanni Crisostomo."

"OK." Dani found the Rialto Bridge on the map and traced her finger along the street they had walked down.

"You will see Strada Nuovo. It is very long street."

"Yes." Dani traced her finger alongside Sara's. Their fingers touched.

"You walk until you see Rio Terra Frisetti. There you see sign for 'Ghetto Nuovo.' Go over bridge and wait in covered area. Prepare for rain. *Ciao.*"

Sara began walking away.

"Wait," Dani called after her.

Sara turned around.

"I mean, what time should I meet you?"

"Four o'clock."

"Great." Dani smiled at Sara. "See you tomorrow then."

"*Domani, ciao,* Dani." Sara turned and disappeared into a dark calle.

"*Ciao,* Sara," Dani whispered almost to herself, enjoying the feel of the words on her lips.

Dani turned and crossed over the Rialto Bridge. She walked past the vendors' stalls, many of which were already closed or closing. She tried to remember the way she'd come. Everything looked different with the store windows shuttered. Metal doors concealed shop entrances and merchandise. There was almost no sign that the shops had ever been there at all. Her eyes searched for a familiar street name. She was relieved when she saw the yellow sign with the arrow that read: LA FERROVIA.

The apartment was close to the train station, and luckily one of the first lessons from the *Learn Italian While You Drive* CD set was on transportation: *barca* (ship), *treno* (train), *ferrovia* (train station). Dani began to make her way back through the maze of alleys, following the arrows on the signs toward home base.

The tiny streets were deserted, and except for the occasional dimly lit bar or a pizzeria that was open, the only other illumination cast was by the gas lamps that flickered in the calli. The squares, so alive with people only a few hours earlier, were now completely empty.

Dani quickened her pace, as before, nervously approaching blind corners and darkened doorways while she followed the yellow signs. And then, she couldn't seem to find another sign for the train station, so she walked towards a bridge that looked familiar. Perspiration formed on her brow.

As she started to cross the bridge, two guys appeared out of nowhere. She didn't get a good look at them. They seemed agitated and were yelling at her in Italian. Dani couldn't understand what they wanted. She took off running. She ran as fast as she could down the cramped alleys. Her only focus now was to put some distance between them and her. She rounded another corner and raced down a street that opened into a small campo with trees. She recognized it. It was the campo near DeLucia's Café.

She got her bearings and ran as quickly as she could to Calle del Figher, the street of her apartment. She hurriedly pulled the keys from her pocket and took the stairs two at a time, not stopping until she was in her flat with the door locked behind her. Drenched with sweat, she leaned against the back of the door, and tried to catch her breath.

Dani peeled off her wet clothes and hung them over the radiator to dry, then she got into the shower. After her shower, she changed into her sweats and took her notebook into the kitchen. She filled a pot with water and lit the pilot light on the stove to heat the water for tea. While she waited for the water to boil, she sat at the table opened her notebook to a clean sheet and began writing about Venice.

Dilapidated bricks of red, pink, gray, and beige bleed through the sienna facades of the three- and four-story buildings that buttress the canals. Each building fills the eyes with innumerable details, symmetrical etchings or grill work of circles, flowers, spirals, vines, cherubs and saints, lions, half wagon wheels, or just terra cotta shingles, each meticulously placed. All the windows are framed by wooden plank shutters painted forest green.

The streetlamps, made lovingly to tease and please the eye, hang on long, black steel vines or are mounted on the walls. They are hexagonal arts of work with green, blue, and orange glass panels housed under a composite of six black metal triangles decorated with black spindles.

My ears are delighted by the vaguely recognizable accents of German, French, and Italian tourists, occasional bells tolling from church towers and the lap and stir of the wake as the boats pass. It is sheer bliss for me and the cats, who do not miss the honking of car horns, or revving of motors, or screeching of wheels. The cat and I bask in the sun, sniff at our surroundings, paying close attention to the flowers, meandering through the streets unmolested by some self-important, harried car and driver.

I make my way through the maze of canals and four-foot-wide cobblestone streets, enchanted when they lead to a large opening, a piazza, or plaza where the young boys kick a soccer ball across the hand-cut, rectangular blocks of stone that carpet the campo. My eyes catch a glimpse of Valentine red flowers from their window box perch.

Satisfied with her new prose, and feeling a sense of the creative inspiration Veronica had promised her she would feel, helped ease the sting of her computer's death earlier in the evening. She turned off the light and thus ended the day.

DICIASETTE

The mournful sound of an accordion caught Dani's attention as she meandered down the dimly lit cobblestone street. She wrapped her coat tighter around her body and followed the sound to a canal. The water glittered from the light cast through the windows of the nearby buildings. She descended the white stone steps to the water's edge and sat down to listen.

The sound of the accordion stopped and she thought she heard a baby whimpering. The cries grew louder and louder, she craned her neck to see where the yowling was coming from. There was a splash and the crying ceased.

In the canal below, she saw a baby floating towards her, its hands outstretched to be picked up. Dani turned to yell for help, but there was no one around. When she looked back the canal was calm. She moved towards the water's edge.

Suddenly a little arm emerged from the water and grasped at Dani. She jolted backwards, slipping on the steps and fell into the canal. It was bone-chilling. She thrashed in the water, thick with green algae that pinned her down. She struggled to free herself, but could not get out of its grip. Finally, she kicked her feet loose and freed her arms, hurling the algae off of her body.

In the next moment, she was back in the bed in the rented apartment, all of the bed covers on the floor. She opened her eyes wide trying to orient herself to what was real. Adrenaline coursed through her body. Her hands trembled. She looked at the clock. It was 7:00 AM. She'd never had so many bad dreams in a row. It was starting to unnerve her.

"Good god. No more ghost tours," she said aloud.

She needed to get some light into the room and break out of the dream's negative energy. She got out of bed and switched on the lights. The heavy stone floor seemed to sag under its own weight. It felt cold through her socks as she quickly walked to the windows and pushed open the green wooden shutters. She was hoping some natural light would help her overcome the feeling of claustrophobia she was starting to experience from living in the cramped apartment and traversing the narrow passageways the locals considered the "streets" of Venice. It was almost useless. The buildings surrounding the apartment were built so close together that only a trickle of light made its way into the room.

She put on her clothes, grabbed her blue spiral notebook and pen, and left the apartment for DeLucia's Café, knowing she would feel more grounded in the presence of other people. She hoped for a seat at the table by the window.

Regina greeted her warmly as she walked in. She looked genuinely happy to see her. "*Buongiorno,* cappuccino?"

"*Sì, grazie,*" Dani said, smiling back. *Maybe I shouldn't close the door on Regina just yet. Straight girls love to experiment, especially before their weddings.* This was something she used to jokingly say to her friends back in San Francisco. It brought up a memory of Michelle, and she suddenly felt a burst of anger.

"You are tired?" Regina asked.

Dani nodded. "I went on that ghost tour last night, so I didn't sleep very well."

"Oh, I'm sorry, I was hoping you'd enjoy it."

"No, I did. I had a really knowledgeable guide and I got to see more of Venice and it is 'even more magical at night,' as the tourist brochures promise." *And creepier,* she thought, but didn't say.

Regina smiled, relieved. She set a napkin and saucer on the counter for the cappuccino she was about to make for Dani. "How is your novel coming?"

Dani rested her elbow on the cold marble counter and held her head in her hand, still trying to steady herself. "Like a slug."

"Slug?"

"It's a slimy little animal?"

"Sorry, *slimy?*" Regina looked perplexed. "I don't know this word."

"Um, like wet and gooey." Dani struggled for words to explain a slimy slug to Regina and tried not to laugh, lest Regina think she was laughing at her. She guessed with the few gardens in Venice, the Venetian slug population was scarce, possibly nonexistent. She still hadn't purchased that Italian/English dictionary which she now concluded her mother had been right about. Then she thought of a word Regina might know.

"OK, I got it . . . like escargot. Do you know escargot?"

"*Sì,* escargot. Your novel is like escargot?" Regina made a funny face at Dani.

Dani laughed through her nose. "Like a snail, slow. Never mind, it just doesn't translate. How about . . . it's coming along slowly?"

"*Sì, lentamente,* slowly, *capisco.*"

"*Malto* slowly."

Regina laughed and set the cappuccino on the counter. "*Molto,*" she corrected.

Dani opened a packet of sugar and poured it into her cappuccino. The sugar crystals sat on top of the thick foam. Dani watched as the foam stood its ground, not giving in to the weight of the sugar. Then, all at once, the foam collapsed and the sugar sank to the bottom of the cup. The frothy white foam surrounded the sinkhole and appeared untouched, like the sugar was never there.

"You seem to be learning *Italiano.*"

"I wouldn't go that far." Dani stirred the coffee with the small spoon.

"Your accent is good."

"Thanks, I studied Spanish in high school. It's *simile.*"

Regina turned the handle on the sink behind the counter and began washing the petite white espresso cups. "Are you going to write today?"

Dani sighed. "I'm going to try this morning. In the afternoon, I'm going on a tour of the Jewish ghetto."

Regina turned off the water and began stacking the cups. "Are you Jew?"

Dani swallowed a sip of her coffee. The question always put her on edge and not knowing Regina's intent made her extremely uncomfortable. If Regina had asked her about her sexuality or why she dressed like she did, she would have answered right away, but this was different.

"Yep, one of the 'chosen people,'" Dani laughed as she said it, carefully studying Regina's expression for a hint of anti-Semitism. She couldn't find it.

"You will like ghetto."

Dani wondered what there could be to "like" about a ghetto. *Italian rappers?*

"Back in the States we try to stay out of ghettos, which are for poor people, rather than take tours of them." She shrugged her shoulders. "Well, I should stop stalling." Picking up her cup, she happily made her way to the window table. She opened her notebook and scribbled out a few ideas before becoming distracted by the sound of someone coughing wretchedly. She turned to see an old man in a beige cap, sitting at the corner table with a cane beside his chair. He alternated between sipping from his cup and coughing up mouthfuls of phlegm and spitting them into a white handkerchief.

Dani felt sorry for the elderly man. Clearly, he was not well. She pegged him for a smoker and thought about her own grandfather who had died from emphysema when she was a young child. She had adored him. He was funny, gentle, and kind, but like her dad, he was taken from her too soon. She felt a pang of sadness and also guilt. Of course, her mother worried about her. She'd already lost so much.

Dani realized that there was no way she was going to be able to concentrate now. She packed up her things, left several euros on the counter and went outside to the payphone to call her mom.

"Hello," her mother answered. She sounded alarmed.

"Hi, Mom—"

"Dani, is everything OK?" her mom interrupted.

"Yeah, Mom, everything is fine. How are you?"

"I'm sleeping. It's two AM." Her mother's concern turned to annoyance. "I wondered when you'd call."

"I'll let you go back to sleep."

"No, that's OK, I'm awake now. How are you?" Her mother's tone was a mixture of genuine concern coupled with her mom's unique blend of Jewish mother guilt.

"Good. It's nice here." Dani looked around at the buildings and bridges over the canal.

"What's that in the background? Is somebody screaming?"

"No, Mom, that's just some kids playing soccer in the square. Soccer is big here." Dani held the phone closer to her ear. The connection was poor and the boys were running in her direction trying to score a goal between two large, free-standing metal billboards in the campo. The billboards were covered with what looked like election posters and the last line of the poster read "*No matrimonio omosesuale.*" She understood the words instantly and felt her stomach drop. "No Gay Marriage." Even in beautiful Italy, gay people were used as pawns to get politicians elected. It angered her.

"Dani, are you there?" her mother asked.

"Yeah, I'm still here."

"Are you sure you are alright?"

"Yeah, Mom, I'm sure, just tired. You know the time difference and such. I'm going to the Jewish ghetto today. Did you know that there was a Jewish ghetto here?"

"Sounds vaguely familiar," her mother said, yawning.

"Yeah, I met a nice Jewish girl and she's taking me on a tour today. Last night I went on a ghost walk tour. Venice is pretty creepy at night. The buildings have these spooky decorations, like weird faces and heads in the facades of the buildings."

"That's nice dear. Is everything alright with your room?"

"Yeah, it's comfortable."

"No one's bothering you, are they?"

"No, no one's bothering me."

"I need to go back to sleep now. I love you and be safe."

"I always am. I love you too, Mom."

"All right then, call me tomorrow."

Despite her intention to be compassionate, what seemed to her to be her mom's neediness made Dani cringe. "I'll call you again in a few days, Mom." Dani hung up the phone quickly before her mother could protest. She watched the boys play soccer for a few minutes, then started walking towards the apartment.

As she went down a narrow alleyway, almost devoid of daylight, she passed a thin guy with short, greasy-looking hair. He made her nervous and she could have sworn that he stopped and was watching her. Being gay and by herself in an unfamiliar city made her more vigilant about her safety. As a precaution, she walked past the turn off for the apartment and continued walking toward the Grand Canal near the Riva Di Biaso *vaporetto* stop to the quay where she and Maurizio had come ashore the day she arrived.

She sat at the edge of the canal and watched the waterbuses and water taxis pass. She took in more of the unusual architecture of the buildings: Corinthian columns, baroque lattice, sculptures of winged lions, and decorative, disembodied heads. What impressed her most was the beauty of the decay and imperfections of the buildings. In the United States, these buildings would be seen as tenements. No owner or neighborhood association with any sense would allow this kind of erosion to continue. It would bring down property values. But here, the faded colors and mixed hues of the buildings, whether freshly painted or baked by the sun and polished by sea winds, seemed to blend together, creating captivating works of art. Venice was genuinely awe inspiring.

Dani looked at her watch. Twenty minutes had passed since she'd seen the weird guy in the alley. She figured he'd be gone by now and that it was safe to walk home to the apartment. She chose a wider, more populated, street for her return.

As she neared the corner, coming from the opposite direction she saw the thin, weaselly man walking with another guy with curly black hair. Most of the Italian men she saw were so well-put-together that in the United States they would be read as gay. They wore colorful pants or expensive jeans with crisp dress shirts or pressed suits with shiny leather shoes. These guys seemed rougher, like drunks who had rolled out of bed and thrown on whatever clothes were lying on the floor from the night before. They didn't seem to take pride in their appearance at all. They made her nervous.

Dani avoided looking at them as she quickly passed by, but she sensed the weasel looking at her. As soon as she was out of their view, she quickly turned the corner and let herself into the apartment.

The place smelled a little like gas. She checked the stove. All the burners were off. She looked at the thermostat. Nothing looked out of the ordinary. She grabbed her blue spiral note-book, took it into the kitchen, and hunkered down to write.

DICIOTTO

The rainfall took Dani by surprise as she started her afternoon trek to meet Sara at the ghetto. The stones in the cobblestone courtyard were painted a slick, grayish black by the rain. She noticed a handful of umbrellas hanging on the metal security framing on the door outside the *tabacchi.* She grabbed a rainbow umbrella, delighted to sport her LGBT colors in Italy, and went inside to pay.

The cramped streets were now almost impossible to navigate as hordes of people with open umbrellas slid in and out of storefronts and through the maze of *calli* on their way to museums or cafés, or wherever else they were going. It reminded her of the jampacked sidewalks in San Francisco's Chinatown, where it is often so crowded that people press against you as they walk from fish market to vegetable stand. By contrast, the sidewalks in Chinatown were bigger than the streets in Venice, which in some places were no more than two- or three-open-umbrellas wide.

Dani crossed over a *ponte* and stopped for a moment to take a reprieve from the frenetic activity in the tiny streets. She leaned on the bridge's ornamental handrailing and watched the canals in her sightline ripple under the soft touch of raindrops. Like everything else she had seen in Venice, the sight was like poetry.

On the other side of the *ponte,* a blue flag with the @ symbol hung in front of a yellow frescoed building, indicating the presence of computers. She crossed the bridge and went in.

An Indian woman wearing an ankle-length blue dress approached her. The woman frowned and said something Dani didn't understand. The woman pointed her finger at Dani, then realizing she was not making herself clear, grabbed Dani's umbrella out of her hand and put it in a garbage can by the door.

"Oh, *mi dispiace*," Dani apologized in Italian, noticing that her umbrella had left huge puddles on the stone floor. She felt her face redden with embarrassment.

"Internet *2.50 euro per quindici minuti,*" the woman said.

"*Sì,*" Dani said, nodding. Fifteen minutes would be enough time.

"*Passaporta?*"

"My passport?" Dani wondered why the woman would need to see her passport.

"*Americano?*"

Dani nodded.

The woman handed her a piece of paper written in English. It explained that due to terrorist concerns all people had to show identification. Dani untucked her shirt and unzipped the money belt under her clothing where she kept her passport and emergency numbers and handed her blue passport to the woman. The woman walked Dani to a backroom with eight computers atop a long table and pointed to the clock on the lower right-hand side of the computer screen. "*Tempo qui,*" she said.

Dani sat down and quickly logged into her email account. There were all kinds of strange symbols on the keyboard. She kept hitting the wrong ones as she typed in Veronica's email address—Goodthyme@EZBaker.com—then she attempted to write an email. She had to go back numerous times to erase the unwanted symbols, wasting her precious fifteen minutes.

Hey V,

You're right. Venice is freaking beautiful! And it would be a great place to write except my computer blew up just when I was getting my groove on. So much for international adaptors. Luckily, I have two chapters backed up on that dinosaur hard drive.

Anyway, I'm glad you kept nagging me, and that I'm a butch-of-my-word, cuz I could not have imagined a more beautiful city in all of my wildest dreams. And speaking of dreams, I keep having weird nightmares. Might be because I went on a ghost tour the other night. The guide was a nerdy, hot Jewish girl. Well, woman to be precise. I'm off to meet her again for a private tour of the Jewish ghetto.

Still can't stop thinking about Michelle and whether or not I should move back to Seattle.

Anyway, ciao for now!

Dani

Before she logged off she Googled "Ghetto Nuovo," where Sara said she would meet her. Apparently this was a neighborhood—on a small island—where all the Jews in

Venice had been forced to move in 1516! Dani logged off and got up from the cold metal chair, paid the woman, and grabbed her umbrella. It was still raining as she continued her trek to Ghetto Nuovo. She felt a sense of growing excitement as she wove through the narrow streets.

Dani was careful to avoid collisions with the potpourri of old ladies walking poodles, stooped old men with canes, and the fast-walking Venetians carelessly dangling cigarettes from their hands. Then, of course, there were the American and German tourists she had to navigate around as they stopped without warning, blocking entire passageways, to window-shop or take a picture of a gondola on a canal.

After about ten minutes of negotiating the foot traffic, she stopped abruptly. Her heart dropped into her stomach. She'd left her passport back at the internet café. She had to go back and get it, but if she did she was sure to be late to meet Sara. *Sara might think I'm blowing her off and leave. How will I find her again if we miss each other?* She didn't want to miss the meeting with Sara, but she absolutely had to get her passport.

Dani turned and darted through the crowd like a fish swimming upstream. She tried to retrace her steps as best as she could, struggling to remember where she'd seen the @ symbol. Everything looked the same: mask stores, Murano glass jewelry, *gelaterria, trattoria,* cafés. She walked briskly down the alleys, turning down various corridors until she found the campo with the blue flag. A metal gate covered the storefront. It was closed. She looked around and glimpsed the Indian woman about to cross the *ponte* on the other edge of the campo. She raced after her, reaching her just as she was about to turn down one of the tiny alleyways.

"*Mi scusi. Mi passaporta, per favore?*" Dani asked, out of breath.

"*Sì, sì, sì.*" The woman nodded. "*Andiamo.*" She turned and slowly waddled back to the internet café.

Dani tried to remain patient as the woman lifted the metal door back up, unlocked the glass door, and switched on the light. It was taking forever. Dani wiped the sweat from her brow.

The woman walked behind the counter and slowly opened a desk drawer, pulled out Dani's blue passport and handed it to her. "*Qui.*"

Dani took it from her relieved. "*Grazie mille, signora,*" she said, bowing to the woman. She lifted up her shirt and unzipped her money belt, put the passport inside and zipped it snug. Then she bolted out of the shop and ran towards the Cannaregio District, map in hand, navigating the streets of Venice.

A memory of her and Michelle flashed into her mind. They were walking through a corn maze at a farm outside of Tacoma, Washington. She remembered how Michelle had freaked out when she went to hold her hand, afraid someone would recognize them. She tried to shake off the bad feeling from the memory.

DICIANNOVE

Dani was grateful to see the sign for Strada Nuovo. It was, by far, the widest street in Venice and, from the map, it looked like it went a greater distance than any other. This afforded her the opportunity to lift her eyes from the map and take in the sights around her.

Strada Nuovo was a refreshing change from the cold, dark *calli* of the Santa Croce District where she was staying. The street was filled with backpack-wearing travelers and purse-swinging tourists perusing the stalls of street vendors and artisans selling their oil or watercolor paintings of the canals, feathered masks, colorful scarves, and "I love Venice" tee-shirts. She loved the bold colors. The playfulness of the scene appealed to her. She threw back her shoulders and walked on, enjoying every moment.

As she was passing an outdoor vegetable market, Dani saw a yellow sign on the corner of a building with black Hebrew letters and an arrow pointing right painted on it. *This must be it.*

Dani followed additional signs until she came to a narrowly enclosed street darkened by tall buildings. She felt a chill as she entered the shadowy passageway and heard the flapping of wings. A pigeon flew directly at her. She felt a gust of air as it whizzed by, almost clipping the top of her head, and causing a surge of adrenaline through her body.

Dani refocused on the arrow on the yellow sign with SINAGOGHE-MOSTRA D'ARTE EBRAICA written on it and followed it to a wooden bridge with a white street sign that read PONTE DE GHETTO NUOVO. She hustled up the steps and crossed over the canal making her way down the bridge to a covered alleyway with another sign that read SOTOPORTEGO. She deduced that *sotoportego* was the name for the tunnel-like passageways that ran under the buildings since she'd noticed the word on other covered streetways she'd seen. She glanced at her watch, relieved that somehow she'd made it in time.

Dani entered the tunnel. It was dark, lit by one light on the side of a bricked wall. It was also cold and dank and damp and smelled of mildew. Something about it smelled familiar. Dani was trying to place the smell when she heard the dripping of water and turned to see a big puddle in a corner and saw a rat scurrying by. *This is where she wants to meet? Crazy Goth. We could have just met at one those cool cafés or gelaterias. Damn, she's committed to her vibe.*

Dani leaned against the brick wall and took a deep breath to settle her nerves. She wanted to be charming, not stressed out, when she met Sara for their possible first date. She looked up at the exposed wooden beams overhead and thought about all the people who had passed through this ancient alleyway and felt a chill run through her. Then she heard the clicking sound of heels and noticed long black boots coming down the wooden steps. She felt a growing sense of excitement as Sara made her way into the *sotoportego*. Sara was wearing a black jacket and a black skirt with a beige flower pattern. *Veronica would love her outfit,* she thought, noticing that even though

Sara wasn't carrying an umbrella she was dry. *She must live close by.*

"*Buongiorno,* Sara." Dani smiled, trying to decide if she looked as good in the daylight as she had under the lamplight. The Gothic look wasn't her favorite, but she was drawn to Sara's brown eyes and her beautiful long brown hair. Dani loved a woman with long hair. She loved pulling back the strands to kiss her lover's neck, or bite an earlobe. It was like pulling back a curtain and revealing a delicious surprise. She loved the scent of shampoo that lingered and the way their tresses or ringlets gathered around her when she kissed the woman. She loved to weave her fingers through the long locks and pull her lover closer to her.

Many gay and bi women, even the femmes, cut their hair short to signify their sexuality. Dani didn't think it mattered. She also found high femmes with short hair attractive. Women with short hair weren't afraid to be bold and brash. They didn't need to hold on to men's approval through their hair. She loved the look of a high femme sporting no more than an inch or two of hair in full makeup and earrings. But ultimately, she favored the powerful femininity of women with shoulder-length hair.

"Did you see any ghosts riding through *campi* on horseback or floating in canals on your way home last night?" Sara asked.

"No, thank god," Dani said, laughing nervously. The thought of seeing ghosts terrified her. "But I did have some weird dreams." Dani stopped short of telling her about the nightmare.

Sara smiled and took Dani's arm in hers and led them inside the square and under a portico out of the rain. "*Andiamo,* we go into ghetto."

It could have just been a friendly gesture. Lots of women walked arm in arm in Venice, it was very European. But this was the second time that Sara had taken her by the arm and Dani felt a surge of energy flash through her when she was touched.

"As I told you yesterday, on Twenty-nine March, in the year Fifteen-sixteen, the Franciscan friars gave an order to move the Jews. Seven hundred Venetian Jews were forced out of their homes and confined here on this little island." Sara pointed to the canal on the right and traced the edge of the ghetto in the air with her finger.

Dani glanced at Sara's hands. They were very feminine, although a little pale, which was befitting for an eccentric ghost-tour guide and poet. Most importantly, she didn't wear a wedding ring. She wondered what kind of poems Sara wrote, and if she would get a chance to read some of them, maybe over cappuccino or *vino* later.

"Ghetto Nuovo ends on the other side of those buildings. Can you see the canal there?" Sara pointed in the direction of two payphones on the edge of the campo. "That was the edge of the first part of ghetto."

"This island is tiny."

"*Sì,* and very crowded. We were over four thousand Jews living here. In 1541, the ghetto was expanded to include a nearby area connected to the island via footbridge. This new area, home to Levantine Jews, was Ghetto Vecchio, which means 'Old Ghetto,' though it was newest part of ghetto."

"Sounds totally intense!" Dani erupted.

Sara turned and looked at Dani. "*Sì,* intense."

Dani felt like an idiot using California slang phrases she'd picked up working in the café. Here she was with an intelligent and beautiful Italian Jewish woman, and all she could think to say was "totally intense." She cringed at the thought that she sounded more like a surfer dude than the distinguished writer she wanted to be.

"You must know, Dani, Jews have traveled to Venezia since Nine hundred-thirty-two, but could not live here. They could stay only for short period, and then had to leave. First Jews were seeking refuge from oppression in Germany."

"Germans hated Jews a thousand years ago?" Dani lifted herself off the wall and stood up straight again.

Sara paused for a moment before speaking and then grabbed Dani's arm and leaned in closer to her. Dani thought maybe she was going to kiss her, but Sara's brown eyes flashed with anger. "Not just Germans. People all over have hated us for hundreds of years. Jews were not allowed in the trades or to own property. These German Jews were pawnbrokers, they were called 'rag and bone men.' Only this, and money lending, could Jews do—and only because money lending was against Christian law, so the *Serenissima* let Jews to make the loans because this prospered Venezia."

Dani tried to follow what Sara was saying, but with Sara's lips so close to her face, her accent, and the flurry of emotion in her words, Dani had completely lost the thread. Dani took a step back. "What is the *Serenissima?*"

Sara's eyes lit up as she talked. She was definitely a passionate woman, especially about history. Besides Veronica, most of the women she'd met while working at the café were passionate only about their next piercing or tattoo. They couldn't be bothered with current events or politics, let alone having any regard for history. Sara was like a Jewish Clio, the muse of history. Intelligence was sexy. She loved women who were educated and well-read.

"*A lora, la Serenissima* was the Venetian government that made contracts with us Jews when it was convenient for them, and broke them when it was not." Sara pointed to the doorway under the portico where they were standing. "This building was once a bank and this one a pawnshop. Christians could not lend money for profit and Jews were forbidden to work or own property. So, Jews lend money to survive, but when we do well, the *Serenissima* would join the friars to blame us Jews for plague, losing war, and sickness. Bad things happen, it's the fault of the Jews. Then they banish us and take the money."

"That's ridiculous!" Dani fidgeted with the coins in her pocket.

"*Sì,* they only allow us to loan the money or to give them money for their rags and broken furniture so they can take money and buy something new. And they say we Jews are greedy."

"People are always looking for a scapegoat, but let me get this straight," Dani mused aloud. "The Mayans invent math,

the Greeks philosophy, and we Jews invent the pawnshop."
She was not sure this was an achievement to be excited about.

"This was *Banco Rosso,* red bank," Sara translated, "because after the banker recorded the amount given for each item the customer was handed red ticket."

Dani looked at the building. It was now an art gallery. She tried to imagine what it might have looked like back then. She wondered how the pawnshops four hundred years ago compared to the pawnshops of today. Did people hock violins and candlestick holders back then like they hock guitars and fancy silverware today?

The rain had stopped and Sara walked into the square. Dani followed her to a brick wall with bronze sculptures hanging on it. These were bas reliefs—long and relatively flat, like picture frames. She looked more closely at one of the frames: It was an image of Nazi soldiers ordering Jews at gunpoint into the notorious cattle cars. It gave her chills.

"You know about the Holocaust, yes?" Sara asked.

"A little," Dani said, looking at Sara.

She felt guilty for not knowing more, but she'd always been more interested in gay history than Jewish history. She knew about Harvey Milk, the openly gay politician of San Francisco who was assassinated in 1978. She knew that Milk's assassin, Dan White, claimed to have gone crazy from eating too much junk food, and was acquitted of the murder. She knew this argument for his innocence had become known as the *Twinkie defense* and had led to the gay community rioting in San Francisco, in what were later called the White Night Riots.

She knew a closeted gay man, Oliver "Billy" Sipple, had saved President Ford by knocking a gun out of would-be-assassin Sara Jane Moore's hand. She knew that Sipple was "outed" in the newspaper and immediately disowned by his family. She knew that President Ford had never given him the recognition a heterosexual hero would have gotten, and that Sipple had died in relative obscurity at a young age, caused by self-hate and social ostracism. Dani knew that no one in 1975 cared that a homosexual had saved a president's life and she felt confident that no one cared in 2006 either. She knew all of that. But all she knew about the Holocaust was the number: six million.

Six million Jews were murdered.

Sara pointed to another bronze sculpture hanging on the wall. It was a bas-relief scene of a firing squad of SS soldiers shooting blindfolded Jews. There were seven bronze panels in total, each portraying the scene of an atrocity against the Jewish people. "These bas-relief sculptures were made by a Jew from Lithuania. He survived and moved to New York after the war, but would come to Venice every year to paint. He made these to honor his mother who perished in a concentration camp, and for all to witness the horrors that have befallen our people."

Dani looked over the horrific images on the bronze plates that hung on the ghetto wall. Her eyes traveled to the letters etched in the corner indicating the artist's name. She read the name aloud, "Arbit Blatas," then paused. "My great grandparents were from Lithuania."

Dani wondered for the first time what might have happened to her great, great grandparents who had stayed in the old country after their children immigrated to the United States. "I'm not sure where my grandparents on my father's side were from. They died before I was born and my father died when I was kid, so I don't know much about that side of my family."

"It is good that you know something of your mother's side. Heritage is very important, Dani." Sara patted her on the shoulder. Dani couldn't tell if it was affectionate or sort of condescending. "We must understand from where we come so that we know where we are going."

Dani pointed to a list of Italian names behind the cattle car picture. "What are all these names?"

"Jews from Venezia sent to Auschwitz in 1944 to be murdered."

Dani read the names. Mario Tedesco. Vittoria Tedeschi. Elena Mariani. Adele Fassel Kohnar. Alberto Pollack. Eugenia Loewenthal Polatscheck, Davide Fishbein. They were Italian, Spanish, and Slavic. There were hundreds of names with their ages listed after their names. It made her sick.

"The Nazis demanded to the rabbi that he give the names of Venetian Jews. He chose suicide."

"That happened just sixty years ago—in this beautiful city? How is that possible?" Dani shook her head.

"Hatred has very thick roots, Dani. Do you see them?"

Dani thought Sara was speaking metaphorically about the roots, but then she saw where Sara was pointing. The "them," were four men who looked like soldiers. They wore gray uniforms with yellow stripes on their sleeves and had guns and handcuffs hanging from their belts. They stood in and around a small guardhouse at the back of the ghetto square.

"What are they doing?"

Sara brushed her hair from her face. "The ghetto is terrorist target for anti-Semites."

"What?" Dani's mouth fell open. "Seriously?"

"They destroy our cemeteries and violate our dead." Sara looked hard at Dani like she wanted to see if Dani understood the seriousness of what she was imparting.

Dani felt like she was getting more than she'd bargained for on this tour of the ghetto. This was not the light afternoon she thought she'd be sharing with Sara. Still, she was intrigued.

"What do you mean, violate our dead?"

"Jews were not allowed to bury our dead in Venezia until Thirteen-eighty-six when the *Serenissima* allowed us some land for cemetery."

"There are tombstones from Thirteen-eighty-six?" Dani interrupted.

"*Sì.*" Sara nodded.

"Why don't we get some sandwiches and a bottle of wine and we can walk there?"

"It's on the Lido."

Dani straightened her shoulders and tried to create a renewed look of interest. "What's the Lido?" Dani asked.

"An island across the *Adriatico.*"

"The Adriatic Ocean?"

"Sea," Sara corrected.

"Can we go there? I love old cemeteries. I find them very peaceful." Dani looked at Sara.

There was an awkward silence. Sara looked at the position of the sun in the sky. "It's getting late," she said.

"Yeah, I should get back to my writing, but all this talk about history is making me hungry." Dani waited to see if Sara would take the bait.

Instead, Sara looked at her earnestly and agreed. "Yes, writing is very important."

This one likes playing hard to get, Dani thought. "Well, thank you for the tour." She pulled out her wallet. "How much do I owe you?"

Sara's smoldering brown eyes widened and she held Dani's eye contact without speaking. Dani could get lost in those eyes. "*Niente.* You owe me nothing," Sara said.

Was she flirting with her?

"Nothing? That's very generous. You must let me repay the favor, Sara."

"Write something of what I have shared with you."

Hadn't Sara listened when Dani told her she was a fiction writer? Dani tried to ignore the faux pas on Sara's part and pressed forward.

"I was thinking more along the lines of dinner."

"Sorry, I'm not hungry," Sara said.

She thought about Veronica. Veronica could always eat.

"Can I see you again?"

Sara took her time considering Dani's request before responding. "Meet me at Levantine Synagogue on the Twenty-ninth at half past ten."

"Yeah, OK," Dani said. It sounded like another history lesson, but Dani hoped that this might lead somewhere soon.

This was unfolding at a lot slower pace than she was used to, but she had time and she really did need to focus on her writing.

"Well, thank you again, Sara, it was an illuminating tour. I look forward to our next adventure together." Dani gave her the best Casanova smile she could conjure.

"You are welcome, Dani. *Buena sera,*" Sara said and crossed a bridge, leaving Dani standing alone in the square feeling a bit perplexed that she hadn't moved her planned seduction further along.

Dani walked home slowly that evening, enjoying Venice's superlative beauty, which contrasted darkly with the things Sara had shared with her about the city's history. She stopped and rested her chin on the cold metal railing of a bridge near the apartment. As she watched the reflection of the colorful frescoed buildings ripple on the water, her mind reflected on the impression left by Sara's beauty, especially Sara's full pink lips, the color of her olive skin, and the memory of her figure under the soft brown sweater she wore the night they met. She was classically beautiful and there something different about Sara that enchanted her. Dani wasn't quite sure what element it was, but whatever it was, she liked it. Sara was intriguing, but a bit too obsessed with history.

Her reverie was abruptly cut short by the sound of Veronica's voice in her head. "Stay focused on your writing, Dani." She slumped under the weight of the imagined words. She'd come here to complete her novel, not find more elaborate and expensive ways to avoid it. The clock was ticking. She walked back to the apartment, heated water on the stove for tea, and took out her notebook.

VENTI

Dani put her teacup in the sink and got in bed with the one book she brought from home—*Take Your Protagonist Shopping*—a book on writing fictional characters for novels. She opened the book and read a few sentences, not retaining any of the content. She was too exhausted for it to hold her attention. She put the book on the bedtable and switched off the lights to sleep.

Her mind wanted to wander back to Sara and the Jewish ghetto. She wondered what it was like to live in Venice and spend your days talking about depressing things that happened in the past.

Dani liked history, but this history was totally depressing. She guessed that Sara was smart enough to be a university professor, but wanted a job that wouldn't detract from her writing time. Dani knew that she herself, as a writer, would likely have to work a shitty day job until she made it big. At this rate, it was going to be forever from now.

As she began to drift, she detected the faint smell of gas again. She was so tired that she didn't want to get up. Then she heard a knock on the door.

"Who is it?" she asked. No one answered. She got up and cautiously opened the door. There was no one there. The smell of gas seemed more pronounced.

Dani put on her jacket and walked down the stairs to investigate the smell. She opened the door to the courtyard and noticed a lit gas lamp. It looked like the one she'd stood under at the Rialto Bridge where she first met Sara. The flame flickered wildly behind the glass.

A figure moved out of the darkness. It was Sara.

"Hey, Sara," Dani said. "This a pleasant surprise."

"There's something I want to show you." Sara extended her hand and Dani caught a wisp of her perfume—and then the gas smell again.

"Do you know if there's a gas leak? It's really strong . . . ," her voice trailed off.

"Come," Sara interrupted and took Dani's hand. Dani felt a chill on her skin as she followed Sara down a long, narrow *calle* and into a dark *sotoportego*. It was so cold. The air smelled dank. It was a familiar smell. She heard the ripple of water against stone in the darkness and then a loud crashing sound. The *sotoportego* closed behind them. It startled, but did not frighten her.

"Where are we going?"

"Shush." Sara insisted.

Dani pulled her jacket tighter around her body. The *sotoportego* opened onto the ghetto square. Men dressed in black coats and red hats with long beards conversed in languages she could not recognize.

"Are they making a film?"

Sara shook her head. She motioned to the edge of the campo.

Dani looked up. All of the windows facing the ghetto were bricked in and the bridge they had crossed over earlier that day was gone, replaced by a solid brick wall. "How do they do that?" she asked.

Sara motioned to follow her.

Dani trailed Sara to a footbridge connecting Ghetto Vecchio with Ghetto Nuovo. A man rowing through the canal in a wooden boat with a lantern hanging on a metal pole to light his way in the darkness yelled at her in Italian. Dani didn't understand him but she sensed an urgency in his tone.

"What did he just say?" She turned to Sara, but Sara was gone.

The campo was suddenly empty. Frightened, Dani ran into the *sotoportego,* where they had entered. The exit was blocked by a thick wooden door. She pounded on it, heaving her body against it, but the door was unyielding. She fell to the cold stone floor exhausted and confused. The smell of gas overpowered her and she succumbed to the darkness.

VENTUNO

Dani entered DeLucia's Café and walked to the counter. "*Come sta,* Regina?"

"*Bene,* and you?"

"I seem to be having a lot of scary dreams since I arrived. I even fell out of bed and woke up on the floor."

Regina brushed her hair back from her face. "*Venezia* can give you bad dreams. I never slept so well as in San Francisco. Here the history weighs on you."

"Really?" Dani looked confused.

Regina nodded.

"I guess that's what it is." Dani's stomach growled. She eyed the pastries in the case. "Can I get one of those jam-filled croissants?"

"*Brioche con mela.*" Regina put the croissant on the napkin and handed it to Dani. "*Bon apetito.*"

"*Grazie,*" Dani said, noticing that Regina seemed different this morning, more business, less friendly. Dani wondered if she was being colder now that she knew she was Jewish.

Regina handed her a copy of the *International Herald Tribune.* "*Ecco,* you might want to read some news in English."

Dani took the paper from her. It was like seeing an old friend again. She wanted to hug the vowels and consonants that made beautiful English words. She opened the newspaper, hoping it would somehow help ground her. Instead, the headline startled her: *"Anti-Semitism at ground level in France."*

She scanned the paper for the date. It was a few days old, dated March 24, 2006. She skimmed the article.

"It's Blacks and Arabs on one side and Jews on the other," read one of the pieces. Another article stated: "After 9/11 someone spray painted 'Death to the U.S. Death to Jews.' Even today there is widespread belief that the attacks of 9/11 were a Jewish plot and that Jews were notified beforehand."

"What is wrong with people?" she said aloud, not caring if anyone heard her.

"What is it?" Regina walked over to Dani.

Dani read a comment cited in the paper to her. "'Hitler would have made a good Muslim. Even seven-year-olds say 'Don't eat like a Jew.'" According to the article, this kind of talk is commonplace in France."

Regina shook her head.

Then Dani read a statistic that chilled her. "Thirty-three hundred Jews from France moved to Israel in Two thousand-five to *escape anti-Semitism,* a thirty-five-year high."

Dani was incredulous. She wanted to tell Sara about the news, but they weren't meeting for a couple of days. It would have to wait. Dani put down the paper and looked at Regina.

"Good thing my friend Veronica didn't tell me how wonderful Paris was in the spring. I might be getting my ass-kicked right now under the Eiffel Tower!"

"I'm sorry, when I was in the United States I missed our paper, and I thought . . ."

"No worries, Regina," Dani said. "Any trips to the *Estati Uniti* in your future? Perhaps your honeymoon?"

Regina laughed. It sounded forced. She spoke in Italian, so Dani didn't understand what she said. It sounded like she was cursing. Regina brushed crumbs off the counter with a dishtowel and tossed it over the neck of the faucet. "Did you like the ghetto tour?"

Dani nodded and picked up the croissant and took a bite. "Yeah, it was really interesting. I learned a lot," she said, her mouth full of pastry. "Like how Jews were treated by Catholic Venetians."

Regina nodded. "Yes, it is true. We were one of only cities that let Jews in, but we are first place in Europe to put Jews in a ghetto."

"I guess someone had to be the first." Dani shrugged. "I also learned that the word *ghetto* was created from a mispronunciation by German Jews of the word *geto,* because the tiny island used to be a metal-casting foundry and the verb *gettare* means to 'cast out.' But *casting out* in English means to 'throw someone out.' An *outcast* is someone who doesn't belong. That's like me my whole life."

Regina gave her a sympathetic glance. "You are smart, and I can see you're good at remembering facts."

Dani lightened when she said that. "Thank you, Regina."

Regina turned toward the espresso maker and began making Dani's cappuccino. "Did you learn that before Napoleon all windows of buildings facing Jewish ghetto were filled with bricks so Christians and Jews would not have contact, like we are having now?" Regina winked and set the cappuccino on the counter. Her hand was shaky and the espresso spoon fell to the floor. "Even the bridges were drawn up at night to keep Jews from leaving ghetto after sunset."

Dani felt a strange surge of energy in her body. Glimpses of what she had dreamed last night came to her and she was about to tell Regina, but then the guy she assumed was Antonio, Regina's fiancé, walked in. Regina mumbled something in Italian and walked away.

Dani practically chugged her cappuccino, anxious to have a productive day of writing. She tried to wave to Regina to let her know she was leaving, but Regina's back was to hers as she stood talking to the guy. She could have sworn he smirked at her. She set the cup on the counter and walked out without a proper goodbye.

It was a sunny day, despite the gray haze that seemed to linger. The weather was similar to the early morning fog in San Francisco. She wondered if Veronica had returned her email. She couldn't remember exactly where the internet café was, but decided to walk in the general direction she had taken yesterday. Dani followed the maze of streets until she recognized the campo surrounded on both sides by narrow canals and saw the flag with the @ symbol hanging in front of the store.

She greeted the Indian woman at the counter as she opened the door and pulled her passport out of her money belt.

"*Va bene,*" the woman said, smiling and waved away Dani's passport. She led Dani to a computer with the number eight taped to the monitor. Dani sat down and typed in the AOL domain and waited for what seemed like forever for her email to pop up. Then she had to search through the sea of spam on ways to "enlarge your penis" to find what she was looking for: a reply from goodthyme@EZBaker.com.

Hi Dani,

I'm so jealous of you! I wish I was there drinking cappuccinos and eating cannoli and gelato with you and not some other "nice Jewish girl." Since when do you like nice Jewish girls? Fact: It's better to have writer's block in Venice than to be in Seattle chasing after some closet case. Remember, you're not there to break hearts. Keep working on your novel. I promise it will come. And have some tagliatelle alla polipo for me.
    Ciao,
    Veronica

How can Veronica be jealous of me? she thought. *She's got a great job and she's already published several books.* Dani began her email, making a mental note to figure out what *tagliatelle alla polipo* was.

My Dear Veronica,

Let me remind you that my computer blew up. How is that not a sign? The good news is that I finally have a name for my protagonist. It's Melandria. It just kind of came to me. Here's what I have so far. Melandria has ditched her family for this dude who came to her village and swept her off her feet. Turns out he's a total douche. She ends up locked in this tower dungeon because he screwed over some royalty and they're holding her captive as collateral for his swindling. Not sure if a tower dungeon is an oxymoron, but it's looking pretty dark for her. There's players and play, and Melandria got played.

Anyway, I don't mean to be a heartbreaker. I can't help it that other people fall more easily than I do. I'm more protective with my heart.

I like the chase.

And speaking of chasing . . . I'm really digging Sara, the nice Jewish girl. She's kind of the sexy librarian type. She has long, wavy brown hair with just a touch of silver, captivating brown eyes, about five foot three, curves in all the right places, and she's ever so slightly older than me. She is a little pale, like the Seattle girls back home who have only ever had a mall tan. She wears these cool, long black boots and these old-fashioned skirts and sweaters. You would dig her fashion. Her look and couture would best be described as retro, a little on the Goth side, but she's a ghost tour guide for god's sake and a poet. Very eccentric! And of course, you can't swing a cat around here without hitting someone wearing a Venetian mask or sporting a velvet cape trying to get attention and make a few bucks with the tourists.

Sara is providing quite the chase through Venice. She gave me a tour of the Jewish Ghetto. She is a veritable encyclopedia Italiana-Judaica. I had no idea that Venice was so rich with Jewish oppression—I mean, history.

Did you know that the origins of making Jews wear badges on their clothes started here like a million years before Nazis? First, it was decorative yellow circles for men and yellow scarves for women. Then the fashion of oppression changed to yellow berets, and then red berets became the "new yellow" to be able to instantly identify who was Jewish and generate new sales. Did you know that this kind of crap was going on way pre-Holocaust?

Well, probably you did, but I didn't until yesterday. I've learned more about Jewish history in the past few days than I have in my whole life. My brain is trying to make sense of it. I keep having crazy dreams. Last night I dreamed I got locked in the Jewish ghetto. It felt so real. Gives me the creeps just thinking about it!

I'm having a good time, feeling a bit more positive about things, especially now that I've met Sara. Nothing like an international romance to cheer you up. I'll spare you my most recent thoughts about Michelle's proposal because I know you don't want to hear it.

Arrivederci,

D

Dani hit SEND.

She perused the internet, checking out the top stories, and was about to log off when a return email from Veronica popped up.

What the fuck, Dani!

I can't believe you're fucking off your writing AGAIN. Get your head out of everyone else's ass and start writing or stop calling yourself a writer and get a real job. I can't waste my time with someone who doesn't take themselves seriously. I'm not kidding, I've had enough of your playing around. Grow up for fuck's sake or I'm done!

Dani starred at the screen stunned.

Her friend was threatening to dump her. *Fuck that!* she thought and hit DELETE. Veronica's email didn't even deserve a response.

Why can't she be happy for me? Why can't she just let me enjoy a real connection? She's just jealous because she's not here having a good time, she decided.

VENTIDUE

Dani paced back and forth in the cramped apartment. Veronica's words had unnerved her. Dani liked Sara. Sara was a nice distraction, but she was more than that. She was a woman that Dani felt she could really connect with. She had ever only felt this way towards Michelle. Dani had hoped to go back to writing but she was too upset and inspiration would not come when she was upset. She left the apartment to go for a walk and promised herself she would go back to writing after her morning jaunt.

As she strolled, she noticed another mask shop. Through the window, she saw a man sitting next to a table lamp delicately painting a mask. Dani opened the door and walked inside.

"*Buongiorno,*" the man said, barely looking up from his work.

"*Buongiorno,*" Dani replied, eyeing the wide variety of masks that hung on the wall. There were masks that just covered the eyes and other masks that were full faces with huge feathers that looked like human hair. She watched the man painting a mask. He spoke to her in Italian.

"*Mi dispiace?*" Dani apologized. "*No parlo Italiano. Parlo Inglese.*"

"*Ah, Inglese.* Handmade," he said. "These handmade one hundred percent. Masks in San Marco, no!" The man waved his hand sharply, accidentally flicking paint across the room.

Dani checked her clothes for paint. She didn't find any.

The man picked up a mask and walked over to her. "The mask of Casanova. One hundred percent handmade. Try."

The forehead of the mask was decorated with red, blue, and green diamonds. It had two eyeholes and a large nose. One side of the face was painted gold and had raised swirls, halfmoons, and stars. The other side of the face was painted with red, blue, and green diamonds. It was quite ornate in color and texture. Dani put on the Casanova mask. The mask came to the top of her upper lip. She was glad it didn't cover her mouth.

She peered at the mask maker through the eyeholes.

The man had put on a black cape and a mask with large, black plumage then begun dancing. He rocked his head from side to side like some sort of possessed demon or madman. His dancing made her feel dizzy. She felt like she needed to sit down.

Dani went to take the mask off. It stuck. She struggled to get it off.

The man stopped dancing and looked at her. "The mask, he like you too much."

Frightened, Dani ripped the mask away from her face. To her surprise, the man was behind the counter, still painting. He glanced over at her. "You like?" he asked. "You buy? *Molto bene, sì?*"

Dani felt lightheaded. *Am I imagining things? Has he been there painting the whole time? Who the hell did I see dancing? What is going on?* She handed the Casanova mask back to him and raced towards the door for fresh air.

She was relieved to be outside and walked as quickly as she could away from the store and those creepy masks. She had hoped the fresh air would stop the dizzy feeling. It didn't. Was she losing her mind?

She followed signs for La Ferrovia back to the apartment and found herself near a large, white-columned building with an official seal carved into the center of the façade. The seal was circular and had the letters S and R on it. The building was alongside a canal, and it had an open cobblestone courtyard in front of it containing a wide staircase that led down to the canal. Several of the steps were underwater and covered with green algae. This area of the canal was wider and intersected with several smaller canals that formed an almost pool like area. Like much of Venice, it had that fresh, crisp ocean smell she loved.

All of a sudden, she had a great urge to jump into the canal. She tried to shake it off, but the pull was strong and her dizziness intensified. Her limbs didn't feel like they were her own. It literally felt like someone or something was taking possession of her body and trying to satisfy its own needs. She turned away from the canal and walked away as quickly as possible before she did something crazy.

As she walked, the dizziness and strange sensations continued. She was even aware of a burning sexual desire. She felt a deep lust in her body that surpassed previous experiences of sexual desire. It took her by surprise. She checked out the female tourists milling around the San Rocco, a big church, and imagined seducing one in a darkened alley nearby. *What is happening to me?* It didn't even feel like her sexual appetite.

It felt almost uncontrollable. She had to get away from there. She headed in the direction of the apartment and away from the San Rocco, quickening her pace, and then suddenly, as quickly as the urges came, they were gone.

Dani felt totally confused. As soon as she got back to the apartment, she lay down to rest. A few hours later she arose feeling refreshed, hoping that whatever weirdness she was experiencing was the result of jetlag or an overactive imagination. She grabbed her notebook and left the apartment to find a new café to write in. She needed to get back to her writing. She hadn't written a single word since her computer blew up. She couldn't let Veronica be right. It was time to stop procrastinating and get back to work.

As she walked the San Polo District, she searched for the perfect café to write in. Cafés in Venice, though, were not like cafés in San Francisco. People didn't sit around on laptops, they went to drink espresso and then left. The perfect café with a table to write at was hard to find. DeLucia's was an exception, and she was grateful it was so close to her rented apartment.

A shop at the end of canal with tarot cards in the window caught her eye. The window displayed pyramids and a statue of a birdman with Egyptian writing on a stone tablet. She knew she should continue her search for a café but was tempted to go inside. Maybe she'd find a book on the Jewish mystical stuff Sara talked about, and she could add to their conversations. The pull was too strong to resist.

She went inside. The place was cramped and dark and smelled of mostly old books, it looked like it had flooded at one point. The room was lit by a red lamp that hung from a black wrought-iron chain. Beneath the red lamp a heavyset woman with coarse, choppy blonde hair sat at a green felt table shuffling a deck of tarot cards. A psychic!

Dani walked closer.

The woman's face looked stern. Her cheeks were ruddy and her eyes bulged like they might pop out of her head. The bracelets on one plump arm jangled as she motioned to a metal parlor chair with red-fringed cushions. "Zit down," she said with a thick accent.

Dani sat down.

"I am Romola," the psychic said.

"Nice to meet you," Dani replied, noticing a wolf pendant the woman wore around her neck. It gave Dani the creeps.

Romola lit a stick of incense and three candles on an altar.

"What is your name?" she asked, studying Dani.

"Dani."

"No, this is not your real name," she scolded.

"It's Daniela, but I go by—"

"Yes, Daniela, you have question, a question about the heart." Romola touched Dani's chest with a stubby finger. "*Amore.*"

Dani nodded, hoping her skepticism wasn't obvious. She figured that most people came to fortunetellers for money, love, and health, so this was not rocket science. Since she was alone in Venice, the city of romance, love was the best guess.

"You touch cards like this." Romola mock-shuffled the cards. "Then cut them three times."

Dani picked up the cards and shuffled them, unsure where she should cut the deck. She closed her eyes and took a deep breath and then cut the deck in three separate places as the woman had instructed.

"*Va bene,*" Romola said, wiping a trickle of perspiration from her brow. "You put them down now."

Dani placed the cards on the table.

"First, we look at your past." Romola began chanting some words that Dani couldn't understand; they didn't sound Italian. As she chanted, she waved her hand over the cards as if she was infusing them with energy. Her hand quivered, like someone with a palsy, only this was intentional. Her bracelets made a loud rattling noise. Then she stopped abruptly, took a sip of her tea, and turned over the first card.

Dani was impressed by this performance. Romola was giving her quite a show.

"The Chariot," the woman said and placed the card at the twelve o'clock position. "You have been in motion, traveling."

Yep, me and the majority of people bustling up and down the narrow streets of Venice, Dani thought. Regina had told her only 60,000 people "lived in Venice," the other 300,000 were tourists. *Obviously, I am traveling.* Still Dani wondered how she'd known which card to pull, she'd have to pay better attention to the next card.

"You think nothing is happening, but below the stillness of water, many things are taking place. You are trying to *realizzare*—how do you say? —complete something."

"Yep." Dani nodded. *Could you be any vaguer?* she wanted to say.

Dani looked blankly at the woman, whose bulging blue eyes seemed to want to burn through her. "Your dreams, look carefully, they tell you next step. You have gift *speciale*. You can see the life before, *la vita pasato*."

"OK." Dani nodded, not knowing what else to say. She'd never had her cards read before and had no idea what the protocol was.

Romola repeated her ritual of chanting and waving her hand over the card, before flipping over the second card. She placed it slightly below and to the right of the first card. The image was unsettling—a tall, ancient building with lightning striking it and two people falling from an open window.

The woman glanced sideways at Dani. She mumbled something Dani couldn't make out and then spoke slowly, "*Adesso*, now, this is your present circumstance."

Dani felt her stomach somersault. "Doesn't look very good, does it?" Dani joked nervously.

"*La torre*. The tower. Old must be torn down. Like damage from *aqua alta*, your foundation is flooded, rotten. Old habits rot foundation. From here you see who you are and what has been your life, like difference between vision in the *calli* and vision in campo. Or like view from *Ca' Rezzonico*, you see, how do you say, big picture. It is the time to let go."

Romola's black cat leaped into her lap and purred loudly.

"*Buona gatinna*. Beauty comes through suffering, through difficult growing you unfold. You walk through world with mask, no more! Remove *la maschera*. *Inmediamento, adesso!* Now! No more lying to you or others. *Soltanto la verità!* Only the truth or your foundation rot again, you fall!"

The woman was emphatic.

Dani felt a chill run up her spine and goose bumps appeared on her skin. Even without telling the woman anything about Michelle, it seemed like the cards were reflecting everything about her current situation. She began to feel queasy again.

"*A lora.*" Romola repeated her ritual: She took a sip of tea, then turned over the third card and placed it below the first. The candles on the altar in the corner of the room flickered. "This is your future."

Dani looked at the card, a picture of what looked like a spiritual person sitting on an elevated throne holding a golden staff. She couldn't make out the gender. They wore a red robe with a white sash decorated with black crosses and a golden headdress. Two bald men stood at their feet.

The card read: The Hierophant. She'd never seen or heard the word before.

Romola smiled, her eyes seeming to want to pierce Dani. "Life is your teacher and there will be many tests. Ah *sì*, they've already begun," Romola said and nodded knowingly at Dani. "Each step will bring light. You are teacher too! You must share what you learn. But first, you must tame your sex. You must be in the present, no clinging like a vine to the past. Clear away the stagnation. Flow like the *Adriatico. No stagante.* Learn from your mistakes. You are here to learn from your past, from when you were here before."

Dani raised an eyebrow. "This is my first time in Venice."

"No," the woman said, smiling a toothy grin that freaked Dani out. "You were here before."

Romola chanted and waved her hand over the fourth card. She turned the card over and smiled as she saw what it was. Romola pointed to the card. "This is resources you possess and obstacles you will face."

"It's good, *va bene?*" Dani asked, looking over the card. A man in a red cape and red boots holding a staff and looking out at the moon over a calm ocean, eight golden cups stacked behind him.

"*Sì, molto bene.*" The woman took a deep breath and sighed. "*Otto de copas.* Time to let go of past and go deeper. From stillness and decay comes new life. Out of swamp we create beauty. You must let go, fall to bottom of murky water, then you emerge like empty vessel to be refilled."

"I had a dream the other night. I went to throw out the trash and fell into the canal and th—"

Suddenly there was a gust of wind and the interior door to the shop slammed shut. Dani sat straight up in her chair. "What the hell?" she blurted out, her heart pounding rapidly in her chest.

"*Va bene, va bene,*" Romola said, attempting to reassure her. "We have many spirits here in Venezia. They will not hurt you. They like to make their presence known. They envy the ones who still have choices and can experience pleasures of the body."

Dani gasped. "I had a sudden urge to jump into the canal earlier. It was like someone else was inhabiting my body. I've never felt that way before."

The woman looked at Dani knowingly. "You were near *frari,* no?"

"Over by the big church, and San Rocco. I thought I was going cr—"

Romola interrupted her, "*Sì, sì.* It is known here. Much mischief near Basilica Santa Maria Gloriosa and the frari. Pazzo. Pazzo. Cortigianas e monacos cattivos. Naughty ladies and naughty monks." She shook her head.

Dani rubbed her temples. She tried to calm down, but adrenaline coursed through her body and she was starting to feel lightheaded again. "I don't feel so well. I think I should go." Dani reached into her pocket and took out some money to pay.

"This is last card I draw for you. It will be enough. It is obstacles you face." She chanted, waved her hand over the card, then turned it over and placed it in the middle of the other cards. "*Sette di* swords."

Dani looked at the card. A man appeared to be sneaking away from a camp with five swords in his possession and two in the ground next to him.

Romola's piercing eyes bored into Dani. "You are running away. You make hasty decisions."

Dani nodded and then averted her gaze.

"You have secret plans that dishonor you. You are doing or going to do something you know you should not. It is about matters of the heart, a secret lover perhaps. We call this card the card of Casanova."

"The Casanova card?" The goose bumps returned to Dani's skin and she froze in her chair like a deer in the headlights. She felt a pit in her stomach. "You can really see that?" Dani asked.

She thought about the Casanova mask at the mask store. There were too many signs even for her to ignore.

"That's how it is written," the psychic said dryly.

Dani rubbed her right temple. The headache was becoming unbearable. She put forty euros on the table.

"This is too much. I get you change." The psychic rose up.

"I need to go," Dani said and stumbled out of the dark store and into the bright sunlight.

VENTITRE

Dani lay on the bed in the Venice apartment. She tried to put together the pieces of Romola's card reading. *What did she mean, I've been here before?* She understood that she needed to learn from her mistakes and contemplated how many years she'd spent not writing and all the things that she'd done to avoid writing: becoming a feng shui expert, a connoisseur of sex toys and women, a barista—however shitty she was at it.

As she lay there in the darkened room, lamenting the time she'd wasted on various pursuits, her mind wandered back to a rainy October night in Seattle when she was nineteen and a sophomore in college. She remembered sitting on her bed surrounded by novels written by the Brontë sisters, Jane Austen, Charles Dickens, and George Eliot. She was working on a paper for her English Lit class at the University of Washington when the phone rang.

"Why are you calling me, Michelle?" she had asked, rhythmically clicking the ballpoint pen she held in her right hand.

"I miss you, Dani," Michelle said, slurring her Ss. She sounded drunk.

"I'm trying to finish a paper," Dani said. She closed her eyes and pressed the phone to her ear.

"What's it about?" Michelle asked.

"It's about the themes of idealism, betrayal, and unrequited love in the works of nineteenth-century female English novelists."

"Bor-ing," Michelle huffed. "I've got something way more exciting for you."

"I'm listening."

"Come over and play with me. I'm lonely."

Dani put her pen down. "Where's Sean?" she asked.

"Trout fishing at Storm Lake in SnoCo with Troy and Kevin."

"Are you schizophrenic?"

"Maybe I am. Maybe I've been thinking about you and it's making me crazy."

"You're married now." Dani was flattered, but her inner alarms bells were ringing.

"Yes, but he's not you. Do you want me to beg, Dani-bear?"

"I thought you were done with me? With anything queer."

"I did what I had to do. You know that."

"Seriously, I need to finish this paper and then I have midterms I need to study for."

"Please, I need you," said Michelle. Her voice was breathy. Dani could easily imagine the pout of her lips and the feel of them on her neck. Michelle loved to kiss her neck, especially when Dani was inside her. "Come get me."

Dani sat on the edge of the bed looking at the receiver of the white plastic phone. She remembered the announcement of Michelle's marriage to Sean had come through that phone over a year ago. *Maybe I can make things right again,* she thought. She put the phone back to her ear. "What's your address?"

"Yeah!" Michelle screeched with excitement. Dani heard her clapping her hands in the background. Michelle was definitely drunk. "Whoops, sorry," she said, slurring her words. "Are you still there? I dropped the phone."

"Yep, I'm still here." Dani tore out a piece of notebook paper and wrote down Michelle's address on the back. Then she hung up the phone without saying goodbye.

"I gotta go see a friend, Ma." She announced to her mother's closed bedroom door, intentionally avoiding contact.

"Which friend?"

"I'll be back tomorrow."

"Make sure you drive safely."

"I will."

"There are so many crazy drivers out there," her mother called out.

Dani had rolled her eyes at her mom's neurotic worries and grabbed her keys from the table where she always put them and left quickly. "I know, Mom!"

As she drove she questioned her sanity. *Why do I still love her after all that she's done to me? Why won't she just come out of the closet and leave that jerk-off?* The questions played in her head. Michelle still had her heart. Dani parked the car and walked up the walkway of the tawny colored two-story suburban ranch house whose address she'd been given.

She knocked on the door. No answer. She waited a minute and knocked again. There was still no answer. Angry, she turned to leave.

The door opened.

Dani turned back to find Michelle wearing nothing but a white bathrobe. She felt a jolt of electricity run through her body. It'd been almost a year since she'd seen Michelle.

Michelle smiled and slid her fingers along the tiger's eye stones on the necklace around Dani's neck. "You're still wearing the necklace I gave you."

Dani's body trembled when Michelle touched her. She ignored her comment, however—or maybe it was more of a question. She felt like a fool for coming to her for a booty call, but in some way, it gave her a sense of righteousness that she possessed the ability to please Michelle in a way Sean couldn't. She walked inside and Michelle locked the door behind her.

"I'm glad you're here," Michelle said and then bit her lip. Her blue eyes looked sparklingly warm.

"We're really alone?" Dani asked.

"Yes, I told you. He went fishing," Michelle replied.

Dani reached out and touched Michelle's face. "I missed you." Dani leaned in and kissed her.

Michelle broke away from the kiss.

"What the fuck, Michelle?" Dani shook her head. "Stop toying with me." Dani headed for the door.

"No, please don't go, come here." Michelle took Dani's hand in hers and led her through an open door into the bedroom where white tapered candles flickered on a rustic oak dresser.

"I need you, Dani," Michelle whispered into her ear. Michelle's hair smelled sweet, like the first time. Dani kissed her, wanting desperately to feel the purity of their once-simple love. She remembered those sweet moments up in Michelle's bedroom when they studied together and laughed with an easiness and innocence that was long gone. She would do anything to get those feelings back or any approximation of the connection the two of them once shared.

That included from that moment on, showing up when Michelle called. Through fishing season and into deer and elk hunting season for over two years, while Sean was off with his buddies, Michelle was hers. Every Saturday night that Sean was away, she'd make the twenty-minute drive to Michelle's house and they'd spend the night making love. Sunday mornings, she'd slip out by sunrise so the neighbors wouldn't see her leaving. The arrangement was far from ideal, but it was better than nothing. For the previous six months, Dani had been exclusively focused on her coursework. She hadn't had time for a regular romance. Now, the fact that they were meeting up again felt good. That they were hiding their relationship created a tension that made their time together even more compelling. Or at least that's what Dani told herself to ease the pain of not having Michelle to herself.

As she lay with her head between Michelle's thighs, she was thinking, *Michelle is mine now, completely mine!*

"Oh god, yes," Michelle groaned. She arched her body and gripped Dani's hair with her hand. Dani felt Michelle shudder and her body softening afterward.

Dani rested her head on Michelle's thigh and edged her tongue around Michelle's swollen honeypot. "You taste so good. Kind of salty tonight."

Michelle reached for the straps on Dani's black tank top and pulled them towards her. "Damn, baby."

"I love you, Michelle," Dani whispered.

"You're so good to me," Michelle whispered back.

"Yeah, I am." Dani lightly smacked Michelle's butt. It seemed fuller. Michelle had gained a little weight since the last time she saw her.

"Hey, I just started writing a novel."

"Really, what's it about?"

"It's a love story." Dani smiled at Michelle, as they lay entwined in each other's arms.

"I can't wait to read it."

"I also applied to an MFA program near San Francisco. I was hoping that—"

Michelle cut her off. "I have news too."

Dani pulled Michelle closer. "You're finally going to come out to your parents and then you can move to the Bay Area with me?"

Michelle patted her stomach and smiled. "I'm pregnant."

The words hung there. Michelle looked at Dani expectantly, waiting for a response.

Dani finally spoke. "You can't possibly be serious," Dani said flatly, her eyes scanning Michelle's body. Michelle's breasts were bigger and her stomach looked harder. She remembered noticing a glow on Michelle's face the last two times they'd been together, but she thought it was because Michelle was happy to see her.

Michelle looked hurt. "I thought you'd notice. Maybe you just thought I'd gotten fat."

"What the hell, Michelle?" Dani said, suddenly feeling nauseous. Why hadn't she noticed the significance of the changes in Michelle's body? She felt like an idiot.

"I'm finally going to be a mom. You know how much I've always wanted a baby and to be a mother."

"You're one fucking mother all right!" Dani kicked the goose down comforter off and jumped to her feet, tripping over her black leather shoes.

"Where are you going?" Michelle asked, pulling the covers back over her naked body. "I thought you'd be happy for me, Dani."

"Happy for you?" Dani gathered up her clothes in her arms. "Are you bat-shit crazy? I can't believe you just let me make love to you and you're pregnant with *his* child." She looked at Michelle with disgust.

"What's your problem, Dani? You don't seem to have any trouble making love to me in *his* bed."

Dani put on her clothes as quickly as she could. "This is totally different, Michelle."

"No, it's not!" Michelle's eyes turned icy again.

Dani ran her fingers through her hair and then held her head in her hands. "I can't do this anymore!" she said. She then finished dressing and left.

That was the last time she saw Michelle. The last image she had of Michelle was her naked body forever changed with Sean's mark. She could no longer pretend that her influence on Michelle was stronger, as he had won in a way she never could.

A few weeks later, when the letter from Mills College arrived, Dani held it in her hand, almost too anxious to open it. She took a deep breath, tore open the envelope, and unfolded it.

"We had many qualified applicants for the MFA Writer's Program, unfortunately we are not able to admit you at this . . ." She stopped reading.

"God damn it!" She kicked the mailbox post and retreated to her room, slamming the door behind her. "I can't stay here," she yelled and threw herself down on the bed.

Dani wanted a new life far from the dull gray of Seattle and the specter of her relationship with Michelle. Grad school or no grad school, she was leaving. She'd figure it out somehow. She wasn't going to stay here and drown.

The day after the semester ended, she packed her shit and made her escape. She didn't bother to wait for graduation. Walking across a stage to receive a piece of paper was meaningless to her. She took her favorite mix CDs, her novels, and her clothes and threw them in the back seat of her car. Leaving the rest of her stuff at her mom's house, she got on the road. It felt good to have pared down her life to just the things that would fit in her Toyota, and only the things that really mattered.

She considered Janis Joplin's definition of freedom in her lyrics to *Me and Bobby McGee*. She certainly had nothing left to lose. Everything she cared for was gone now. All of her dreams were officially dead. She put her car in drive and headed south on Interstate 5 to the gay promised land: San Francisco.

Dani had hoped for a fresh start in San Francisco, but it was only a temporary escape from the heartache she had run from. Here she was in Venice, years later, and she still couldn't free herself from the hold Michelle had on her heart.

VENTIQUATTRO

Dani crossed over the bridge by the train station and turned left on to Rio Terà Lista di Spagna. She passed multiple stores catering to tourists selling Carnival masks, paintings of gondolas, and clothes with the word *Italia* and a picture of the boot of Italy painted on them.

She also passed at least a dozen stores filled with blown-glass figurines, vases, pitchers, drinking glasses, and ornate chandeliers. One store's window display caught her eye. Next to a sign that said "MADE IN MURANO, NOT CHINA" were several figurines of male Jews with long beards, black hats, and long noses, holding scrolls. *The Torah,* she thought. She knew that the scrolls were the Jewish bible, but she'd never seen one. She'd never even been to a synagogue. Her parents were Jewish but did not practice the religion.

Another Jewish figure held a baby upside down with one hand and a knife in the other. She knew that is was supposed to represent the circumcision of a baby boy, but it looked sinister. She tried to compare the Jewish figures to the non-Jewish figures. The Jewish figures had larger noses for sure. Dani noted a figurine of Pinocchio in the same glass case where the Jewish figures were kept. *Was Pinocchio's nose growing longer when he lied some sort of racial suggestion that Jews were liars?* The thought pissed her off.

Dani walked quickly until she came to another bridge and saw a sign with the Star of David, Hebrew lettering and an arrow pointing left. She crossed the bridge and walked down the wide sidewalk alongside the canal. There was a market on her left with stands of fish, octopus, and even sea snails. It smelled like the sea lions at Pier 39. The fishmongers waved away seagulls drawn to a pool of water on the sidewalk formed from the thawing ice the fish were packed in. She kept her distance and veered towards a bakery on her right—its rich smells of coffee and croissants filled the air.

Dani would have missed the entrance to the Ghetto Vecchio altogether if there hadn't been a bright yellow sign with the word SINOGOGHE above the entrance to a very dark sotoportego. It looked cave like and creepy even on a sunny morning. It hammered home how this area had once been separate and off-limits.

Dani walked through and continued down a dark street with what seemed to be the tallest buildings she had seen thus far in Venice—some at least seven stories tall. She came to a tennis-court-sized campo with a gray cistern in the middle. *This must be it,* she thought. She looked at her watch. It was 10:30 AM.

Dani turned when she heard the clipping sound of heels on the cobblestone. It was Sara. As she walked, her long brown hair bounced at her shoulders and glimmered, almost translucently in the morning light. Each step was punctuated by a staccato echo on the cobblestone. Sara looked regal, like a noblewoman from the Renaissance, only in a beige sweater and a black lace skirt.

Dani was breathless. *This woman is as beautiful as she is smart.*

"Buongiorno, Dani. I hope I haven't kept you waiting long."

"Only, all my life!" she wanted to say. "I just got here," she said, instead.

"March Twenty-ninth. Do you know why this date is important? Because the day before March Twenty-nine we were Venetians, and the day after we were Jews. On that day Four hundred and ninety years ago, the friars convinced la Serenissima to lock us in ghetto. Come, we go now to hidden synagogues."

"Hidden synagogues?"

Sara held a finger to her lip. "You must promise to be very quiet."

"I'll try not to make trouble for you, but I can't promise." Dani winked.

Even as she flirted, the painful memory of getting fired from Common Grounds was still fresh in her mind and she felt a wave of concern for Sara. She didn't want Sara to lose her job like she had. Regina had told her that only retired people with a lot of wealth were able to own apartments in Venice, which was why she, and most young people, lived with their parents until marriage. Newlyweds typically had to move to the mainland in Mestre or one of the surrounding islands like the Giudecca or the Lido, where rents were cheaper.

"Come, I will show you *Scola Canton,* the corner synagogue, first," Sara said, taking Dani's arm in hers. Dani felt butterflies in her stomach when Sara touched her. She hadn't shivered at a woman's touch since Michelle. It stunned her.

This mysterious tour guide awoke something within Dani she thought was dead.

Sara led her over a metal footbridge into the larger ghetto square. From there they walked to a corner where there was a three-quarter-sized, narrow door. Sara opened the door and ushered Dani in, closing the door behind them. Sara put her finger on her lip, reminding Dani to remain silent. They walked up three flights of stairs and then Sara opened a door and a cold rush of air filled the hallway. Dani wrapped her scarf around

her neck.

Sara beckoned her inside.

The walls were decorated with reliefs of vines and fruits carved into the wooden panel with ornate detail and painted gold. Dani was awestruck by its beauty.

Sara looked pleased. She pointed to an elevated platform with a table on it. "That is the *bimah*."

"*Bimah?*" Dani asked. She'd never heard the word before.

"On Shabbat, the rabbi opens the Torah scrolls to read the daily portion. You see, they take it out of the ark and then they spread it out on that flat desk."

Dani looked at the ark. It was flanked by two beautiful wooden columns encircled by hand-carved vines. The synagogue windows were framed by bright red curtains. One window was simple stained glass with what looked like a yellow fan against a blue background, two decorative red diamonds, and three small green circles. It was simpler than any decoration she'd seen in a church.

"These Jews were Ashkenazi from France. They built this synagogue in Fifteen-thirty-one."

"I thought the Ashkenazi were from Germany?" Dani whispered.

"Jews were expelled everywhere they went." Sara shrugged. "From France in Eleven-eighty-two, England in Twelve-ninety, and Spain in Fourteen-ninety-two. Jews wandered all over Europe looking for home. Jews from Spain, the Orient, Germany, France, and parts of Italy lived in ghetto here in Venice. For many, this ghetto was a place of hope where they could live and worship in some safety."

"In the closet," Dani interrupted, shaking her head, "hidden from view."

"Much of our history is." Sara sighed. "Look up, you see stars in *cupola?*" Sara pointed to a small circular area with five windows that let in the light. "These Jews also studied the Kabbalah; stars are the sign of Kabbalah."

Dani looked up. "Yes, I see them. What's the *Kabbalah* again?"

"Jewish mysticism."

"You see these pictures?" Sara pointed to a series of framed three-dimensional images, like sculpted pictures. Dani couldn't tell what the images were. "These are passages from Torah."

"Where are the pictures of the rabbis?"

"In Jewish law, you cannot show images of people."

"I didn't know that." Dani looked at her shoes. "You must think I'm an idiot."

Sara gave her a sympathetic look. "No shame in ignorance, only in refusing to learn or remember."

Dani nodded. "Well said." She looked up at the images. "What does the one with the waves mean?"

"It is Jews crossing the Red Sea. And one with hand." Sara pointed to a depiction of a hand reaching down. "This is God giving Jews *manna* from heaven while they are wandering for forty years in the Sinai Desert after fleeing Egypt," she explained.

"What's the one that looks like water sprouting up from the ground?"

Sara smiled. Dani could tell her questions were pleasing to Sara.

"This is the water spilling forth from the rock that Moses struck with his staff."

"Sorry, I'm biblically illiterate. I don't know anything about Moses or the Jews fleeing Egypt," Dani said apologetically. "My parents never taught me anything about their culture. I only knew we were somehow different than Christians."

Admittedly, Dani could have studied Judaism in college, but she had no interest in religion, Jewish or otherwise. Religion caused war and was used to justify the oppression of others.

"Sorry, the only Mana I know is a Mexican rock band. I love their music. Have you heard of them?"

"No." Sara shook her head. "I prefer Solomoni Rossi and Palestrina."

Dani shrugged her shoulders. "Never heard of them. I'll Google them later."

"Where was I?" Sara asked.

"Manna."

"*Sì*, manna. It is special food from God that God gave to Jews, telling them, 'I will give you what you need day by day.'"

"I rarely meet women with your passion for history." *Like, never!* Dani thought.

"It is our story, Dani. And many people would like to erase us or to convert us to their ways with kindness or violence. Come let me show you the first synagogue ever built in ghetto, at least legally," she said, winking.

Sara closed the door to the Canton Synagogue and they crossed the hallway and went down another flight of stairs, passing through another door and into an alcove.

"This is the *Scola Grande Tedesca*—the Great German Synagogue." Sara opened the door to a room significantly larger than the first. The opulence shocked her. She hadn't expected such architectural treasures hidden in an unassuming tenement building.

Dani noted the room's distinctive oval shape. There were wooden benches built into the walls. The upper parts of the walls were marble. The bottom half of the walls were handcrafted with dark wood in an almost Star of David pattern.

Dani's eyes were drawn to an extravagant golden balcony, embellished with many bronze torch chandeliers. There was another bimah with eight golden Corinthian columns supporting it. Dani ran her fingers over the grooves, admiring the intricate details of the designs.

"This is incredible! I can't believe they had to hide their synagogue in an apartment building."

Sara put her finger to her lip, hushing Dani and pointed. "The balcony up there is where we women sit. We are not allowed to be among the men."

"God forbid." Dani rolled her eyes.

"Yes, that's exactly what they say," Sara laughed.

Dani laughed too. "That marble is so beautiful!" Dani said, stunned by the riches of the synagogue.

"Not everything is as it appears, Dani," Sara said and smiled. "This is wood that's painted to look like marble. Marble is heavy and costly."

"Really? It doesn't look like wood at all. It looks like stone." Dani turned her neck trying to take in the synagogue completely. She noticed the floor looked like it was sinking under the weight of the decorations. It was clear that a room full of ornate decorations packed with people worshipping in secret over the centuries had caused the floor to sag.

"*Andiamo,*" Sara said and ushered her down the staircase.

Once they were back in the ghetto square, Sara pointed to the top of a building. "Look up. Do you see those five windows there?"

Dani could make out Hebrew lettering at the very top of a five-story building. It blended almost imperceptibly with the white ornamental fringe on the rooftop. Dani's eyes scanned down the building and she saw a set of five windows. "OK, I see them."

"Those are the windows of the synagogue. Five windows for synagogues. Jews know to look for this."

"Amazing!" Dani exclaimed.

"Now look to your right."

Dani turned to see where Sara was pointing. She saw a yellow building with five coffin-shaped windows—each one shuttered with forest green shutters.

"Behind those windows is *Scola Italiano.*" Sara grabbed her arm again. "Come, there is more to see."

Sara took Dani to three other synagogues: the Italian and two others, one she called the *Scola Luzzatto* and the other the *Scola Spagnola.* Each one was ornamented with faux marble and garland columns and had exotic fabrics adorning its walls, ornate chandeliers, and featured breathtaking woodcarvings. The textures and textiles swam in her head.

"Can we rest for a minute? I'm feeling kind of dizzy."

"I have just one left to show you," Sara insisted.

Oh, thank god, we're almost done, Dani thought. *I've never been to a synagogue in my life and now I've seen five in one day. Veronica is not going to believe this if she ever talks to*

me again.

Dani reluctantly followed Sara into another building and up several flights of stairs. She was completely exhausted. She wondered if Sara had an off button when it came to Italian Jewish history. She loved Sara's enthusiasm for her subject, but was now ready to talk about something else. *Anything else!*

Sara opened the door to a narrow alcove. It was like a catwalk above the synagogue. Sara motioned to a few wooden chairs that lined the catwalk. "The Luzzatto, which was a family name, is now called the *Scola Levantina.* The few Jews who live in Venezia come here in winter months to pray."

Dani peered through the rectangular holes of the brown crisscrossing wooden screens, she could just barely see the bimah below. Mostly she could see the tops of the windows and the chandeliers.

"This is *matroneum*, an area mandated for women to sit in."

"You can hardly see anything from here."

"*Si*, we women sit up here gossiping while men sit down there at wooden desks or *daven* and recite Torah. We barely see them. And they barely see us."

"What does *daven* mean?" Dani asked.

Sara shook her head. "It is Yiddish word, from your Ashkenazi ancestors who roll in their graves because their culture is being lost. It means 'to pray.'"

Dani tried to change the subject and pointed to the reddish-orange tapestry that lined the walls. "God, that's beautiful. When was this synagogue built?"

"Luzzatto Fifteen-forty-one, Spagnola in Fifteen-forty-eight, and Italiano in Fifteen-seventy-five."

"So ancient." Dani exhaled. "You know, I never cared about this before."

"You mean your heritage?"

"I was raised atheist."

Sara looked confused. "You were raised to believe that there is no God? How is this possible? What does it mean to be Jew with no belief in God?"

"I'm trying to figure that out. And I do appreciate you sharing all of this with me. It's very illuminating. There's a lot of similarity between how Jews and gay people have been treated throughout history. Anyway, can we get out of here and get something to eat?" Dani had seen enough for one day.

"We wouldn't want you to starve to death, even though you're spiritually and culturally malnourished." Sara grinned.

Dani might have appreciated Sara's sarcasm if she wasn't feeling so lightheaded and aware of her growling stomach.

Sara took her arm. "Come, let's get you something to eat."

Dani and Sara strolled along the canal taking in the sights: the gondolas filled with smiling tourists, the restaurants and bakeries. Dani was grateful to be out of the cramped ghetto buildings. They made her feel claustrophobic. She spotted a trattoria alongside the canal that looked perfectly romantic. The tables covered with pink tablecloths and petite vases with sprigs of red flowers delighted her. "This is perfect. Let's stop here," she said.

The waiter held up his index finger.

"Per due, vicina la canal per favore," Dani said, hoping to impress Sara with her developing Italian skills.

The waiter hesitated, then waved his hand at the empty table closest to the canal.

"Do you have any favorites?"

Sara shook her head. "I'll have whatever you have."

Dani looked at the menu. "I think I'm going to get the *fettuccine con verdure*. And how about *una bottiglia de vino rosso* and some *acqua minerale*?"

"*Parfeto*," Sara said.

Dani set down the menu and leaned in towards Sara. "Tell me more about you?"

Before Sara could respond the waiter was back to take their order. *"Prego?"*

"Una bottiglia de vino rosso e una bottiglia de acqua minerale natural e due fettuccine con verdure."

"Due?" the waiter asked. He looked at her disapprovingly.

Dani wasn't sure if he was disapproving of the fact that she was ordering for Sara or that they were eating the same dish.

"Si, due." What's with these waiters? Dani thought, remembering the waiter's complete disgust with her request for ketchup with her French fries a few days ago.

The waiter scribbled the order and walked away.

"Was my Italian that bad?" she asked, hoping for Sara's approval.

"No, Dani." Sara looked into her eyes. "You have a strong intellect. And you learn quickly," she added.

Dani nervously looked away. "So, you were going to tell me a bit about yourself?"

"Si, but first I tell you about the friars and the constant threats we Jews faced."

"Go ahead." Dani sighed. She hoped the story would be quick, but she was getting the feeling that Jewish history might be Sara's main interest and maybe her real interest in Dani was simply to convince her to practice Judaism. She didn't think Sara was with the Chabad, an Orthodox sect of Jews from America who wore all black and whose major focus was on converting people to Judaism, but she couldn't be too sure.

"The Franciscan friars blamed us for public poverty."

"Vino e acqua." The waiter placed the bottles on the table.

"Why?" Dani turned their glasses over and poured the wine.

"Franciscans believed the Jews' moneylending and charging interest caused poverty in la Serenissima because people had to pay more than they borrowed. Now, remember how I told yo—"

Dani interrupted. "Jews could only be moneylenders and pawnbrokers. Yeah, I remember."

Sara smiled. "Good, you are listening to me, not just humoring me."

Dani's face reddened. She was humoring Sara. Her whole focus now was how to get her in bed. She hoped it wasn't obvious.

"The Franciscans blamed the Jewish money-lending practices for causing poverty? That's absurd, what else were Jews supposed to do to make a living?" Dani sipped her wine and tried to compensate for her transgressive thoughts.

"Jews were also allowed to be doctors, but in Fifteen-sixty-seven the laws changed and only doctors who took the Christian oath *professio fidei* could practice. They said we treat the body, but damn the soul."

"What kind of oath?"

"An oath to their virgin, and to belief in Jesus as the one true God. An oath to reject our religion."

"*Permisso, fettuccine con verdure.*" The waiter placed the plates on the table with a delightful presentation.

"*Grazie.*" Dani admired the food and then rolled her fettuccine with her fork onto the spoon to gather it up and took a bite. "Mmm, this is good."

Sara looked past her food and kept talking. "Jews were blamed for many things by Christians. For Bavarian plague in Thirteen-forty-eight. They said we spread it through wells."

As Sara spoke, Dani ate self-consciously, frequently wiping her face with her napkin, hoping that she didn't have anything in her teeth. She studied Sara's features; her olive skin, her brown eyes, the shape of her nose. She was captivated. How had she never been attracted to Jewish women before? Sara was certainly converting her into a lover of Jewish women. She wanted to touch Sara's face, to kiss her, but she usually let the femmes make the first move; that way she couldn't later be accused of unwanted advances or "misunderstood kindness" by bi-curious straight girls. Dani gazed into Sara's eyes.

"Did you want to say something, Dani?"

"What?" Dani's face reddened. She hoped Sara couldn't read her thoughts. "No, just thinking about what you said. You've hardly touched your food, Sara. Didn't you like it?"

"No, is good. I am not hungry."

Dani was surprised that Sara wasn't eating anything. *Is she just being polite? Maybe she is with the Chabad. They can't eat anything unless it's from a kosher restaurant. Or maybe she's just trying to watch her weight.* Dani pondered all these things while Sara went on and on with the history lesson.

"Franciscans blamed us for plague of Sixteen-thirty, though four hundred and fifty Jews died."

Dani felt a strange sensation, like she was remembering a dream. She could see herself and Sara standing over a white rock with the number four hundred and fifty on it. "That's really weird," Dani exclaimed.

"I do not know that word . . . *weird?*"

Dani wasn't sure how to respond. She didn't want to tell Sara about the déjà vu feeling she was having lest she think that she was crazy or making it up.

"*Finito?*" the waiter interrupted.

"*Sì,*" Dani said, relieved.

"*Cappuccino? Dolce?*"

No grazie, il conto per favore." Dani took out her wallet. "My treat," she said.

"*Grazie,* Dani."

"*De nada,* whoops, I mean *prego.* I should have gone to Spain, at least I know the language there."

Sara shifted in her chair. "You'll find much of our history in Spain too."

"You mean the Inquisition?" Dani wanted to roll her eyes.

"Yes, I do. In Fourteen-ninety-two . . ."

"Columbus sailed the ocean blue," Dani interrupted wryly.

Sara shot her a serious look. "Jews were expelled from Spain and came to Venezia. Some believe that is why Columbus left on his voyage for India on the last day Jews were allowed in Spain in October Fourteen-ninety-two."

"Really?" Dani sat up in her chair. She'd never thought about Columbus being Jewish or being forced to leave Spain because he was expelled by the Catholic monarchy along with all the other Jews. That certainly added an interesting twist to history.

Sara nodded.

"God, I'd hate to have that hanging over my head with my Native American friends," she murmured.

"What?"

"Nothing." Dani wondered why Sara was so obsessed with history when they could be on a gondola ride enjoying the evening. Sara was beautiful, smart, well-educated, but a little prudish.

"Andiamo." Sara got up from the table.

"Where are we going?"

"Back to my apartment."

Dani practically jumped up from the table. *Now we're talking,* she thought.

VENTISEI

Sara and Dani walked to Campo Ghetto Nuovo. Dani followed Sara into one of the tall apartment buildings in the Ghetto Vecchio. They climbed several small rickety-wooden staircases before proceeding down a dimly lit, constricted hallway no more than two feet wide and six feet tall.

"Why are these hallways so narrow?"

"Thousands of Jews were living here in ghetto. We had to find ways to fit. One floor became two, hallways were narrowed to make more rooms. Hallways here are smaller than anywhere else in Venezia."

Dani could see how the hallways were tightly tapered to make more room inside of the apartments.

Sara opened the door to her apartment. It looked like an upgrade on a sixteenth-century prison cell. It was sparse and dark. The furniture looked ancient. Dani felt like she was going to hit her head when she followed Sara inside the cramped apartment. It made her rented studio in San Francisco seem like a mansion in comparison. The room was furnished with a twin bed, a bedside table, a wooden chair, a table the size of a TV tray, and a built-in wooden shelf with two dozen leather-bound books and what looked like a stove. The walls were painted yellow and the bedspread was bright with flowers.

As small as it was, the bedroom doubled as a living room and dining room.

Dani felt like the walls were closing in on her. She really understood now what Regina meant about how expensive it was to live in Venice. This must be all she could afford on a tour guide's salary. Dani was glad she had insisted on paying for dinner.

"Please sit," Sara said, motioning to the chair.

Dani sat on the wooden chair and Sara sat on the bed. Dani wondered if there was enough room for the two of them there.

The place smelled musty. The only natural light in the apartment was coming from a tiny window that was practically useless because it was no more than two feet away from the adjacent tenement style building.

"I hope you have listened to what I told you today, Dani," Sara said, her tone paternalistic. It made Dani bristle. The librarian thing was sexy, but only to a point.

"Yes, I've learned so much, thank you. You really are an exceptional guide. Your boss must love you. How about sharing some of your writing with me? I'd love to hear your poems."

Sara smiled as she considered Dani's request. "I write sonnets."

"Seriously? I love sonnets!"

Sara got up and took one of the leather-bound books from the shelf. Then she sat down on the bed and opened it. She paged through the book several times before deciding what to read.

"They are all in *Italiano.*"

Dani leaned back in the seat, interlocked her fingers, and cupped them against the back of her head. "Even sexier."

"*Sì, Italiano es molto sexy,*" Sara said. "English sounds like bar bar bar bar bar."

"Bar bar bar," Dani imitated and laughed.

Sara held the brown leather-bound book in one hand and began to read, the other hand moved in time like a conductor with the flow of her words, staccato at first; then becoming more erratic as her voice rose and her pace quickened.

"O di vita mortal forma divina,
E dell' opre di Dio mèta sublime,
In cui se stesso e 'l suo potere esprime,
E di quanto eí creò ti fe' Reina . . ."

Though she didn't understand any of it, Dani was enjoying the rhythm and rhyme of what she was hearing.

"Mente che l'uomo informu, in cui confina
L'immortal col mortale, e tra le prime
Essenze hai sede, nel volar da l'ime
Parti là dove il Cielo a te s'inchina . . ."

Dani tried to focus on the words as they formed on Sara's full lips, but she was distracted by the gap of the lace shirt and the swell of Sara's breasts.

"Stupido pur d'investigarti o cessi
Pensier che versa tra caduchi oggetti,
Che sol ti scopri allor ch'a Dio t'appressi.

"E per far paghi qui gl'umani petti,
Basti saper che son gl'Angeli stessi
A custodirti e a servirti eletti."

"Wow, that was beautiful," Dani said, clapping. "What does it mean?"

Sara pulled a lock of hair behind her ear. "It is about immortality of soul."

"Can you translate it?"

Sara pursed her lips. "I try, but my English is not so good."

"That's OK." Dani leaned over Sara's shoulder as Sara slowly translated. "O mortal form of life Divine, God expresses its power, because He create you in faith a queen."

This Sara really turned her on. Dani had an urge to kiss Sara's neck.

"Mind of man borders immortal with mortal, flying in from time where Heaven bows to you: It is enough to know I am same angel who has elected to watch over and serve you."

"'Flying in from time where Heaven bows to you.' I like that." Dani smiled. "And the part about the angel. Very cool. You guys are big on angels here, huh?"

"*Sì,* Venetians are fond of archangels and saints, especially beloved San Marco, the winged lion."

How did I not see it before? The winged lion? The candle? Dani looked like a deer caught in the headlights. "Sara, fate led me to you."

"*Scusi?*"

"Before I came to Venice, I went to a store and this woman, a psychic woman, gave me a candle with the winged lion painted on it. I asked her to help me with my luck and she gave me the candle. It was good luck because it led me to you."

Sara got up from the bed. "Would you like some tea?"

"Sure," Dani said, embarrassed she'd revealed so much. Sara must have thought that was the cheesiest pickup line ever.

She filled a kettle and placed it on the stove then lit a match and sparked a flame on the burner. "Once I had a very beautiful home here in the ghetto."

"What happened?" Dani asked, trying to cool it with her *blurtations,* her crosses between flirting and blurting out the strange synchronicities she was putting together in her mind.

"Things change," Sara said wistfully.

Dani couldn't wait for Sara to come to her any longer. She got up and took Sara's hand in hers, readying for a kiss. Sara peered deeply into Dani's eyes. Dani loved Sara's intensity, but the look in her eye knocked her off her game. It wasn't a look of passion towards a lover, it was more of a look of concern.

"Is something wrong?" Dani asked, confused by the change in Sara's demeanor.

"Dani, it's important for you to remember who you are."

"What do you mean?"

The kettle squealed and Dani released Sara's hand. Moment gone.

Sara turned off the stove, poured the hot water into a mug with a tea bag, handed Dani the mug, and then sat on the bed. "You've lost your way."

"It's that obvious, huh?" Dani said, forcing a laugh.

"We each have a soul purpose."

She wondered where this was going. "You mean like the one thing we're here to do?" Dani asked.

"Close," Sara said. "Our soul's purpose. What we came here to do. It's not just one thing."

"Like, I'm here to be a writer," Dani said and took a sip of the tea. She loved how deeply thoughtful Sara was. "What's your soul's purpose, Sara?" she asked.

Sara pursed her lips, considering the question carefully. Then she abruptly got up from the bed. "Let me walk you home."

What the hell? Clearly the question had struck an uncomfortable chord in Sara. Dani looked at her mug. She'd barely taken two sips.

"No need," Dani said, pulling the map out of her back pocket. "I've got the *Idiot's Guide to Finding Your Way Around Venice.*"

Sara didn't seem to get her joke. "Venice is so confusing at night that even Venetians sometimes get lost. Everything looks different at night. I will walk you home."

Dani finally understood that Sara wanted to go to her place with her. She tried to hide a guilty smile. "OK, thanks."

The night air felt good on Dani's face as she and Sara walked alongside the canal on their way back to her apartment in the Santa Croce District.

"It's so peaceful here," Dani said, and exhaled deeply. "And romantic."

Just as Dani wondered if Sara might let her hold her hand, Sara paused at the water's edge. "This is canal where Jews would bring our dead from ghetto to take to cemetery on Lido. Christians would throw trash at bodies as we pass."

Way to kill the romance! Dani turned so Sara couldn't see her mock smack herself in the head. She was trying to be understanding, reminding herself that she'd met Sara on a ghost walk tour and that Sara made money telling people about the history of the island. *She definitely gets the Goth award for morbidity.*

"Yeah, I remember you telling me about the cemetery. Maybe we can go next weekend?"

Dani thought she saw Sara smile, but she couldn't tell. Sara took her arm in Dani's and they continued walking.

"Here we are," Dani said, turning into the small courtyard of Calle de Figher and putting the key in the lock on the ground floor entrance leading to the apartment.

Sara's eyes sparkled in the lamplight. "Dani, our ancestors live on through us. We honor them when we live our lives fully, since they could not."

"Then let's give them something to enjoy." Dani leaned in, kissing Sara full on the lips. She felt a current of energy pulse through her body. It was electric.

Sara broke the kiss.

"There's nothing to be ashamed of. Sara, please, come inside."

Sara turned towards Dani, her lips only inches from Dani's. "I . . . ," she hesitated. "This is not what you need."

Dani pulled Sara to her. "I can decide what I need." Dani leaned in and kissed her again.

This time Sara gave in to the kiss. It felt good to finally kiss her, to feel Sara's body next to hers. She pulled Sara closer, enjoying the conquest, but something felt different. She couldn't put her mind to it, then it registered: Sara's lips were cold. Ice cold.

Sara broke away from the kiss with finitude. "No, is not possible. I must go now, Dani," she said, and bolted for the stairway.

Dani chased after her.

"I'm sorry. I failed you," Sara said.

"It's fine. Goodnight, Sara," Dani said, her face unable to mask her disappointment that the night was over and her mind puzzling at how cold Sara's lips were. She watched Sara turn down the alley and fade into the darkness. Then she walked back to the apartment building and went inside. Dani closed the door to her apartment, resting her back against the door and let out an enormous, disappointed sigh. When she took her next breath, she was aware of the lingering scent of Sara's perfume. She closed her eyes, lamenting her failed seduction. *Well,* she reasoned, *we've only spent a few days together and she is a good Jewish girl. Always tomorrow.*

But even as that thought crossed her mind, she realized that it felt off. The kiss felt awkward, clumsy. Between the psychic's comments and Veronica's scolding, she was starting to feel like she was losing her finesse. *Maybe I'm not reading Sara right. Is Sara really straight?* That hadn't stopped Dani before. She'd been with many bi-curious straight women. *Maybe Sara hasn't been with anyone in a long time? Maybe she just needs more time to warm up to the idea of being with me? Or maybe it's something about her lips. Does she have some sort of condition? Tomorrow I'll Google what makes someone's lips ice cold.*

VENTISETTE

Dani got into bed with a book. She struggled to keep her eyes open, but sleep overtook her. The book slipped out of her hands and rested gently beside her.

Suddenly, she was startled awake by the sound of footsteps. There were always the sounds of voices and footsteps traveling up from the alleys below, but this sounded closer.

"Come to your senses, Sara?" Dani called out. But there was no answer.

She heard the noise again, only this time she was sure it was coming from outside the bedroom. She jumped out of bed and looked around for an object to protect herself with. There was nothing. She grabbed the pen on the nightstand, held her breath and walked slowly to the door. Gripping the pen in her right hand she threw open the bedroom door with her left. She scanned the narrow hallway leading to the kitchen and the bathroom—it was empty—but the front doorknob of the apartment began to turn. Her heart raced and she could feel her mouth going dry with fear. She was too afraid to scream.

The door crept open. A hunched figure appeared in the doorway. Dani held her breath then she saw it was a petite elderly woman working her keys out of the lock. The hunched woman disappeared into the outer hallway, but returned with a set of white towels. She walked into the apartment and saw Dani standing there in her pajamas. She offered the towels to her.

What in God's name? Is this the landlady coming in here at ten-thirty at night?

"*Señora,* you almost gave me a heart attack," Dani said, clutching her chest.

The woman held out the towels to Dani and spoke in Italian. Dani didn't understand what she was saying. The elderly woman shuffled past Dani into the bedroom and put the towels on the bed. Then she mimed mopping motions.

"You want me to mop?" Dani asked.

The old woman shook her head and pointed to herself.

"You want to mop now, *ahora*—I mean *adesso?*"

The old woman shook her head again. "*En la mattina.*"

"In the morning."

The woman nodded.

"OK." Dani nodded, clutching her arms around her stomach. *What if Sara had spent the night and this old lady came busting in while they were having sex? What was she was thinking?*

The old woman shuffled to the door and let herself out.

Dani got back in bed and picked up her book, her hands shaking. She took several deep breaths and thought she smelled gas. She wished she had asked the old woman about that. She wrapped the blankets around her, picked up her book, and went back to reading.

VENTIOTTO

Dani sat at the desk wrapped in the bedspread, her notebook opened to a fresh page. She picked up her pen to write. She felt a sharp pain in her hand, like something had stung her. A scorpion scurried across the desk and under a crack in the window ledge.

Startled, Dani looked at the site of the sting. A red mark erupted on her skin. It began to spread. It started to look like a letter, a cursive letter. It burned and began to spread across her hand. They were letters, in a sixteenth-century Italian cursive. They curled up like a vine around her arm, turning from red to black as they cooled like metal. They were the words of Sara's poem branded into her arm.

"It was just another bad dream," she told herself, pulling the blankets tight around her and sipping a cup of hot tea. But it didn't help. Her mind was fraught with too many thoughts and questions. Venice was so peaceful and beautiful and yet, it had a darker side, a side that seemed relentless in haunting her with its history.

Sara had told her that the friars had played to stereotypes and lies about Jews to fan the flames of anti-Semitism. And how they accused Jews of poisoning Venetian wells to kill Christians, part of their bigger crusade to strip the Jews of their homes and rights and lock them on the tiny island that would become the world's first ghetto.

It was here in Venice where Jews were forced out of their homes and into a ghetto, forced to wear yellow stars on their clothes to identify them, and restricted in their employment and ways of making money—all roadmaps leading, centuries later, to Hitler's Holocaust. Only Italy wasn't the only place Hitler got his ideas. The U.S. doctrine of manifest destiny surely inspired him too, which justified taking possession of land and property from the Native Americans and justified death, deportation, and enslavement of those considered inferior. *Hitler had invented nothing. He had only borrowed ideas from previous playbooks on oppression and genocide.* The puzzle pieces came together forming a dark and sinister picture.

Dani remembered reading an article in the *Bay Area Reporter,* a local newspaper serving the lesbian and gay community in San Francisco, about marchers being attacked during a gay pride event in Poland the previous summer. Officials wouldn't give the marchers a permit and stood by while the All-Polish Youth, a right-wing group, pelted marchers with bottles and rocks, and yelled, "We'll do to you what Hitler did to the Jews!" Instead of arresting the All-Polish Youth for assault, they arrested 175 peaceful marchers. She felt disgusted by this.

Dani had never been interested in Jewish history before, but now she was seeing parallels between Jewish oppression and gay oppression and it infuriated her. She wondered if there were closeted Jews too, hiding their cultural heritage, like Michelle had hid her sexual orientation.

She looked at her watch. It was 7:00 AM. She kicked off the covers and beelined for the shower, excited to see Sara again and share what she was learning with her and the connections she was making.

As she showered, she imagined walking hand in hand with Sara along the quay. Then she pictured them sitting outside a café near the Rialto Bridge watching the boats row by on the Grand Canal while Sara read poetry to her in Italian and translated it for her. Perhaps in the evening, they would stroll through the calli eating gelato and stop to listen to street musicians playing accordion and violin. She had fallen in love with both instruments on this trip.

Dani believed Sara was into her. She had felt it the night before when she kissed her, though something about the kiss unsettled her, she just couldn't put her finger on what. *Sara is probably coming to terms with her same-sex attraction to me,* Dani told herself. *She needs a little more time to get comfortable with the idea.* Sara was old-fashioned and older than Dani, she would need more time to romance her. Tonight, she would call her at work and invite her to dinner.

VENTINOVO

After her shower, Dani dressed quickly and left. She walked across the bridge and down the steps to DeLucia's Café. Regina was at the counter squeezing orange juice by hand.

"*Buongiorno, Dani. Succo?*" Regina handed her a glass of fresh orange juice.

"*Sì. Grazie.*"

"Sit, I will bring you, cappuccino."

Dani sat down, opened her notebook, and began writing. Ideas started coming to her almost out of nowhere. She filled page after page of the notebook.

Regina brought her a cappuccino. "How is the writing?" she asked.

"I think I'm on to something," Dani said, smiling. Without realizing it, she rubbed her hand where the scorpion had stung her in the dream.

She sipped her cappuccino and wrote furiously. An hour later, she got up to stretch her legs and ordered a sandwich from Signore DeLucia. By three o'clock, she had spent close to eight hours in DeLucia's café outlining her novel in her notebook. She'd drained two bottles of Acqua Panna, sucked down four cappuccinos, and eaten three *tramezzini,* petite finger sandwiches, while she worked.

Dani felt like things were finally coming together because she was able to detail several new compelling characters, a gripping climax, and was crystal clear on the direction she wanted to take the novel. She had painstakingly outlined each chapter of the novel in her notebook.

Dani fist pumped the air.

Regina walked over. "*Va bene?*"

"*Sì, molto bene!*"

Antonio, who had come in for a cappuccino about an hour earlier, looked up from his newspaper, took a sip of his coffee, and lit a cigar.

Dani thought he was leering at her, but she wasn't sure; there were all kinds of subtleties of Italian culture that she didn't get. *Maybe he thinks Americans shouldn't bother speaking Italian,* she thought.

"Would you like another cappuccino?" Regina asked.

Antonio's cigar smoke wafted in her direction. It was a pungent smell she didn't care for. "No, thanks, Regina. I'm good for today." She picked up her things to leave.

Regina smiled at her. "*Domani.* See you tomorrow."

"*Domani.*" Dani smiled and waved goodbye.

Dani looked at her watch. She still had time to kill before going to find Sara to invite her to dinner, but she didn't want to go back to her dark, claustrophobic apartment. The crazy landlady was going to come clean it and she wanted to avoid another encounter with her. Her shoulders were still practically up to her ears from the previous night's shenanigans and the onslaught of bad dreams they had triggered. She felt like an exposed nerve. Even the streets felt like they were closing in on her again.

Dani noticed the gondola tied to a wooden pier in the canal near DeLucia's Café. The *gondoliere,* dressed in a white-and-black striped shirt and black pants sat at an outdoor table and sipped his coffee waiting for his next fare.

"*Gondola, gondola, gondola,*" he called out to a passing Japanese couple who shook their heads no. He shook his head back and lit a cigarette.

Dani felt something urge her towards him. "*Cuanto?*" she asked the gondolier.

"*Ottanta euro,*" he said, exhaling the smoke from his cigarette.

She translated it and did the conversion. *Eighty euros—that's like a hundred-twenty dollars. I can't afford that.* She peeked in her wallet. She only had eighty left and didn't know when she'd make it to the bank again or how low her checking account was since she didn't really understand the conversion rate. She couldn't put this purchase on her credit card like she'd done with the others. Still, she felt drawn to the gondola and envious of the tourists she'd seen gliding through the canals in them.

"*Sessanta euros,*" she bargained.

"*Si, per che no?*" he said and crushed out his cigarette. He held out his hand to assist her into the gondola, which was similar to entering a canoe, although stepping into it was more precarious than boarding a water taxi. She made her way carefully toward a padded love seat with red velvet and golden stitched flowers in middle of the gondola. The seat looked like something one might find in a king's throne room, regal and luxurious. Besides this movable bench, there were two petite black-lacquered wooden chairs with matching red and gold velvet cushions to accommodate additional passengers. She was thrilled to have the boat all to herself.

"*Italiano?*" he asked.

"*Inglese, per favore,*" she said.

"My name is Luca," the gondolier told her as she sat down on the velvet red and gold loveseat. She noted that on each side of the sleek black boat, where one would expect to see oarlocks, there were two gold-plated ornamental horses.

"I'm Dani," she answered the unspoken question.

"Where are you from, Dani?"

"California."

"Your first time in *Venezia?*" Luca asked.

"In this lifetime," she said. "A fortune teller just told me I lived here in a past life."

Luca smiled. "What do you think? *Bellisima, no?*"

Clearly, the man had no idea what she had said. He walked on the edge of the boat to the back. He took the long wooden oar out of the oarlock. It looked like a twisted tree branch glued to the side of the boat.

"*Sì, bellisima.*" She smiled in return.

Luca pushed the boat away from its mooring and into the center of the canal with his oar. He then began rowing the boat through the sparkling blue-green water.

"The gondola was created special way with weight and shape to be rowed by one person. If it was regular boat, it would go in circles," he explained.

"Been there," Dani mumbled under her breath.

"There are about two hundred and thirty-two palaces in Venice. We call them palazzos. Many of them are from the fourteenth, fifteenth, and sixteenth centuries."

Dani felt her body begin to relax as they glided past the ancient palazzos. *If they can weather this much adversity and still retain their integrity, so can I,* she thought.

"Venezia is made of one hundred-eighteen little islands made by one hundred and fifty canals that are in this lagoon, which is not so deep. There are almost four hundred bridges, one for every one hundred and forty-five Venetians. As you see, that one is out, so we go another way." Luca pointed to a bridge with a red and yellow sign that showed a picture of a boat with a red slash through it.

"Every year the water rises, and soon we won't be able pass under many bridges."

"Why?" Dani asked, distressed by his dire prediction.

"The ocean, she is rising."

Global warming, liberal conspiracy theory, my ass, she thought.

"More than three meters and whole parts of the city will be underwater." Luca looked sad as he said this.

Dani shook her head. She couldn't imagine how horrible it would be for such a beautiful city to be destroyed.

Luca turned the boat around and it slipped through the canal passing under several lines of hanging laundry. He pointed at the laundry and grinned. "Venetian decoration."

Dani smiled back, endeared by the way Luca embraced the simple joy of his job.

"On your left, we have the Byzantine Palace. Very beautiful, no?"

"*Sì.*" Dani studied the building façade ornately decorated with camel carvings, detailed white moldings, and arched windows. "Mesmerizing." *Two points for you, Veronica,* she thought. She imagined what it would be like to live in a Venetian palace where you'd have a street entrance and one that opened on to a canal. *If I ever make it as a writer or win the lottery, I'm buying a palazzo.*

"Venice is built on marble, Istrian stone. If it weren't for that, no Venice."

Dani appraised the stone. "Yeah, I've seen it everywhere and wondered what it was. The Rialto Bridge is made of Istrian stone too, right?"

"*Sì.* Rialto was built in fifteen hundred, so it is tall for big boats. We have twenty-four shops and three lanes for walking. Rialto Bridge is like a highway to Venetians." He recited his tourist facts for her.

"*Hoy!*" Luca yelled out as they turned to pass under a different, lower bridge. The light from the water below danced its reflection on the underbelly of the bridge. The sun felt warm on her face and the boat rocked gently as the water glided underneath them. She rested her tired body against the soft padded seat of the gondola. She had needed this.

Luca rowed them through enchanting canals lined with breathtakingly handsome buildings featuring exposed red bricks and eroding hues of brightly colored stucco—their plant boxes bursting with spring flowers. Luca began to hum quietly to himself then broke into song. His voice a perfect accompaniment to the sound of the waves lapping against the ancient buildings.

"Do you see the eclipse?" Luca suddenly asked.

"Excuse me?"

Luca took off his sunglasses and handed them to her. "The eclipse," he repeated.

It was perfectly sunny out. She wondered how there could be an eclipse. She put on his sunglasses and glanced at the sun.

"Wow, half the sun is missing." She took off the sunglasses and handed them back to Luca.

"Not everything is as it appears to be," he said, putting the glasses back on.

Dani remembered Sara saying that same thing in the synagogue, and wondered what he meant by it and whether it was a Venetian saying. She imagined it might be because everything seemed otherworldly in Venice. Magical almost.

Dani glanced at her watch. It was already after four o'clock. She couldn't believe a whole hour had passed. She could do this forever. She reluctantly got out of the boat and paid Luca, thanking him in Italian. He kissed her on the cheek. The kiss took her by surprise. She failed to return the first kiss, but when he kissed her on her other cheek, she kissed his cheek back. She was endeared by his sweetness and getting the hang of the Italian customs, so different from those of Americans.

The thought entered her mind that maybe Sara was just being friendly by kissing her goodbye on her cheek. Maybe she'd read too much into the gesture.

Nah, she thought, *she digs me.* Dani remembered an old joke about the difference between a lesbian and a straight girl— *more wine.*

TRENTA

Dani searched the apartment for the Avventure Serenissima brochure. She finally found it folded up in the pocket of her black slacks. She walked to the payphone and dialed.

"Pronto, Avventura Serenissima."

Dani hesitated, unsure how to ask to speak to Sara in Italian. *"Ciao, e Sara qui?"*

"Sara?" the man's voice echoed back to her from the other end of the phone.

"Sì, Sara Sullam?"

"No Sara qui."

Damn, I missed her! Dani tried to find the words in Italian.

"Quando Sara . . . work?" she asked, hoping the man would understand her question. She couldn't hear his response because a mother with a screaming child walked by. He hung up before she could ask him to repeat what he'd just said.

Dani walked back to the apartment and grabbed her scarf, plaid jacket, and well-worn notebook. She was proud of the notebook's crinkles and coffee stains, and that it was now full of chapter outlines, plot elements, character arcs, and three new chapters of her novel. Finally, she could see the light. She was going to resurrect this project from the dead. Because the novel was finally coming together, she couldn't wait to share her work with Sara.

Dani felt a chill come over her as she left the apartment. She wrapped her scarf tighter around her neck to shake it off. She crossed over Ponte de Cannaregio de la Guglie and strolled alongside the canal where she and Sara had eaten their dinner the other night. People sat outside the cafés drinking coffee and smoking. She was so engrossed in watching them that she almost missed the sotoportego to Ghetto Vecchio.

As Dani approached the covered walkway, she looked for the holes in the wall that Sara had told her about. These holes were from the days when fortified wooden gates with thick wood bolts were used to seal the ghetto off from the rest of Venice. Dani found the indentations in the side of the building and slid her hand around the edges of the holes. It was hard to believe that this mark of oppression from more than five hundred years before was still clearly visible in the wall. It reminded her of something she'd dreamed about a few days earlier.

Dani wandered through Ghetto Vecchio and tried to remember which apartment building was Sara's. She found the well and the Levantine synagogue where they had met, but was unable to recall which building Sara lived in.

They had visited so many places, traipsing in and out of the ancient structures, traversing from one building to the next, up and down staircases, through hallways and all sorts of cramped little passages, that she was now completely confused about which one Sara lived in.

Dani walked to the central ghetto square and found the corner with the door they'd used to enter the Scola Canton. It was sealed up with concrete. *That's weird,* she thought. There was a sign that read: *in costruzione.*

The Jewish Museum was open. Sara hadn't taken her there. As Dani entered, she found a cluster of teenagers with backpacks sprawled out on the black-and-white checkered floor of the museum hallway. The teens clogged up the staircase to the museum and impeded the path to the bookstore where Dani was headed. She eased her way through them.

The bookstore was filled with postcards of the synagogues, a display of Jewish music, and stacks of books in Hebrew and Italian. She wished she knew Hebrew and was sad that her parents had hidden their Jewishness. She understood why, the Pacific Northwest wasn't known for cultural diversity.

A matronly woman behind the counter with chestnut curls, wearing a colorful purple scarf, stood at the counter and rang up postcards and books for a group of Israeli students. Dani waited for them to leave and then approached her, hoping that she could help her find Sara.

"*Mi scusi.*"

The woman turned towards Dani, who noted that her purple eye shadow matched her scarf perfectly.

"*Parlei Inglese.*"

"*Sì.*" The woman smiled; she had a kind face. "How can I help you?"

"I'm looking for Sara Sullam. Do you know her?"

The woman came from behind the counter and walked to a book display. She picked up a thick, navy-colored paperback and handed it to Dani. It was written in Italian. Dani tried to translate the title, *La Bella Ebrea Sara Copio Sullam poetessa nel ghetto di Venezia del 1600*. She recognized a few words: "poet of the ghetto of Venice."

"Wow, she's published," Dani said, excited to be holding one of Sara's books.

Sara was so modest. She hadn't mentioned she was a published poet. Dani flipped through the pages. The print was small and the book looked more academic than a typical book of poems. *Sara probably prefaces her poems with Jewish history, since she is a veritable encyclopedia,* she thought.

Dani read on, looking for Italian words she might recognize. The beginning paragraph on page thirty caught her eye.

"*Quando, nel 1618, Sara Copio iniziava Ansalda Ceba la corrisponenza . . . ,*" she read the sentence again, doing her best to translate it. "When, in 1618, Sara Copio initiated correspondence with Ansaldo Ceba . . . " She thought it must be some kind of typing error. She'd noticed multiple misspelled street names and typos on her map of Venice. Then, it dawned on her. *It's the year of the Jewish Calendar.* She took the book and sat down at one of the tables in the bookstore café and continued her attempt to translate from Italian.

"*Scusi,*" a young man interrupted her and said something in Italian she didn't understand.

"*Ingelese?*"

"You must order to sit," he said.

Dani got up and pulled her wallet from her back pocket. "*Cappuccino per favore.*" She paid him and went back to the table to decipher the book.

She continued flipping through the pages of the book. She thought she found the poem Sara had read to her the other night. It was entitled "Sonetti VIII." The words were as beautiful on the page as when Sara had read them to her. She began to read them aloud.

"O di vita mortal forma divina,

E delle opre di Dio mèta sublime…"

The young man brought her a cappuccino. "La Bella Ebrea's poem of immortality. *Bellisima, no?"* he asked.

"Immortality, that's what it's about?" Dani smiled. "*Sì, bellisima.* What year are we in the Jewish Calendar?" Dani asked him.

"My English not so good," he apologized.

Dani got up from the table and walked to the front counter where the woman with the purple scarf was organizing receipts. "What year is 2006 in the Jewish calendar?"

"Five thousand-seven hundred and sixty-six," the woman said.

Dani looked confused. "I don't understand, this says Sixteen eighteen?"

"That was Fifty-three-seventy-eight," the woman replied.

Dani struggled to do the math; it didn't make sense. "But that's almost four hundred years ago."

An older German couple walked up to the counter. Dani waited while the woman rang up a Yiddish music CD and a book called *History of the Jews* for them. As soon as they left, she approached the woman again. "I'm looking for Sara Sullam, the person, not the book. Can you tell me her address?"

The woman came out from behind the counter and picked up a large paperback. She opened the book to a specific page and handed it to Dani. "Go to the Venetian Jewish Community. We don't do those tours here."

"Oh, that's who she works for," Dani said, relieved. She looked at the page the woman pointed to and saw a picture of a headstone with a footnote that read: "*La Tomba di Sara Copio Sullam al Cimitero Ebraico di San Nicolo del Lido.*"

Dani flipped through a few more pages and read.

Sara Copio Sullam, 1592–1641, poet and guiding spirit, received Jews and non-Jews in her abode in the ghetto. In 1621, she found herself up against a difficult contentious issue with Baldassare Bonifacio, a priest, poet, and the Archdeacon of Treviso, who accused her of not believing in the immortality of the soul.

It sounded like her Sara, with the exception of this woman being dead for over 350 years. Dani grew more confused and annoyed. *What is going on?*

"I'm looking for Sara Sullam. I was at her apartment yesterday. She has brown hair and works as a tour guide here in the ghetto."

"You buy the book or no?" the woman asked. She then turned to the young man and joked, *"Abbiamo un altro pazzo che vede i fantasmi di Sara."*

The young man laughed. *"Lei sempre aggira per la vulnerabile,"* he replied, laughing.

"What are you laughing at?" Dani demanded.

"Someone is playing tricks on you. Sara Sullam is dead," the woman said.

"What?" Dani felt sick with betrayal and confusion. "What do you mean?"

The woman in the purple scarf shook her head and walked away.

Who the hell is this woman I've been spending time with and why is she pretending to be a dead poetess? Dani dropped the book and pushed her way through the crowd of teenagers rushing for the door. She felt like she was going to throw up. She had to get outside and far away from the ghetto's bricked walls with barbed wire that she felt closing in on her.

Dani walked briskly, almost running out of the ghetto. She didn't know where she was going at first. Then she turned and headed for the Rialto Bridge. She walked at a clipped pace, following the yellow signs that read "Per Rialto" passing windows of Murano glass necklaces and pastry shops with chocolate eggs and marzipan bunnies. A men's hat store with red berets in the window caught her eye. She remembered Sara telling her that Jews were forced to wear yellow berets, and then red berets later, to distinguish them from Christians. She shook her head. *Why would anyone want to impersonate a dead Jewish poetess? It made no sense.*

Dani saw a woman in a cape with long brown hair speaking to tourists at the top of the bridge. It had to be Sara. Dani climbed the steps and pushed her way through the crowd and tapped the woman on the shoulder. "Excuse me, Sara, or whatever your name is," she said.

The woman turned around. "*Scusi,*" the woman said in a thick accent.

It wasn't Sara.

"Um, I'm, uh, sorry," Dani said flustered. "I'm trying to find a tour guide named Sara. I thought you were her. She does ghost tours."

"There is no one like that," the tour guide said.

"I know, it's not her real name," Dani said, agitated. "I don't know what her real name is. She dresses in old-fashioned clothes and pretends to be Sara Copio Sullam as she gives ghost tours."

"*La poetessa Ebrea*? The Jewish poetess?" the guide asked. She seemed a bit startled by Dani's agitation.

"Yes," Dani said, relieved. "Where can I find her?"

The guide's eyes widened. "I have heard of this."

"Who is she and where can I find her?" Dani insisted.

The tourist group started to grow impatient, restless for their tour to begin.

The tour guide held up a finger to her tour group and began speaking. "Around the anniversary of the Jewish ghetto, the ghost of Sara Copio Sullam is said to—"

"Wait, wait, wait," Dani interrupted. "Did you just say ghost? Are you serious?"

The tourists crowded in closer.

"*Sì*, the ghost of Sara Copio Sullam, a Jewish poetess, is rumored to appear to lost souls to help them find their way forward." The tour guide turned to Dani. "You must be one of her lost souls."

The tourists stared at Dani. Then they started taking pictures of the crazy lost soul who'd seen a ghost. Cameras and phones clicked and whirred.

"What? No, no. I don't understand," Dani stuttered. "Venetians are crazy!" She yelled and ran down the Rialto steps, her heart raced as she pushed through the crowd retracing her steps from the night of the ghost walk. She entered a narrow alley with protruding bricks and walked into the sotoportego with wooden beams that led to Campiello del Remer where Sara had first taken her.

It was empty.

She walked to the edge of the canal and stood on the wooden pier looking up at the Rialto Bridge. *What the hell is happening?* She thought back to the night of the ghost walk. She didn't remember seeing any paperwork or other identifiers linking Sara with the Avventure Serenissima Tour Company. Sara, or the woman who said her name was Sara, had approached her when she was standing at the Rialto Bridge.

"I've gone fucking mad!" she said aloud.

Tears fell as she watched the boats pass by.

Dani took out the pen from her pocket and opened her journal. She sat at the edge of the canal and started writing. The words came easily. Then she read it out loud.

"Sara, you come to me in dark of night,
Capture my heart under the gas lamplight.
You woo me with your wisdom and beauty
and fill my head with ancestral duty.
Yet, here I stand alone dismayed
From lust to love I am now betrayed.
'Twas once my goal to come and claim my quill.
I search but only find I am your fool."

She shook her head. "A ghost? How is that even possible?" she muttered. Dani took out the ghost tour brochure from her jacket pocket, tore it into a million pieces and threw it into the canal. "What the hell was in that candle?!"

TRENTUNO

A clock tower chimed nine times. It was dark now. The sun had set about an hour before. Dani knew she needed to get back to the apartment. She picked up her notebook and began walking through the throngs of tourists over the steps of the Rialto Bridge and towards the Ferrovia signs that led to her apartment in the Santa Croce District.

The streets were dark and nearly deserted. Dani walked briskly searching for familiar buildings. She relaxed when she entered Campo de San Giacomo dell'Orio, which was close to the apartment and DeLucia's Café. *Oh, thank God,* she thought, as she continued left, past the church and down the street that led to the café and her apartment. She knew her way from here.

Dani heard a commotion and turned to see Antonio stumbling out of a taverna. He tripped over the uneven walkway. A man rushed out of the establishment, grabbing Antonio by the arm before he fell. *"Facilmente, Antonio."*

Dani recognized him right away. It was the curly black-haired guy she saw the day after the ghost walk.

"No me tocco, Marcos!" Antonio yelled at him. He looked drunk. Then the weasel guy walked out of the taverna.

Dani tried to get out of the three men's way.

The weasel looked in Dani's direction and said something in Italian. Antonio looked up. He pushed Marcos off him, almost knocking Marcos's black stocking cap off of his head, and staggered to his feet. "*Paulo,*" he said, appearing somehow more alert, his senses sharpened. "*Lesbica Ebraica da America,*" he bellowed.

Dani tried not to make eye contact with the men. She surveyed the area and realized that the only way she could go was through. She felt her heart pounding rapidly in her chest. Traversing dangerous terrain was an all-too-familiar game. She'd played it unwillingly with Sean and the other jocks back in high school. She took a deep breath, stood up straighter, and began walking directly forward, hoping to get through it quickly.

"What's this?" Antonio grabbed at Dani's blue notebook. She struggled to keep it from him, but he tore it from her hands. He opened it up. "*Lesbica* love poems?"

The men laughed.

He began reading in a thick accent. "You capture my heart under lamplight."

"Give that back to me!" Dani grabbed at the notebook and fought hard to get it from him.

The men laughed louder. Antonio tightened his grip on the notebook, keeping her from it and everything it contained.

The scene was so familiar to her that she could have written it even better than the scenes she was trying to write in her novel. Men like Antonio were predictable in their violence and she knew things were only going to get worse.

"I got something else to give you," Antonio said, grabbing his crotch firmly. He whipped the notebook into the black darkness and came for her.

Dani heard a loud splash. He had tossed the notebook into the canal.

"No!" she cried out, devastated. Antonio had murdered her creation. Everything she'd been working on to finally piece together her novel was in that notebook—everything for which she'd come to Venice. All of her hard work gone in an instant to a watery grave.

But there was no time to grieve this unexpected death. The notebook was only *prima patti,* the first course; Antonio and his pals were hungry for more. She was at risk of a beating or worse. Dani knew that look of violence anywhere. She had to pull it together and figure out how she was going to get out of this situation.

The men closed in on her. "Get away from me," she yelled.

"Paulo," Antonio said, motioning to the guy who looked like a weasel.

Paulo grabbed a hold of Dani's jacket at the collar and jerked her back towards him. It tore as Dani struggled to get free. She swung her fist hard at Paulo but Marcos grabbed her arm before it could make contact with Paulo's face.

Paulo grabbed Dani's other arm and pinned her. The two of them held on tightly as Dani fought unsuccessfully like a fly caught in a spider's web. Antonio stepped forward. Dani could smell the liquor on his breath.

"You like to look at my Gina?" Antonio interrogated, his face only inches from hers. She could feel the angry spittle on her flushed cheeks. She did not respond. Dani knew that any response would evoke more violence. She struggled to free herself from the men's grip without further tearing her father's jacket.

Frustrated with Dani's silence, he asked again, waving his hands in the air. "You like to look at my Gina?"

This time he didn't wait for an answer. He spat in her face. Dani blinked her eyes against it. The mucous burned her eyes as it dripped down her face. She wanted to wipe it off, but Paulo and Marcos held her tight. She prayed that the attack would only be a physical beating and pushed the other thought from her mind. Antonio grabbed the lapel of her jacket with both hands.

"Let me go you asshole!" she shouted and tried to fight him off.

"*Cosa succede?*" a voice rang out.

Dani recognized the voice, but not the Italian words.

"*Antonio e tu?*" Signore DeLucia stood in the doorway of the restaurant. He was wearing a red-and-white striped bathrobe.

"*Sì, Carlo e me,*" Antonio replied. He glared at Dani, then he let go of her and turned around.

"*Venga qui, Antonio.*"

Antonio stepped out of the shadows.

"*Cosa succede?*" Signore DeLucia asked Antonio again. Dani saw Regina appear by her father's side in pink pajamas.

"*Niente,*" Antonio lied.

The grip on Dani's arms loosened a bit.

"*Cosa succede, Padre?*" Regina asked her father, then glimpsing Antonio she called out to him, "I heard screaming."

Regina recognized Paulo and Marcos in the shadows. "Paulo, Marcos, *cosa succede?*" she demanded.

"*Non ti preoccupari,*" Antonio said calmly, intending to lull the DeLucias back into their apartment and beds without any further questions.

Paulo's grip tightened on Dani's arm, the pressure of his fingers nearly cutting off her circulation. He muttered something to her in Italian. She knew she had to say something before Regina and her father went back upstairs. The words stuck in her throat, "Hey Regina."

"Dani? Dani is that you?" Regina called out in English." She put her hand to her eyes and squinted. "Paulo, Marcos, *sei con l'Americana?*" she interrogated.

Paulo dug his fingers harder into Dani's arm.

"Yeah, it's me," Dani yelled from the dark corridor by the canal, the words breaking as she fought to hold back tears.

"Dani, are you OK?" she asked.

"No," Dani said, her voice clearly cracking.

"Dani, what's going on?" Regina walked towards her and Paulo. Paulo discreetly let go of Dani's arm and Marcos lit a cigarette. Antonio walked up to meet Regina before she could make it to Dani.

"Antonio, *cosa succede?*" Regina questioned him, looking in his eyes for the truth.

"*Niente,*" he lied again, trying to block her from going any further towards the canal where Paulo and Marcos had been holding Dani. "Everything is fine," he lied in English and held out his arm to embrace her. "*Sei ubriaco? Naturalmente siete!*

Ll'odore di alcol sul tuo respiro. I hate it when you are drunk. Get out of my way!" Regina pushed past him.

Antonio looked like he wanted to grab her, but aware that Signore DeLucia was watching, he reluctantly let her pass.

"Dani, *mio Dio!* Your jacket is ripped!"

Dani wiped Antonio's spit from her face.

"And they spit on you? Who spit on you?" Regina's questions rang out one after another, demanding answers, but everyone was silent.

Regina turned to face Marcos and Paulo "*Come hai potuto.* How could you?"

"No—" Marcos started.

"*Silenzio!*" Antonio yelled.

Regina held up her hand up to Antonio. Her gentle eyes looked angry. "*Basta,*" she said. She turned to Dani. "Dani, who spit on you?" she insisted.

Regina's fierce protectiveness surprised Dani. Tears of gratitude fell from her eyes. Michelle had minimized what Sean had done to her and they had been lovers. The only claim she had on Regina was a claim to the kindness of a stranger. She didn't need to say anything to Regina, as Regina got the picture.

Regina turned back to Antonio. "*Che tipo do animale sei, Antonio?*"

"*No, non e cosi, Gina.*" Antonio went soft. His voice seemed no less menacing for it.

"*Parta!*" Regina yelled at Antonio commanding him to leave. "*Vada via!*"

Regina hooked her arm through Dani's and led her to the apartment door. As she came out of the shadows and into the light, Signore DeLucia gasped when he saw the expression on Dani's face and how disheveled her clothes were. He opened the door for Dani and Regina. He stared unblinking at Antonio and locked the door behind them.

Regina and her father ushered Dani upstairs and urged her to sit on the sofa. Dani's body shook from the adrenaline that coursed through her veins. Regina brought her a blanket and then went into the kitchen with her father. She made tea and they spoke softly in Italian. Dani was grateful Signore DeLucia and Regina showed up when they did. She felt lucky to be alive.

Regina brought tea to Dani. The cup shook in her trembling hands.

"You will stay here," Regina said, bringing more blankets over to the sofa.

"It's fine, the apartment is—"

"*Per favore. Ferma qui,*" Signore DeLucia interrupted.

Dani looked up at Signore DeLucia. His friendly face looked sad and concerned. He gently placed his hand on Dani's shoulder and gave it a little squeeze. "Stay."

Dani nodded her head accepting their invitation.

"*Buonanotte,*" Signore DeLucia said. He lightly patted her shoulder then excused himself to his bedroom.

Dani pushed back into the sofa pillows trying to steady herself and stop the shaking.

Regina walked down the hallway then returned with a tangerine-colored sweatsuit. "Here, these are more comfortable for sleep."

"So my color," Dani said, trying to lighten the situation. She went to the bathroom and changed into the girly tangerine sweatsuit.

Dani returned and sat on the couch next to Regina. "Thank you, Regina, I—"

Regina interrupted. "I'm sorry Antonio did that to you."

"He thought I was coming on to—"

"So, what if you were?" Regina interrupted her again. "No *scuses* for his behavior. He was wrong. I can't have man like that as my husband!" Regina said something else in Italian that Dani did not understand.

"You're just mad. You'll work it out."

Regina looked at Dani's head. "Did they hit your head?"

"No, thank god."

"If you didn't hit your head, perhaps you are crazy? You can't work those kinds of things out!"

"But you don't even know me?"

"I know you enough. You are good person."

Regina's words struck a chord. Tears streamed down Dani's face. "No, I'm not. You don't know me." Dani began to babble about her relationship with Michelle, the loss of the book, and meeting a Venetian tour guide named Sara whom she'd fallen for, and who had suddenly ghosted her.

Regina looked at her confused, unsure of how to help her or what to say to comfort her. "I don't understand, but I know it will be better in the morning. Please, sleep now. You are safe." Regina reached out her arms to hug Dani.

"I'm 'cool.'" Dani turned away and wiped the tears from her face.

"*Basta.*" Regina put her arms around Dani and hugged her. "I'll see you in the morning."

Dani shook out the blankets and lay down on the sofa to sleep. Her body still struggled to get warm. She pulled the covers over her head anxious for the light of day.

TRENTADUE

Dani sat at a wooden table, eating soup. Normally, she would have enjoyed a place like this, with its yellow walls softly lit by candles. But now, as she swallowed warm bites of carrots and potatoes, all she could think about was home. She wondered what Veronica was baking and how Veronica would love this minestrone. Each bite made Dani miss Veronica more. It became too hard to swallow, the homesickness was so acute.

Even the kindness Regina and her father had shown her for the past week couldn't make up for the fact that Dani was ready to leave, to go home. But where was home, Seattle or San Francisco? And what was she going back to? Michelle? Unemployment? Failure?

She was no closer to finishing the novel than when she left San Francisco. All of the details she'd outlined and those first few chapters were gone. What would Veronica say to her? If she ever even talked to her again. She'd probably tell her it was her fault for chasing after a woman instead of focusing on her writing like she'd come here to do. Her pride stung her like a swarm of angry bees.

As she took the last bite, a familiar song came on the radio. John Waite's "Missing You." The song had always made her think of Michelle whenever she heard it. She put down her spoon and closed her eyes as the words echoed in her ears. Each plucked at her heart strings. She sang along. The analogy about sending a message to someone's soul stuck in her head.

Her mind drifted to the woman who called herself Sara. She couldn't explain it, but she felt like Sara was sending a message to her from the beyond. She didn't understand their strange connection. Or why this woman had chosen her.

She didn't know if it would bring her any clarity, but when the song ended Dani knew what she had to do. She had to see it with her own eyes. She knew that seeing would at least bring some closure to her encounter with the stranger, and the strangeness, she had found herself caught up in.

TRENTATRE

It was a cold, rainy day when Dani went to visit the cemetery in the Lido. She'd forgotten her umbrella, so by the time she reached the vaporetto stop at Piazzale Roma, her stringy wet bangs stuck to the side of her face. She entered the hull and took the steps leading down to the passenger cabin and took a seat in the front. The waterbus was crowded and mostly submerged. It stunk of cough drops and bad breath. The young woman sitting next to her was dressed in evening clothes, clearly returning home after a wild night in Venice. She thought about all the girls she'd been with and felt a little guilty for leading them on. Something was different in her since she'd met Sara, she could see that now, but didn't understand it.

Even as the boat traveled across the lagoon, she wasn't sure how this was going to stop her obsessive thoughts or answer her questions, but she had to make the trip. Dani had lied to Franca at the Jewish Community Center. She'd claimed to be writing a historical novel about the Jewish ghetto to get into the Jewish cemetery. Franca had insisted advanced appointments were required. Dani had assured Franca she had emailed months earlier to confirm her request and that it must have gotten lost. She felt bad for lying, but her need to understand what had happened haunted her, and she knew if she didn't take this step she'd never be able to put it to rest.

The boat banged into the floating dock of the vaporetto stop at Santa Maria Elisabetta on the Lido. The man named

Adamo said he would meet her at 9:00 AM. She had thirty minutes to kill. She saw a café across the street and walked toward it. A car swerved to avoid hitting her. The driver honked the horn violently. She'd forgotten there were cars on the Lido. She'd forgotten what it was like to be around cars altogether, but she hadn't missed them a bit.

Dani sipped a cappuccino at the café counter. This was her last day in Italy; tomorrow she'd be back in San Francisco. As she left the café, she noticed a flower shop next to it with white buckets of roses, assorted colors of Gerber daisies, pink and white tulips, and carnations.

Dani's eyes were caught by a simple bouquet of yellow flowers. She picked up the bouquet and went inside to pay for it. Then she walked back across the street and waited for Adamo to arrive. A gray car pulled up and an older man, wearing a black cap over his shocks of white hair and a long black coat, stepped out of the car. He had bushy white eyebrows and kind eyes.

"Adamo Azzo?" she asked, sizing him.

"*Sì, Senorina* Riman?"

"*Sì.*" She held out her hand to shake his. "Thank you for taking the time to show me the cemetery."

"Please come," he said in a thick accent and opened the car door on the passenger's side.

"So, you are here for research?" he asked as he started the car.

"Yes," Dani lied.

"You are studying Sara Copio Sullam, no?"

Dani nodded.

"Where are you from?" he asked.

"San Francisco, California."

"Oh, San Francisco." Adamo smiled. "I was stationed there when I was in the merchant marines."

Dani looked out the window as they drove trying to get a sense of the Lido. "How long have you lived in Venice?"

"Since I was boy. Only when I was in the merchant marines and when my family was hiding from the Nazis was I ever away." Adamo's eyes appeared watery.

"You had to hide from the Nazis—that seems so long ago."

"Yes, Nazis came to Venezia when I was a boy, and we had to hide for many months. I am seventy-five years."

Dani was surprised. He didn't look what she imagined seventy-five would look like. He seemed youthful. Still, she felt bad about dragging a man of his age out in the rain and for such an unorthodox reason.

"And you?" Adamo asked "How many years do you have?"

"Twenty-five."

Adamo laughed. The edges of his mouth turned up and then quickly back down. He had a classic Italian look and was quite handsome.

"Here we are, Jewish cemetery."

Adamo parked the car and they got out. He walked over to the gate and unlocked it. Dani followed Adamo into the cemetery. The rain continued to fall, pelting the top of her umbrella. It sounded like pebbles being tossed into a pond. Dani held the umbrella over her head and tried unsuccessfully to cover Adamo. Thankfully his hat and coat seemed to be covering him well.

"Where is Sara buried?"

Adamo looked at the flowers in Dani's hand. "You brought her flowers?"

Oh God, he thinks I'm crazy for bringing flowers to a woman's grave who has been dead for almost four hundred years.

"Yeah, I didn't want to come empty-handed," she explained.

Adamo nodded approvingly of her intentions. "We usually bring rocks to Jewish graves." He paused for a moment. "Well, Sara was a modern woman for those times. I'm sure she would appreciate that." Adamo reached out and patted Dani's shoulder.

Dani felt relieved that she hadn't mucked the whole thing up with her ignorance of traditions and was struck by the thoughtfulness of Adamo's comment.

"Can we go there?" Dani asked, unsure what it would mean to look upon Sara's grave. She was still trying to figure out what had transpired.

Regina told her people in Venice liked to masquerade around as famous dead Venetians, even after Carnival. *But where had the woman who called herself Sara gone and why?*

Dani still couldn't comprehend why she felt so intensely for a woman she'd just met anyway. She hadn't allowed herself to care about anyone since Michelle. Sara, or whatever her name was, had brought up real feelings in Dani, feelings she couldn't explain. Those feelings were now clouded by feelings of shock and betrayal toward the woman impersonating Sara Copio Sullam. *And why would someone impersonating Sara have spent all that time trying to teach Dani Jewish history?* She couldn't make sense of it. *Had her mind been playing tricks on her? Had she really met a Sara impersonator?*

It was the only logical explanation unless . . . The thought was unimaginable, otherworldly. Dani felt like seeing the grave would tell her something. She just wasn't sure what.

"Please, I am in no hurry. You are Jewish, no? You want to know story of cemetery?"

"Sure," Dani said, not wanting to insult his kindness, but impatient to see Sara's grave.

Adamo clasped his hands. "On Twenty-five September Thirteen-eighty-six, the Venetian government leased this land to the Jews to bury our dead. Before it was cemetery, it was beautiful beach, then vineyard, then food garden for wealthy families."

Dani pretended to listen while her eyes searched the headstones, wondering which was Sara's.

"That is monastery. Do you see the walls there?" Adamo pointed. "The Benedictine monks that lived there were angry about Jewish cemetery. They felt this was their land and they would invite Venetian—how do you say in English? — hoodlums, to come and visit. The monks encouraged them to eat their lunches in the cemetery and desecrate the Jewish graves since they couldn't do that themselves."

Dani nodded. "Sara told me."

"Excuse me?"

Dani corrected herself quickly. "A friend was telling me about how Jews were treated in Venice. It's so horrible."

"*Sì, sì, sì,*" he said, shaking his head. "In Thirteen-eighty-nine, walls were built to stop the people coming in and knocking over *tombas* and digging up graves."

"Why did they do that?"

Adamo reached out and cupped Dani's face tenderly in his hands for a moment, "They hated us," he said matter of factly. He turned and pointed to the water. "You see, the Jewish cemetery used to go all the way to the lagoon, but now there is road. They dug up our bones and moved them and the headstones. And over there, in Eighteen-eighty-four, they built a shooting range over the bones of our ancestors."

Dani shook her head at the indignities the Jewish people of Venice had experienced. She also thought about how the Spanish missionaries had done something similar to the Indigenous peoples of North America. They had built Dolores Park and the San Francisco Mission over a sacred Ohlone burial ground. And only a few years earlier an outdoor mall and an Ikea store were built on top of another Ohlone burial ground in Emeryville across the Bay Bridge from where she lived. *There's even a hierarchy for the dead. White bodies get preferential treatment and other bodies get treated like dirt,* she thought.

Adamo pointed to a decorative headstone. "You see over here we have the *tombas* of the Castilian Jews—from northern and central Spain. Can you see the knight and the coat of arms?"

Dani squinted her eyes at the figure and then made out the shape of a knight's helmet and what looked like a shield with a lion in the middle. It was interesting, but she wasn't here for a history lesson. Though she was sure that Sara, or the woman pretending to be Sara, would have approved of Adamo's lessons. She needed to see Sara's grave, she needed to know if she was going crazy. *What if I am? What if . . . ,* and the thought chilled her to the bone, *I have been visited by the ghost of Sara Copio Sullam?*

"These ones are from Jews expelled from Spain during the—"

"Inquisition." Dani finished his sentence.

Adamo smiled and continued walking through the cemetery. Dani followed him from grave to grave through the muddy cemetery. An inch of mud caked the bottom and sides of Dani's shoes. Adamo stopped suddenly and gave her a funny look. "You didn't bring anything to write your notes in?"

Dani stood frozen like a deer caught in headlights. She thought of her notebook drowning in the canal. "Well, um," she stammered, then tapped her head. "I have a memory like an elephant."

Adamo nodded approvingly. "You see here the praying hands, they represent the priests, the *Cohens,* and the jug represents the *Levis,* who washed the priest's hands." Dani noted the carvings in the headstone.

He brushed leaves off the headstone. "Jews were never allowed to own this land. They had to rent it. The Lido was critical to defense of Venice, so burials were suspended from Sixteen-seventy-one to Sixteen-seventy-five to fortify the island during war with Turks."

"But how could the burials stop? People had to be buried somewhere, right? What did they do with the bodies?"

Adamo grinned. "We found ways to sneak the bodies in. Come."

Dani followed Adamo through the cemetery tracking huge amounts of mud on her shoes as they walked through the ivy and clover moving from headstone to sarcophagus.

Adamo paused in front of a headstone with a scorpion and ladder on it. "Here is Sara."

Dani couldn't read the name on the headstone because it was written in Hebrew. The dream she had of being stung by the scorpion flashed in her mind and goosebumps formed on her arms.

"What do the ladder and scorpion mean?" Dani asked feeling a lump suddenly form in her throat as she stood before the grave.

"*Copio* means 'Scorpio' and *Sullam* means 'stairs' or 'ladder.'"

Dani's mind raced, trying to put the puzzle pieces together. "When did she die?"

"You can't read Hebrew?" Adamo asked.

"No." Dani felt a hot wave of shame spread across her face. "But when I get home, that will be remedied."

"Sara died Fifteen of February, Sixteen-forty-one. That was, of course, according to the Christian calendar. It was the sixth day of Adar in Five-thousand-four hundred-one of the Jewish calendar."

"Sorry to ask so many questions, but what does *Adar* mean?"

"'Strength.' It is the last month of the Hebrew calendar, the twelfth month, and it is known as the month of good fortune for Jewish people."

Dani shrugged. "Some luck for her."

"Would you like me to read you her epitaph? It was written by Leon Modena."

Dani remembered Sara telling her about Modena the night of the ghost tour.

"The rabbi?"

"*Sì.*" Adamo nodded, impressed. "This is the stone of the distinguished Sara, wife of the living *Jacobbe Sullam.* The angel of death sent the arrow that mortally wounded Sara, a woman of great gifts, who was wise and a supporter of the forsaken."

Dani eyed him. "It says all of that?"

"There's more." Adamo took a breath and continued reading aloud. "Although presently the worms are preying on her, she will rise on the day chosen by the Lord. Come back, come back, oh *Sulamita!* Ceased to live the sixth day of Adar of the Jewish era. May her soul enjoy eternal happiness."

"She will rise on the day chosen by the Lord," Dani repeated. "If he only knew how powerful his words were."

"*Mi scusi?*" Adamo asked, looking concerned.

"Powerful words. Very beautiful," Dani said, shaking her head.

"Yes, he was also poet. Come, I will show you his grave. But first perhaps you would like to give Sara your flowers."

"Yes, I would like that very much."

Dani unwrapped the flowers from the paper. She set the flowers down on the earth in front of Sara's grave. Adamo intervened. He grabbed a stick and dug a little hole in the ground and then planted the stems in the earth. They brightened the gray tombstone.

Adamo placed his hand on Dani's shoulder. "Come, I will show you where my brother and I used to play when we were boys."

"You used to play here when you were a boy?" Dani asked, teary eyed.

Adamo continued. "*Sì,* my brother and I played here before the Holocaust. The *cimetero* was the only place where we could be Jew and not have to worry about someone hurting us."

"Can I have a moment?" she asked him.

"*Sì.*" Adamo bowed and walked over to tend to an area overgrown with ivy.

As Dani stared at Sara's grave and the hundreds of other ancient tombstones, she finally realized what Sara had been trying so hard to impart. The stories of real-life Jews, like Adamo, were much more important than any romantic fantasy she was trying to invent. She remembered Sara's words. "Write about what I have told you."

Dani's eyes filled with tears. "I will," she whispered.

A raven flew overhead. It circled back and landed on Sara's headstone. It cawed three times. Dani stared at the headstone. She still didn't know if she'd met the ghost of Sara Copio Sullam or someone pretending to be the Jewish poetess. It didn't matter anymore. She was simply grateful to answer this new call she'd been given.

Dani walked over to where Adamo was carefully removing the ivy from a headstone. "Let me introduce you to Rabbi Leon Modena," he said, smiling.

"*Ciao,* Rabbi," she said. "*Piacere.*"

Adamo looked amused. "I thought I was only one who talked to the dead."

"Nope." Dani burst into a laugh almost choking and tearing up. "Adamo, how did you survive the Holocaust?" she asked, trying hard to swallow the lump in her throat now overcome with emotion. Adamo reminded her of her own grandfather, what she remembered of him. Adamo could have easily perished like so many others, but here he was now taking her hand and sharing her history with her, something that before she met "Sara" had no value to her. Only now, it was like finding a chest full of precious antiques and heirlooms. She had never felt more grateful.

"My family was very lucky. We were taken out of Venezia by a Catholic family who hid us in their barn in the countryside near Rome."

"That's incredible!" she said, wiping back the tears.

Adamo smiled and touched Dani's chin. "Yes, it is the only time, except for when I was in the merchant marines, that I was away from the Lido and this *cimetero.* I have worked here all my life. Come, I will show you my most important work of art, my Mona Lisa."

Dani followed Adamo to a meadow where all of the headstones were bright white.

"Do you see these?" Adamo pointed proudly. "I call this my fifth child. I have spent my life in restoration of these beautiful headstones. It has taken me years to repair them, to find the missing parts, and glue them back together. They were in pieces from the elements, and the hoodlums who desecrated them.

Dani took Adamo's arm in hers. "They are beautiful, Adamo. Thank you for sharing them with me."

"*Prego,* Dani, it's a pleasure so see a young person so interested to learn about our history. So many are not."

Dani patted his hand and smiled. She knew her father would have been proud too.

"Come," Adamo said, and they walked on together arm in arm.

TRENTAQUATTRO

Dani bought a bottle of water then walked over to the terraced steps of the Rio de San Stin at the edge of the canal. The sunshine was warm and inviting. She sat down and took a sip of the water, charmed by the sounds of opera and clinking wine glasses spilling out of the open windows from the building across the canal.

A pigeon flew over to where she sat. When Dani failed to offer it anything it hopped down to the canal steps and pecked at the algae-covered stone.

Dani gazed into the reflection of the buildings in the murky green water and thought of Michelle. Within seconds, she felt a cold wind on her neck. She pulled her collar up, her hand brushed against the necklace. She remembered how beautiful Michelle looked the day she gave it to her. How her blue eyes had sparkled and her blonde hair shimmered in the light of the winter sun. Then she thought about what the fortuneteller said. This was all she would ever have: an empty canal reflecting her loneliness and a simple relic—a rock on a chain around her neck—that kept her believing in a love that would never be hers.

A man appeared in the open window in the building across from her. He glanced at her. She felt slightly self-conscious. He shuttered the windows and it became so still that all Dani could hear was the water lapping against the bricked buildings.

Michelle's words echoed in her mind. "Sean is traveling all the time for work. We could spend at least two nights a week together. You would just need to be out of the house before my son wakes up."

Dani considered what being with Michelle with her son in the house would be like. Michelle's proposal sounded significantly less appealing then when she'd first whispered it to her over the phone. Dani realized how starved she'd been for Michelle's love—almost willing to give up everything to have another taste.

She imagined what it would have been like if Michelle hadn't cared so much about what other people thought. *What if she had just come out and been honest about her feelings for me instead of marrying Sean?* It was ludicrous, like wondering what Heathcliff would have been like if Cathy had chosen him in Emily Brontë's *Wuthering Heights.* Michelle had made her choice.

Dani reached up and unclasped the necklace and held it in her hand. Her fingers massaged the green agate and tiger's eye necklace, studying the stones. Michelle's words echoed in her mind. "When you wear it you'll feel my love for you."

Dani balled up the necklace in her fist then brought the stones to her lips and kissed them. "Goodbye, Michelle," she whispered and then hurled the necklace into the canal. There was a small splash and a wave of expanding ripples in the middle of the canal and then nothing. Her reflection blurred in the ripples and then slowly became clear again. She could see herself clearly in the calm water. It was done. The spell was broken.

On her walk back to the apartment, she stopped at the canal near DeLucia's Café where her novel had died. It was dark now and the lights from the streetlamps glittered like diamonds on the water's surface. She felt at peace with what was.

TRENTACINQUE

It was Dani's last night in Venice. She strolled through San Marco Square, eating gelato and enjoying the vibrancy of Venice: the tourists, the musicians, even the pigeons. She felt free, really free. She couldn't remember a time when she'd felt so liberated.

Dani found a beautiful restaurant along a canal and decided to stop there for dinner.

"*Per uno?*" the waiter asked.

"*Sì,*" Dani replied.

"*Prego,*" he said and took her to a table overlooking the canal. She sat down and ordered a glass of wine. Her eyes watched the lights flicker on the canal. It was exquisitely beautiful here. *So romantic.*

She turned and recognized the newly engaged couple she'd seen when she first arrived. The ones that had triggered her with their public displays of affection. They were seated at the table two up from hers. They were smiling and happy. Her animosity towards them was gone, replaced by a different feeling. She signaled the waiter.

"*Prego?*" he asked.

She pointed to the wine list.

He nodded approvingly and went inside.

Dani felt a deep peace in her heart.

The waiter returned with a glass of a wine and a bottle of champagne.

"*Per loro,*" Dani said. She motioned for him to take the champagne to the couple, grateful that she'd picked up more Italian words.

The waiter smiled and took the bottle to the young couple. He pointed to Dani. They smiled at her.

Dani raised her glass to them. *I really am free,* she thought.

Her eyes lighted on the sparkling canal, the reflections of the evening canvas shimmered on the water's surface. It was nothing she could put into words; however, she understood on a new level Veronica's wish for her to be inspired. Venice was living inspiration. She took another sip of her wine breathing in the sea air and enjoying the caress of the *aria fresca* on her face. She watched the boats move silently across the water.

TRENTASEI

Dani zipped up her suitcase. "I still can't believe I was breathing in all that gas at the apartment . . . and that crazy landlady. Thank you for letting me stay here," Dani said to Regina.

"Yes, that is not usual, Dani. Some of the older people have *demenza,* and because their children live on the mainland they don't realize how bad it can become. I'm glad you were not hurt. The gas is not good for your brain."

That was clear, Dani thought. She figured the gas was causing her bad dreams. *But could it have caused severe hallucinations?* she wondered.

"Do you have everything?" Regina asked, looking around the apartment.

"Yup."

"I'm going to take the *alilaguna* with you to the airport."

"You don't have to do that. You've helped me so much as it is."

"I know." Regina grabbed her coat and purse. "I want to."

"Doesn't your father need you at the café?"

"He'll be fine."

"I hope you'll come visit me in San Francisco."

"I'm planning on it." Regina smiled.

Dani's suitcase clicked over the cobblestone street as they made their way from the DeLucias' apartment to the waterbus stop.

"I'm going to miss the canals and these tiny little streets," Dani said, getting one last look at Venice. "It will be weird to be back in San Francisco with noisy cars and traffic."

Regina nodded silently at Dani.

"So much for writing my novel. At least it was better than Gustav von Aschenbach's trip. Only, my book died in Venice." Dani turned to Regina to see if she knew the reference from the book *Death in Venice.* Dani was disappointed to see that she did not. It made her appreciate Veronica even more.

"What happened with that tour guide, Sara?" Regina asked.

Dani pursed her lips. She had no idea how to explain to Regina that Sara wasn't real. Well, she had been real 400 years before. The whole thing was too bizarre. "It's a long story," Dani said and left it at that.

"Relationships are not fairy tales." Regina smiled a half smile, fighting tears. "Sometimes when Antonio drank . . ." Regina looked down. "He had temper and he . . . when I saw what he did to you . . ." Regina covered her face with her hands.

"I get it." Dani put her arm around Regina's shoulder.

The boat banged into the side of the dock and throngs of people crowded on board. Regina and Dani found a place in the middle of the boat and held on to a railing.

"Can I ask you something personal?" Regina asked, wiping tears from her face.

"You've already seen me in a tangerine sweatsuit." Dani smiled.

Regina looked at her deeply. "What do you want?"

"You mean like to make my flight on time?"

"No, *nel senso grande*—in the bigger sense?"

"That's not what I was expecting." Dani turned and looked away. "I just want a cappuccino."

Regina laughed and elbowed Dani. "*La verita*. Truth."

"I don't know," Dani said. She shrugged and took in the colorful Venetian buildings as the alilaguna made its way through the Grand Canal. "I thought to write a novel, I guess to prove something, you know? Maybe to prove that I was good at something or that there was a point to my life, but now I don't know. I think I'm supposed to do something else."

"What did you decide about Michelle?"

Dani sighed. "I can't live my life like that anymore. For a long time, I was willing to settle for any little thing she'd give me, but I can't do that. I have to let her go."

"So, I ask you again." Regina looked at her more intently. "What do you want?"

"OK, OK." Dani laughed. "I get what you're asking." She pursed her lips and took in the question. "It may sound simple, but I want to be happy. And I want to write because I love writing, not because my whole self-worth depends on it. I think I want to learn more about Jewish history too, though I have to say it's a smidge depressing."

Dani took in a deep breath of ocean air. The boat clipped at a faster pace as it was crossing into the open channel of the Adriatic Sea in the direction of Marco Polo Airport, leaving the colorful city behind. She searched for the right words. "And I want to find love again. A love that is a constant flame, a love that doesn't self-consciously diminish itself when it meets a stranger's gaze. I want to be with a woman who loves me as much in public as she does behind closed doors."

"*Bellisima!*" Regina said, impressed.

Dani smiled at her. "What do you want, Regina?"

"I thought to marry Antonio and start a family, but when I met you and you told me you had come all the way from United States to write book, not knowing Italian, not knowing anyone . . . seeing you do something so *impulsivo,* so brave, it made me to think about my life."

Dani laughed. "You think I'm brave?"

"You took risk. That's brave. I can't go back to how it's been," Regina said, her eyes tracing over the water.

"You mean with Antonio?"

"More than Antonio. You show me, go after what I want."

The waterbus pulled up to the dock at Marco Polo Airport and the passengers grabbed their luggage and disembarked.

Before she got out, Dani said, "Thank you, Regina, I'll never forget your kindness." She went to hug Regina.

Regina held out her arm. "No, Dani."

Dani took a step back and almost tripped. She tried to regain her balance. Her cheeks flushed red. "OK, bye," she said, hurt and confused by Regina's rejection.

She hadn't expected Regina to be homophobic in this way. She thought Regina was different. She turned and walked off the boat, trying to shake off the sting.

Dani suddenly felt a hand on her shoulder and whipped around to confront whoever was touching her.

It was Regina.

"What?" Dani asked defensively.

"I'm coming with you." Regina grinned. "If you'll let me?"

Dani felt like she might laugh and cry all at once. "What are you talking about? I'm not smuggling you in my suitcase."

Regina pulled her passport from her purse.

Dani was confused. *Is this why she didn't want to hug her goodbye?*

"But what about your clothes, you have nothing to wear."

"Can I stay with you?" Regina inquired, looking a little less sure of herself now.

"You're serious?" Dani asked, still in shock at this turn of events.

"*Sì.*" Regina nodded and put her hand in Dani's. "If I don't go now, I'm never going to go. I've broken with Antonio. I want to be free. I want to see the world. I start by visiting my cousins in America."

"Wow." Dani smiled, impressed with Regina's pronouncements. "You're sure?"

"*Andiamo.*" Regina locked arms with Dani and they made their way up the walkway to the airport. She hadn't been wrong. *Regina's kindness and friendship are authentic.*

Dani checked in for her flight while Regina booked her ticket on the same flight. "I'm going to get us some cappuccinos," Dani told Regina, then headed in the direction of the café. She changed course when she saw the airport bookstore and had a light-bulb moment. She went inside the store and bought a green spiral notebook with her last euros, then slipped into the café queue.

Regina joined her in line. "Everything OK?" Regina asked.

"Yep, I feel the Universe just sent me a message." Dani smiled. "Now, about that cappuccino."

An hour later, while most of the passengers slept in the darkened cabin, one reading light remained on—the one above Dani's seat. Dani, wide awake, wrote feverishly while Regina slept in the seat next to her.

Sara had helped her get out of her own way. The writing was easy now. The words flowed effortlessly onto the page. Sara had been her muse.

They deplaned in San Francisco around 11:00 PM and Dani knew there was something she needed to do. She and Regina walked out of the airport doors from Baggage Claim and Dani hailed a cab.

They rode in silence. Regina still groggy, slept most of the way.

"This is it," Dani said to the cabbie when they arrived at Valencia and 21st. Dani gathered her belongings from the trunk and paid the driver. Then she woke Regina and they ascended the steps to Dani's studio.

"It's small, but you're welcome to stay as long as you want." Dani opened the door and invited Regina in. "You can have my bed tonight and I'll sleep on the couch."

Regina looked concerned. "No, I don't want to cause you trouble."

"No trouble at all, *amica,*" Dani said, smiling. She put her luggage down. "Let me give you the grand tour." Dani stood and pointed to the various corners of the studio. "Kitchen, bedroom, living room, that door leads to the bathroom, and this is Fern," she said, introducing Regina to her plant and glad to see Veronica hadn't killed her.

Regina smiled. "Hi Fern."

Dani opened a closet door and grabbed a pillow and blanket for herself and threw them on the couch. Then she reached into her dresser drawer and pulled out her Nokia Flip phone and a key chain of a Trolley Car. "Here are the keys to the apartment. Make yourself at home. I need to go see someone. Don't wait up for me."

TRENTASETTE

Veronica, half asleep, opened the door to her apartment wearing a leopard pattern bathrobe, her cleavage visible. "What are you doing here?" she asked. "I . . . I thought you were still in Venice."

"I was . . . I just . . ." Dani was distracted by Veronica's cleavage. "Um, a . . . your girls are . . . uh."

Veronica looked at her confused.

Dani motioned with her eyes.

Veronica looked down and saw her breasts slightly exposed. She wrapped her robe tighter around her.

"I just got back and I want to apologize for acting like a big dick. Well, I'm not sure if it was an act."

"It's OK."

"No. You've been a great friend and, well, I haven't. I appreciate all that you've done to support me."

"What happened with your novel?" Veronica asked.

Dani looked at her sheepishly. "It drowned."

"What?"

"It's not important. I was writing it for the wrong reasons, but now I'm writing another one for the right reasons."

"OK."

"Listen, it's late. I should go."

"Are you hungry?"

"I could eat. I mean, it was a long—"

"Flight and airplane food, right?" Veronica interrupted.

Dani grinned. "Yeah, airplane food."

"Come in, I'll fix you something."

"You sure?"

"Sit," Veronica said and walked to the kitchen.

Dani sat at the table. She watched Veronica, noticing for the first time Veronica's beauty. Her smoky brown eyes, her long auburn hair, the perfect curves of her body that were visible through her robe. And there was something sexy about the way her lips parted when she smiled. All of the sudden, even the freckles on Veronica's face were sexy.

Veronica brought her a bowl of Greek yogurt with fig slices and drizzled honey.

Veronica placed the bowl in front of Dani, then unexpectedly tousled Dani's hair.

"I really missed you. I can't imagine what it's going to be like when you go back to Seattle." Veronica looked at Dani and then looked away.

"I—" Dani began, but was cut off by the ringing of her cell phone. She took it out of her pocket. There were multiple missed calls, all from Michelle.

"It's Michelle. I've got to get this," she said to Veronica.

Veronica, visibly upset, went into the kitchen.

Dani answered. "Hey, Michelle."

"I've been calling you for weeks now," Michelle said, the irritation in her voice plain. "Why didn't you answer?"

"Yeah, I was in Venice, Italy. I didn't have my cell with me. Why are you calling so late?"

"Sean is out of town."

"OK."

"So, when are you coming back?"

"I'm not." Dani sighed. "I'll always care about you, but—"

"But what?" Michelle screeched. "What are you saying, Dani?"

"I'm saying goodbye, Michelle." Dani hung up the phone and exhaled deeply. She stretched out her arms and the heaviness lifted from her body.

She heard a loud banging noise coming from the other room. She walked into the kitchen and found Veronica ferociously scrubbing a pan. Dani took the sponge out of Veronica's hands and wrapped her arms around her. "I'm not moving," she said and brushed back a wisp of Veronica's brown hair from her face. Dani thought she felt Veronica tremble a little as she held her.

"You're not moving?" Veronica studied Dani.

"Nope." She smiled, wondering if Veronica could see a difference in her. "I'm staying right here with you."

Dani leaned in and kissed Veronica, rough at first, biting her lip, then softer, kissing her more tenderly. Veronica kissed her back with a fierce intensity that matched Dani's.

It felt good to kiss Veronica, but something was different. She felt it in every part of her body—a longing to feel her body as one with Veronica's—like the flames of two candles dancing together, yearning to become one blaze.

TRENTOTTO

Dani woke up to the smell of coffee. She sat up in bed, pulling the comforter tighter around her body. She'd slept hard.

Veronica sheepishly entered the room and handed Dani a steaming mug of coffee with cream. Just the way she liked it.

She took a sip of the coffee. It was perfect.

Veronica sat on the edge of the bed with her own coffee mug in hand. "That was weird," Veronica said, breaking the awkward silence.

"I've just been through a whole lot of weird. That wasn't weird." Dani gave her a flirty grin. "It was unexpected."

It was fun, but it's no big deal." Veronica shrugged. "Doesn't need to change anything between us."

Dani took the cup from Veronica's hands and placed it on the nightstand next to hers. "It is a big deal. It changes everything," Dani said and kissed Veronica.

TRENTANOVE

Dani sat behind a table at City Lights Bookstore, her back to the bookshelves. A poster of a cover for a book entitled *Flowers for Sara* was clipped to an easel.

Eighteen months had passed since she returned from Venice, and here she was, signing books and chatting with the crowd.

An attractive young brunette with blue eyes and full red lips in a tight white blouse and flowy skirt approached the counter. "Will you sign this for me?" she asked, handing Dani her copy.

Dani noticed the girl's tattoo with the Chinese characters on her wrist. It was Hello Kitty, but grown up and without the nose ring. More natural.

"I loved the book," Hello Kitty said. "Such a beautiful homage to those who came before us and the question of immortality. It totally reminded me of that William Wordsworth poem.

"Our birth is but a sleep and a forgetting:
The Soul that rises with us our life's Star,
Hath had elsewhere its setting,
And cometh from afar:
Not in entire forgetfulness,
And not in utter nakedness,
But trailing clouds of glory do we come
From God, who is our home. . ."

"That's beautiful and kind of mind-blowing," Dani said, impressed by Hello Kitty's elocution. "Who should I make this out to?"

"Katarina." Hello Kitty smiled.

"Nice to see you again, Katarina." Dani signed the book and held it out for her.

Katrina took her book and read the inscription. "'We honor our ancestors by living our lives fully.' Nice. You know, I went back to the café the next day, but they told me you didn't work there anymore. I'd love to have coffee with you."

Dani looked over to where Veronica was waiting patiently for the crowd to disperse. "Maybe in another lifetime," Dani said, smiling. "I'm kind of spoken for."

Katarina's blue eyes called to Dani. "Don't you want to live your life fully?" she asked, undaunted.

"Mmm." Dani smiled and contemplated her invitation. "I think I am." She took Katarina's hand and shook it. "It was really nice to see you again. Thanks for coming."

"If you change your mind." Katarina winked and walked away.

Dani finished signing the books for the people in line and signed the last copies for the bookstore.

"Ready?" Veronica asked.

"Almost," Dani said, gathering her belongings. A book suddenly fell off the shelf. It seemed to almost jump off the shelf. She picked it up. She couldn't believe her eyes.

The book was entitled *Salonica, City of Ghosts: Christians, Muslims, and Jews 1430–1950*. She randomly opened it to page 56 and scanned the text. Her eyes caught the number

"1545" midway down the page. The passage talked about the "overcrowded Jewish quarters" with "smells and noise."

She turned to see the publication date in the front of the book. It was published in 2006, the year she went to Venice. The year she met Sara. She got chills. It was like Sara was speaking to her from beyond the grave. It was an absurd thought.

"Ready now," she said to Veronica, putting the book with her other stuff.

"What's that?" Veronica asked.

"Just a book that jumped out at me," Dani said.

She walked to the counter with the book.

"Great having you here tonight," the bookstore clerk said. "People really loved it."

"Yeah, I was pleased with the turnout." Dani handed the clerk the book. "I'd like to get this."

He looked it over. "Hmm, never seen this one before. Looks interesting."

"If you're a Jewish history junkie, this is top shelf. In fact, I think that's what shelf it fell off of," Dani said, jokingly.

The clerk gave her a funny look. He began to ring it up, but stopped to turn up the radio. "Oh, I love this song," he said.

She listened. It was an old Hall and Oates song, "Sara Smile." She shook her head and chuckled. She felt certain Sara was speaking to her. It gave her gooseflesh and a giddy feeling inside, like she was right where she was supposed to be.

"Enjoy," he said, handing her the book and receipt.

Dani walked over to Veronica and put her arm around her. "Let's go get some dinner, baby."

"What do you have in mind?" Veronica asked as they descended the staircase.

"Definitely Italian." Dani smiled at her. "My treat."

Veronica stopped her just before they exited the bookstore and kissed her on the lips. "You're my treat and I'm so proud of you. You did it!"

Dani reached into her pocket and wrapped her fingers around the velvet jewelry box inside, just making sure it was still there. "That reminds me," she said beaming, "there's something I've been meaning to ask you."

EL FIN

ACKNOWLEDGMENTS

Thank you, Shaul Bassi, for taking a chance on a random American and meeting with me for coffee in 2006 to discuss Sara Copio Sullam. Our meeting was a mitzvah that blessed my life and helped me learn more about the history of our people. Thank you for your openness and kindness, and also for connecting me even more deeply with the city of Venice through the 2008 National Endowment for the Humanities (NEH) Summer Institute on Venice, the Jews, and Italian Culture, and Venezia's citizens, especially Fabio Bozzato and Delia Vaccarello, who helped me contribute to the Italian discourse on LGBTQ equality. It has been a great honor to know you.

Special thanks to Aldo Izzo, who touched my heart with his personal stories of growing up Jewish in Venezia and his absolute joy, kindness, and hospitality as he shared his life's work with me. His stories and his care of the inhabitants of the Jewish Cemetery on the Lido are worthy of celebration. When I was younger, as a masculine nonbinary person, I often felt vulnerable in the presence of elders, but I felt a deep connection with Aldo, a man who was forward thinking and extremely respectful. Meeting him was a blessing. He is a true mensch.

Thank you to Murray Baumgartner, who accepted me into the NEH Venice and Jews of Italy program and widened my studies of Italian Jewish history.

Thanks to the young woman tour guide who took me on a spooky ghost tour through Venice at night. I don't recall your name, but I will never forget the stories you shared or the cool places you took me that I would not have found on my own.

I wish to acknowledge my writing teachers, mentors, and colleagues, especially Martivon Galindo, Ericka Lutz, Philip Eisner, Charmaine Colina, Collin Watts, Adam Burch, and Shannon Kenny who have read and reread this and other projects.

Also, I wish to acknowledge my amor, Diana Martin Del Campo, and bonus son, Dominic, who always help me with book cover design ideas and encouragement on my projects; and my family, my mom, my dad and stepmom, my Ant and Unk, my siblings and their spouses, and my nieces and nephews, for their support in all my endeavors. Special thanks to Tara May and my cherished friends who know who they are and whom I've acknowledged in other books.

Thank you to my editor and book packager, Stephanie Gunning, and cover designer, Gus Yoo.

And thanks to Sara Copio Sullam, who called to me
from beyond the veil to write this story.

ABOUT THE AUTHOR

Davina Kotulski, Ph.D., is a licensed clinical psychologist, sought-after speaker, and award-winning author with a thriving therapy and international life coaching practice. She facilitates workshops and webinars on past-life regression, mysticism, meditation, spiritual growth, self-empowerment, and authentic living.

Dr. Davina received notable awards for her LGBTQ civil rights advocacy, including the Saints Alive Award from the Metropolitan Community Church, the Michael Switzer Leadership Award, and Grand Marshal, San Francisco LGBT Pride Parade. As a respected leader in the LGBT equality movement, Dr. Davina has appeared in dozens of documentary films, been a guest on television (notably on CNN) and on National Public Radio and the talk shows of numerous other radio stations, and has been featured in print publications, like *Newsweek, USA Today, San Francisco Chronicle, L.A. Times, Oregonian,* to name a few.

Dr. Davina has been interviewed on Good Morning La La Land, Wake Up to the Sound of Transformation with Michael

Bernard Beckwith, and numerous radio shows, podcasts, and online summits. She was a guest therapist on the show *Please Understand Me* produced by Sarah Silverman. In 2020, Dr. Davina's past life regression work was featured on the Sky Life Channel and the India-based web-show *OK-tested.*

Dr. Davina's previous books include *It's Never Too Late to Be Your Self: Follow Your Inner Compass and Take Back Your Life, The Manna Paradigm Shift: Creating the Consciousness of Abundance and Freedom, Why You Should Give a Damn about Gay Marriage, Love Warriors: The Rise of the Marriage Equality Movement and Why It Will Prevail,* and the novel *Behind Barbed Eyes.*

Behind Barbed Eyes was a Nautilus Gold Medal winner in 2016 and a 2019 Reader's Favorite Finalist in Fiction Audiobooks. *It's Never Too Late to Be Your Self* won the 2018 Nautilus Silver Award in the category of Inner Prosperity and Right Livelihood and was a 2019 International Book Awards Finalist in the category of self-help and a Finalist in the 2020 Next Generation Independent Book Awards in the Motivational Self-Help category. Her writing has been featured in periodicals, anthologies, online magazines, and blogs.

DavinaKotulski.com

ABOUT RED INK PRESS

Founded in 2016, the mission of Red Ink Press is to uplift our readers with inspirational and entertaining fiction and nonfiction that empowers them to move beyond fear and perceived limitations to be their best and highest selves and create a world where love prevails. Our catalog includes books in the categories of personal growth, self-empowerment, spirituality, and psychology.

At Red Ink Press, we are committed to supporting authors who have a powerful message to share through their stories of transformation and redemption. Our aim is to feature characters and give voice to topics that are underrepresented in mainstream media.